To Sarah,

Happy reading!

Mountain Shadows

Laurie McLure

LAURIE McLURE

Mountain Shadows
Laurie McLure

Copyright 2024 by Laurie McLure

All rights reserved. This book or any portion thereof may not be produced or used in any manner whatsoever without the express written permission of the author except for the use of brief quotations in a book review.

The characters and events in this book are fictitious. Any similarity to real persons, living or dead, is coincidental and not intended by author.

First edition: 2024

ISBN 978-1-73811-790-1
ISBN eBook 978-1-73811-791-8

Fiction / Mystery / Crime / Suspense

To Bob and Lindsay, my everything.

Also, to Jenny and Michaël, for their unwavering support

And in loving memory of my wonderful Mom and Dad for always believing in me.

I love you.

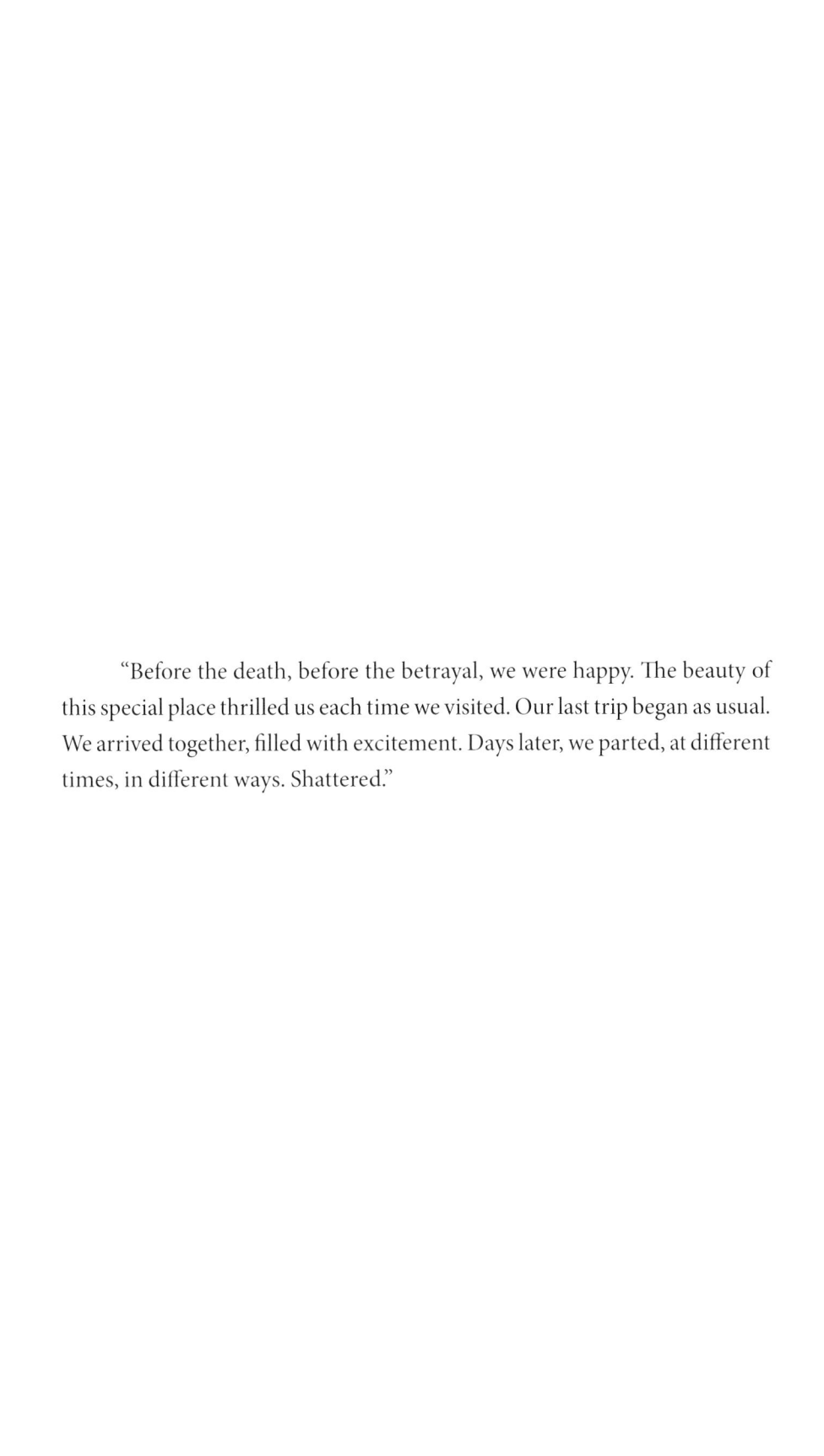

"Before the death, before the betrayal, we were happy. The beauty of this special place thrilled us each time we visited. Our last trip began as usual. We arrived together, filled with excitement. Days later, we parted, at different times, in different ways. Shattered."

PROLOGUE

She crouched between bushes at the edge of a narrow path and tried to calm her breath. No one saw her leave. No one knew she was out here. No one was looking for her. Everything hurt, but she had to keep moving.

She had to get back to the lodge. She knew the evidence she placed in the perfect hiding spot would provide all the answers.

Would anyone find it?

Now it was her turn to find a hiding spot. Her head was spinning. How could she escape? She knew she couldn't double back. Her only hope was getting to the shoreline. A failed text notification pinged on the phone in her hand.

Too loud.

She inhaled. She'd try again when she got close to the water, where she might be able to get a signal. Her text might go through there. It had to.

Covering the glow from the screen, her fingers flew across the small keyboard. One sentence. It was the name of the person trying to kill her and the reason why. She secured her phone in her pocket and heard approaching footsteps.

A random memory flashed through her mind. It was of a television interview with a security expert who addressed a studio audience. The room was filled with women of all ages, hyper concerned for their personal safety. He warned the riveted audience members to never let an attacker take you to a second location. That is where most victims die.

She already managed to get away from the first attack on the way to her cabin. This *was* the second location. She had to keep fighting. Her body shook, and she stifled a scream.

As she stood, her thighs burned, her head throbbed, and her vision blurred. She tested her weight on her twisted right knee. It held her. Blood trickled down her temple. A faint beacon of moonlight helped her see a possible escape route. She once was a fast runner. She had boxes of faded ribbons from long forgotten track and field days to prove it. She summoned what was left of her strength. Like a starter in a race to the finish line, she catapulted forward and ran through the bush. She ignored the pain. She was dizzy. Branches she didn't see whipped her face and slashed her neck. She plummeted from the hilltop toward the beach. Her bare, bloody heels dug into the ground. She fought to maintain her balance while she galloped forward.

The slope gave way. She fell.

A sharp rock sliced her knee, and she felt the warm blood spill down her shin. She crawled for a few feet and then righted herself as she half-sat, half-tumbled down the remainder of the slope.

Keep going.

The beach was close. Worth the risk. She could hear the sound of water gently breaking on shore. If she could get there, maybe the lights from the lodge would be bright enough for someone to see her.

She hadn't noticed the curve in the shoreline until she was near the water. No one could see her, and she was too exposed.

Change of plan.

Back up the hill, she ran, slower now, toward the cabins, toward the cover of safety. She grabbed chokecherry branches while forging her way through the brush. Though they shredded her palms, they helped her balance.

Keep climbing.

She didn't see the cloud of mosquitoes until she swallowed half of them. They were in her nose, eyes, everywhere. She swatted the air. She couldn't see.

Snap.

Her head jerked backward. A brutal force pulled the hood of her jacket. She twisted loose and faced her attacker. The entangled bodies hurled over tree roots, dirt, and rocks. The death grip somersault ended with her on her side.

Too late.

Her breathing was heavy, and exhaustion overtook her body. She ached all over but still had to fight. She rolled onto her back and fanned both hands along the ground in the darkness. She felt something. A large, jagged rock on the ground next to her. As her fingers curled around it, a hiking boot came down hard on her forearm. The overwhelming pain ended all hope. No need to be quiet now. What was supposed to be a yell came out as a moan. Was that horrible sound coming from her? Was it loud enough for the others to hear?

Injured and exhausted, she held her arm and struggled to stand as her attacker watched. Her knee gave out. Her legs slid away, and she was on her back again. She looked up into the face she had been fleeing. A horrible smile, on a face she once thought so attractive, looked back. Cold eyes, filled with hate, bored through her. Her gaze drifted past the face, past the shadow of trees and mountains as she watched as a curtain of clouds opened to reveal a million stars. . . beautiful, shining diamonds.

Something else appeared. Her eyes blurred. A glint of light bounced off the rock she was unable to reach. It was now floating above her head, getting bigger.

Closer.

Then nothing.

CHAPTER 1

THURSDAY

Nicola Henderson began each day, for the past three months, with the same mantra. Protection. As she slid the shower door open, she whispered, "Today is the day it will end."

She stepped in and tilted her head toward the spray hoping to combat the fog of another sleepless night. The hot water pelted her face until it turned cool, far too soon. Turning the taps off, she looked past the unmade bed, through the open window, into a blue sky day. Her fluffy, only-for-company, towels were folded in the linen closet, ready for unnamed visitors who may never arrive. Her every day, threadbare bath towels were in the dryer in the basement. What was left for her was on the floor, damp, used by Alex after his morning run.

She bent to pick up the towel, flinching at the coolness as she wrapped it around her. Nicola lifted her head and caught a glimpse of a shadow from across the room, outside her bedroom window. She heard a whirring sound from outside the window, left open to let in fresh air and birdsongs. A blue jay landed on a branch of the old ornamental crab tree, planted long before the

Hendersons bought the house. The bird was on the closest branch, staring at her. Nicola could almost touch it. She jumped when it screeched and flew off.

Nicola closed and locked the window, and her thoughts focused on her work to-do list. She pulled black pants, a white shirt, and gray blazer from her closet and made her way downstairs. Court attire. Her curls were still wet, but she was dressed and almost ready for the pandemonium of a weekday, school rush morning.

Evidence of breakfast recently consumed was in the form of milk and cereal spilled across the quartz counter. The morning anarchy included a rushed coffee-flavored kiss from her husband, Alex, on his way out the door. He was always in a hurry to escape.

Nicola, cleaning up the spills and wiping toast crumbs from the counter into her hand, yelled up the stairs, "Kyra, hurry up, time to go."

The clock was never on their side, especially this morning. But, Nicola thought, at least it wasn't like last week when Barnaby, their Labrador, threw up on the kitchen floor and her son, Bennett, slipped and fell in it. Unlike her daughter Kyra, Nicola's son took everything in stride and climbed upstairs to change clothes. All Ben cared about was Barnaby's sloppy kisses, unwavering devotion and the understanding the dog would secretly eat vegetables Ben hated. Last week's mishap was the latest of many Barnaby messes and Ben was unfazed.

With a quick kitchen clean-up, and a mad scramble to the bus stop, the kids were out the door with their backpacks slung over one shoulder. Nicola waved and watched them hop up the steps as the school bus was about to pull away.

Everyone was gone. Exhale.

Ready for work, Nicola paused to do her ritualistic glance around the house. Stove off, faucet off, lights off, back door locked. Deep breath. Nicola stood outside a moment to deadbolt the front door. Out of the corner of her eye she spied a colored piece of paper peeking out of the lid of her mailbox. It was probably another invitation to some kid's birthday party. Without looking at it, she pulled it from the mailbox and threw it in her cavernous carry all bag. Much later, in solitary moments, Nicola would ask herself if that action was where everything went wrong.

But, for now, all she thought about was the work waiting for her at the office. Funding for the Victim's Services Program was minimal and existed under the continuous cloud of potential cut backs. As a not-for-profit program, funding only covered a modest salary for Nicola's position and minimal funds for insufficient compensation grants to victims of crime. There was never enough money, but the municipal police detachment offered up a small storage room area as an office along with some minimal administrative support. Nicola loved her work and managed to serve her clients well under challenging circumstances.

Her tires crunched on the gravel as she pulled into the parking lot sending up a cloud of dust from her car. She turned off the ignition and, along with it, the comfort of the air conditioning that provided temporary relief from the early heat of the day. Heat made people crazy. Sometimes violent. Not good in her line of work.

"Hey, kid," the Inspector paused by his car and smiled.

His eyes crinkled when he said, "You keep speeding through here. I'll check to see who I assigned to traffic this week. They might be paying you a visit." He was carrying an oversized rectangular item with numbers on it.

Nicola beeped the lock on her fob, walked across the parking lot, and waved, "Morning, Inspector. Sorry about that. Running late, as always. What in the world are you carrying?"

Inspector Glen Lancaster laughed and held up an electronic contraption that looked like a cross between a 1970s digital clock radio and a bomb.

"It's my wife and kids' idea of a joke. It's a countdown clock to my retirement. New Year's Eve will be my last official day. Nothing like the wildest night of the year to end my career. Sheila thinks she'll work an additional six months and then we'll both be retired."

Glen was a great police officer, a respected Inspector, and a father figure to Nicola. She wasn't a member of his staff, but she knew he considered her a member of his unofficial team. She was always included in professional development events when appropriate, family picnics, and the annual Christmas party. Nicola knew he admired her work ethic, sense of humor, and commitment to helping her clients. He was a valued community member and a well-liked boss. He believed in catching his staff doing things right instead of always finding fault. It made for a great workplace environment, with one exception. But, in every workplace, there's always at least one pain in the ass.

Nicola and her family were relatively new to the town of Hillside, having moved there two years prior. When she and Alex discovered the picturesque, sleepy, little community, with green rolling hills covered in summer wild flowers, they knew this was where they wanted to raise their family. Hillside was located at the base of a dramatic mountain range. During the summer months, the population increased with the arrival of those who were fortunate enough to own vacation homes in the surrounding area. Crime rates were low, but no place is exempt.

"That thing looks more like a doomsday clock. . . T-minus and counting. What are we going to do when you're not around here keeping us all in line?" He smiled at her and held the door open as they entered the one level, brick building with few windows and poor ventilation. They were greeted by two things—the sound of the photocopier rhythmically spewing out documents at an annoyingly loud decibel and by a waft of burnt coffee lingering in the air.

"Don't worry," Glen said. "My family has plans for me. My wife has been speaking to a landscape company to get price quotes on re-doing the backyard come summer. My kids are already scheduling me for next year as a free babysitter. God help me, it sounds like more work than being here. But, no fear, I'll be one of those lost retired old guys who keep coming back to the office well past their sell by date."

"You're hilarious. That's the last thing you'll do."

"I'll hit the switch on July 1st to start the countdown for 184 days, six months, to New Year's Eve. Let's, you and I, see how much fun we can have between now and then. Good morning, everyone. Hello, Yvette." Glen greeted the frumpy but efficient receptionist who beamed back at him. Yvette was always one step ahead of everyone's administrative needs but could never manage to keep her straggly gray hair in her unflattering bun.

Nicola put her purse in her bottom desk drawer and switched on her computer to tackle the overnight emails. Her clients ranged from seniors who were tricked into giving up life savings, to those whose property was damaged or taken and, heartbreakingly, to victims of assault whose innocence was stolen. She met her clients on the worst day of their life. For victims of major crime, she knew they would go on to define their lives for the remainder of their existence as either before, or after, the event. All of their lives were forever changed on the day she arrived to help them.

The light on her phone blinked, and she poured her third coffee of the morning before listening to her messages with voices outlining the terrible things human beings did to one another. The first was a message from Children Services providing a positive update on an earlier case, and the second call was a hang up, one of dozens she had been getting lately. The calls always came in after office hours. She assumed it was someone who managed to dial the number but was still trying to muster the courage to speak to her. Phone call data, including date and time records, indicated, like all previous hang up calls, this one was made in the middle of the night from a blocked number. Nicola was patient. She'd be ready to listen when they were ready to talk.

The good news was today there was no note waiting for her. Over the course of the spring, three previous notes arrived in the mail, all addressed to Nicola at the police station. They were identical, each handwritten, black felt-pen, capital letters on white stationery.

Each note read, *SEE YOU SOON*. Each ended with *XO XO*. Hugs and kisses.

Bizarre.

Her colleagues were mystified, and, while the notes were relatively harmless, Nicola didn't like the feeling of dread that engulfed her every time one appeared. It needed to end.

Nicola stood at the edge of the reception desk and rummaged through Yvette's bundle of office mail yet to be dispersed.

"Bonjour, Nicola, no note?" Yvette asked as she pulled out her chair, blew on her steaming mug, and replaced her head set.

"No note." Nicola smiled. "I'll be in and out of the office all day, but I'll have my cell phone, except when I'm in court later this afternoon."

"Okay, à bientôt."

Nicola froze. She looked at the receptionist who was busy on the phone, unaware of Nicola's stare.

French . . . for see you soon.

That afternoon, Nicola was scheduled to accompany one of her elderly clients set to testify that his caregiver conned him into financial ruin. Elder financial abuse was on the rise in every community. She'd helped the gentleman with an overview of what to expect in court and with the preparation of his Victim Impact Statement. She'd be in the court room when he testified.

Next on Nicola's to-do list was confirming the professional decontamination crew to clean and sanitize the mess an arsonist made of a young family's attached garage. Insurance agents already assessed the damage. The family was lucky no combustibles were present at the time of the fire, and it hadn't spread inside their dwelling. No one was injured. The smell of smoke, however, permeated the house, and it was deemed unsafe. Luckily, they were able to stay with nearby relatives. This marked the third arson incident that summer, and it was only a matter of time before someone was hurt. There were no doorbell cameras in the neighborhood and no leads yet.

Nicola settled into her chair and picked up her phone. Her busy day was underway.

Eight hours later, she was in her kitchen, wearing her favorite comfy loungewear set, emptying untouched lunch bags and starting supper all while listening to Ben share about his fun day. She must have missed yet another email from the school announcing a special event that neither she nor Alex attended. Ben wasn't upset as he described all his accomplishments at various competitions, how much he ate at the pizza party and that he had no homework. Kyra's description of the day would likely differ, but she had stomped upstairs and slammed her door upon arriving home.

Nicola was chopping onions. It was spaghetti night, her kids' favorite.

"Hey, Mom, can I have some gum?" Ben asked.

Nicola reached for her purse and handed a piece of sugar-free bubble gum to her son saying, "Make sure it hits the garbage can when you spit it out. Go upstairs and play in your room or watch something until supper is ready."

Returning the gum to her carry all, Nicola spotted the light blue envelope she threw in her bag that morning. She wondered whose birthday party she would need to buy a gift for and how much time she had to do it. Why was it always on her shoulders to ensure their children had friends and a social life?

There was no writing on the outside of the light blue envelope. Inside the note read:

LOOKING GOOD, NICOLA!

Something fell out of the envelope.

A polaroid picture.

It showed Nicola that morning, exiting her shower, barely covered in the wet towel she retrieved from the floor. Exposed.

The outside frame of the master bedroom window appeared at the edge of the photo. As did a few branches of the ornamental crab tree next to it, leaving little doubt how the picture was taken.

She stifled a scream, as she didn't want to scare her children. She could hear her kids arguing about what to watch in the windowless den. They were safe. While they were both upstairs, Nicola tore through her house closing curtains and blinds and locking windows and doors. Her eyes filled with tears from frying onions but, more so, from fear. Someone was watching her while she showered and got dressed. The gut punch realization that she had a stalker took the air from her lungs.

Nicola sensed anger radiating from the note she held. This one was different.

Specific.

Menacing.

The others were delivered to her workplace, but this one came to the place that protected her and her loved ones from a frightening world. Her sanctuary. Where her children slept. This note changed everything, triggering her heart palpitations and creating a sense of doom she now carried.

She had no doubt this was work related. While dealing with perpetrators often encroached into her work with victims, this breach and threat to her personal safety changed everything. She supported battered women as they testified against their abusive partners. She helped support Crown Prosecutors as they prepared cases on behalf of very young and very elderly victims, society's most vulnerable. She had a list in her head of those who may want to harm her ranging from petty thieves and slum landlords to gang members and more than one sadistic psychopath.

The kids were oblivious, still upstairs, watching television.

Alex arrived home a few minutes later to find Nicola on the kitchen floor, huddled against the corner cupboard doors, with the note and the picture, still gripped in her hand.

CHAPTER 2

FRIDAY

Nicola's hands shook as she looked at the photocopy of the note for the hundredth time. A shiver kissed the back of her neck. She never expected to be in this position. Somehow, the helper was the target of a lunatic.

She had a digital copy of the note on her phone, but holding tangible proof of the threat to her safety in her hands made it more real. The polaroid and the original note were entered into evidence and secured. When she handed the sensitive picture over to the female detective who recently started working in Hillside, Nicola felt her compassion. It was unspoken, but everyone involved realized the note and picture were a clear indicator of escalation in her case, never a good sign.

The home delivery of this particular note was a turning point that filled Nicola with panic and dread. The increased threat level highlighted the need for the Henderson family to leave their home temporarily. Her two children were told they were going on an impromptu family adventure. Bennett, eight, was all for it. Fourteen-year-old Kyra pushed back at the thought of not being with her friends as summer holidays began. Only Nicola's husband, Alex, was fully aware of the danger and made all arrangements.

MOUNTAIN SHADOWS

On the advice of the few work colleagues who knew the situation, the Hendersons packed a duffle bag each and then checked into a hotel the same night the note was delivered. The next day, the family of four arrived at the secluded Mountain Shadows Lodge. No one who knew of the harassment dismissed it as a harmless prank. Those who worked in law enforcement were cognizant of the fact that Nicola's circumstances could escalate. It was the reason she and her family fled their home.

Nicola was relieved the authorities were already involved. When one of their own was threatened, they all were threatened. In the family's absence, cameras were installed throughout their property, and surveillance cars patrolled the Henderson's neighbourhood. Off-duty, vetted, security guards, disguised as exterminators, entered their home and made all the necessary security upgrades. An infestation would explain the family's absence if someone was watching the house. She trusted the police to find who it was, and then they could return to normal.

Nicola answered all the questions the small investigation team asked her. No, she didn't have an enemy, she had no grudges against anyone. No neighbourhood disputes. Nothing involving her kids, or their school, or Alex's work. To her knowledge, she hadn't done anything to make someone want to terrorize her. The common consensus was the stalking was likely related to her victim advocacy.

She viewed the previous notes, and the hang ups from the calls to her work phone made in the middle of the night, differently now. She wondered if the reason for no verbal threats was that she would recognize the voice. His voice. Or was it her voice? Nicola always thought of her note writing stalker as a male but had no reason to come to that conclusion.

She reported all notes at the time, but they still kept arriving. The notes were untraceable, no fingerprints, common stationery, previously white now blue, sold at every office supply store. She didn't recognize the handwriting. Block letters, proper punctuation, black Sharpie pen.

Then the notes stopped, briefly, until this last one. If she could not identify who was terrorizing her, what could possibly be done to stop it?

She documented the harassment and recorded the delivery time and content. She compiled a short list of possible suspects based on her recent work. Potential suspects Nicola encountered through work would be interviewed. Her clients' violent exes, identity thieves, local troublemakers. Cop haters. Neighbourhood assholes. Local troublemakers. The usual nutso whack jobs.

Her life was good prior to this nightmare. She was finally content. Growing up as a child not knowing a lot of love, all Nicola ever wanted was a family of her own. She dreamed of a man who loved her and an SUV filled with happy kids in wet bathing suits or wet snow suits. She visualized it, she pursued her dream, and she made it come true.

Now she had to deal with this crisis. Her only option was to temporarily disappear and take her family with her. Time and distance would help, and maybe, when it was evident no one was home to incite a reaction, the stalker would move on to some other poor soul. Or they'd be caught.

She organized a last-minute leave of absence from work citing a family emergency, placating the co-workers who didn't know about the threat. Alex booked vacation time, and, with their kids and their yellow lab Barnaby in tow, the Henderson family vanished.

At first, Nicola wasn't thrilled with where they ended up, at a remote mountain lodge only a couple of hours from home. They told no one in their personal lives where they were going. Was it far enough away? Would anywhere on earth be far enough?

She hoped they'd travel to a tropical resort with ocean breezes, not end up in the middle of nowhere on a wilderness adventure. Alex made the plans, and, while she appreciated his support during this nightmare, she wasn't thrilled with him for bringing her to this bug-infested forest, located half way up a mountain of granite, with cliffs so steep it made her stomach flip.

Now, for the first time since the notes arrived, Nicola took a deep breath. She reached back and stuffed the wrinkled copy of the last note into the pocket of her jeans. She stood at a safe distance from the edge of a small cliff with a treacherous pathway that led down to the lake. She did a panoramic scan of the property surrounding the secluded lodge, hidden deep within a coniferous forest, and liked what she saw.

The lodge and its surroundings were gorgeous. Wooden barrels of bright red geraniums, with ivy spilling over the side, bookended the main entrance. Little white flowers filled the spaces in between. Spillers, fillers, and thrillers. Somebody knew the gardeners' motto for potted plants. A tidy gravelled circular drive welcomed vehicles. Adding to the quaint vibe was a white, hexagon-shaped wishing well, perfectly placed in the centre of a patch of freshly mown lawn. The website description of the Mountain Shadows Lodge was accurate. The splendour and the grandeur were all on display. The problem was, while Nicola dreamed of an escape with housekeeping services and pool boys included, her main concern was Mountain Shadows Lodge's proximity to home. She also hoped for a secure, gated resort, and, so far, she hadn't spotted anything like that here.

There was no denying the beauty of the landscape and the majesty of the surrounding mountain range could take one's breath away. The combination of crystal-clear water and icy blue colored mountains surrounded by a lush green forest, made her heart soar. A row of small cabins, made of stone and wood and painted burgundy with bright white trim, was nestled amongst the mountain terrain. The cabins were surrounded by a dense forest of pine and spruce trees, now more like dry tinder due to the recent lack of rainfall. Nicola felt a hint of serenity, and a sense of protection, in the quiet of nature's beauty.

From a distance, Mountain Shadows Lodge was an imposing structure. Once she got closer to the building, Nicola could see the need for another coat of paint, noticed the odd loose deck plank around the back of the building, and thought there was an imminent need for a new roof.

She guessed the resort had seen better days, but it felt surprisingly tranquil given its dramatic setting situated on a ledge against a jagged cliff leading down to the lake below. The terrain began to slope just below the main lodge deck next to a rickety looking staircase. Below, a circular lake appeared with glass-like water mirroring the mountains and forest. It was as if the lake was placed in its perfect spot by a landscape painter. Local folklore, recounted by generations, shared the belief that the body of water was divinely placed in the perfect spot to please the eye and quench the thirst of visitors, both wild and human.

The website mentioned the water was cold, clear and inviting during warm summer days but dangerously cold when the sun slipped behind the neighbouring mountains. The location reflected beauty befitting a tourist brochure, yet Nicola hadn't heard of the place. It was secluded. A perfect hideaway. Alex knew someone who visited and mentioned it to Nicola as a safe haven for their family. Alex said when he made the booking, it sounded as though the owner hoped it would remain a secret.

Both Nicola and Alex were relieved to learn only seven other guests would be staying at the lodge on the weekend. While it was seven more than they would have preferred, it was manageable. They were told the guests included a cabin for three young men on a guys' getaway weekend, three young women enjoying an annual reunion trip, and a middle-aged woman on a retreat. The lodge had two staff members, the owner named Otis McIntyre and a summer student named Tyler Donahue.

It was a gorgeous day with the blinding sun reflecting mirror-like flashes from the circular lake below. The local birds were practicing their scales with gusto. Nicola took a few slow, deep breaths to shake off her anxiety. It calmed her. The heat defied all the shaded areas, and the warmth of the sun brought comfort. She paused a moment and tried to capture the feeling of well-being summer always brought her, but it didn't work.

While Alex and Kyra went to check in, Nicola was playing hide and seek with Ben. She was covered in dirt with a twig sprouting out of her curly, light brown hair. Ben was a rambunctious child, and, after a couple of hours in the vehicle, he needed to burn off some energy. She ducked down next to a deck on the lake side of the lodge and held her breath. Her knees hurt from crouching so she stood on wobbly legs and forged her way through the brush. She decided to head toward the lake and circle back up top. It was a longer route, but it might work. She stubbed her right toe on a tree root.

"Geez, damn, for the love of . . . ouch." Nicola fought the urge to holler a series of spectacular swear words but, instead, hobbled forward. She was embarrassingly out of breath. Her forty-four-year old body needed less wine, more cardio. Somehow, she managed to beat Ben back to the starting point probably because the boy was easily distracted.

Nicola looked down at her filthy flip flops to assess the damage to her toe. Purple, more like indigo, was a pretty colour. On a toe, not so pretty. She'd had enough. She caught a glimpse of her son running toward a path with a sign warning of rugged terrain ahead.

"I surrender," Nicola yelled.

"Gotcha, Mom, I won," His blond curls appeared from the slope above. Nicola wondered how he got up there so fast and then acknowledged he's stealth, lean, and eight years old, that's how.

"C'mon, kiddo. We must be all checked in by now. Let's find Dad and Kyra."

Ben picked up a stick and drew BB, for Ben and Barnaby, in the sandy dirt and looked farther to his right.

"Hey, is that bear poop?"

"God, I hope not," Nicola muttered examining the substantial specimen. "No, it's probably from when Barnaby jumped out when we got here. Good thing your Dad caught him, and clicked his collar onto the leash at the wishing well. You need to get a bag from the van and dispose of it properly like you promised."

But Ben didn't hear her and was already running ahead looking backward, his hands raised in victory. A vehicle approached on the left but Ben didn't see it. The little boy was too busy celebrating his hide-and-seek victory. Two middle-aged people were standing talking on the slate steps near a car next to the stone pillared entrance. The man had his back to the scene, but the woman's eyes widened as she looked past the man in front of her. She saw what was happening and waved her hands as she ran forward letting out a warning scream.

"Stop, look out!"

The young man driving the Jeep heard her scream and braked barely missing the little boy's left arm as he came to a full stop. Ben was running too fast to stop in time, and he fell forward into the stationary vehicle. The kick up of gravel sent choking dust everywhere.

The lab, tied to the wishing well in the grassy middle of the circle drive, barked and strained to reach the boy.

A spew of curse words exited the Jeep along with three college-aged young men and a few empty beer cans. Roadies.

Nicola ran to her son, scooped him into her arms, and checked that he was okay. His left shoulder had made contact with the rubber bumper when he tripped, but the vehicle had stopped by then, saving him from serious injury. Ben was crying from fright, and the driver looked like he was about to join him. Even though it amounted to Ben barely bumping into a parked vehicle, it was closer to disaster than it needed to be due to the driver's speed and carelessness. Nicola exploded.

"You, idiot, you could have killed my son." Her voice shook as she fought back tears.

Otis McIntyre, the lodge owner and the guest who screamed, ran toward the scene. They saw the boy's mother approach the men and could tell words were exchanged but none they could hear.

"Are you okay, sweetheart?" The elegant, middle-aged woman approached and patted Ben's shoulders.

"Uh huh." He nodded to her, wiping his tears on his tee-shirt. She reached out a diamond adorned hand with a Kleenex and dabbed the tears running down his cheek as his mother embraced him. She knew he was trying to be brave.

"Holy shit, Carter you almost hit that kid." One of the three young men shook his head and asked, "You okay, little buddy?"

"I'm okay," Ben's response was shaky.

Nicola saw the beer cans in the hands of the two passengers and a second wave of fury engulfed her.

Carter looked through the dust from his friends to the woman, put his hands up in defense and stated, "I wasn't drinking. I just dropped my phone. I was searching Google Maps to find the entrance to this place, I promise. Those other cans have been there since last weekend. I didn't have time to clean out my van. You can breathalyze me if you want."

"Why were you even on your phone? You can't get a clear signal here, and distracted driving is illegal. And on these dangerous roads." She shook her head in disgust.

"What happened?" Alex coughed from the dust hanging in the air. Kyra rubbed her eyes as the two of them approached.

"Your son was almost run over." Nicola said.

"What? Are you okay, Ben? What happened?"

Nicola left Alex to deal with the young men. She held Ben's hand and walked across the outside entrance to the woman who saved the day with her scream.

The woman, in her late forties or early fifties, approached. She was stunningly beautiful, and her casual clothes looked elegant and expensive.

The older woman met her half way and said, "Hi, I'm Victoria Shae. You must be so shaken up. Are you okay?"

"No, I'm not okay. I'm Nicola Henderson, and this is my son Bennett. Thank you for saving him from getting hit." She looked down at her son clinging to her side, and fresh tears appeared.

The older woman took Nicola's hand, "Here, come with me." Victoria led them both to a bench next to the lodge entrance. "You need to sit and get your bearings."

"I think we should call the police." Nicola said.

"Well," Victoria spoke softly, "We could but . . ."

"No, Mom, we'll get them in trouble. I wasn't watching where I was going, and I'll get in trouble too." She held his worried face and said, "Okay, we won't call them."

Victoria's smile was warm and gentle. "I'm so glad you are okay, Bennett. Nicola, does anyone ever call you Nicky?"

Nicola recognized Victoria's attempt to change the subject and went along with it. "Sometimes, but I don't care for it. Does anyone ever call you Vicky?" Nicola smiled.

The woman laughed and brushed her hair over her shoulder. "Yes, they do, but I'm like you. I don't care for abbreviated names either. Or nicknames. Except for my husband. I used to let him get away with it. He used to call me Fancy Pants. Can you imagine? He always gave loved ones nicknames and that was mine." She looked down at her hands, and Nicola noticed a sizable ring on her left hand.

Nicola knew that Victoria was trying to distract her from what just happened. She glanced at Victoria's white eyelet top, tan capris, gold jewelry, and matching purse and sandals. Perfect makeup, perfect hair. Casual but a bit over the top for the rustic setting. Nicola smiled to herself and thought the nickname fit. She hoped she had been successful spot cleaning the coffee stain on her own tee-shirt from the spill on the drive to the lodge. Her hands shook ever since the stalker's note appeared at her home, and the caffeine she craved did nothing to calm her nerves.

"Is your family joining you?" Nicola asked noting Victoria's sizable wedding ring.

"I'm here on my own. I really wanted to be in this beautiful spot this weekend. It's what my soul needs. Self-care is important, doing something just for yourself. I bet that's not easy with your busy family. I hope you have a wonderful stay and look at the spectacular day we have to enjoy. I saw you playing hide and seek earlier. Looks like the path you and your son took was very steep and maybe a bit treacherous." It was obvious the woman was continuing to change the subject for Nicola's benefit.

They remained outside the entrance of the lodge. Nicola nodded but didn't know what else to say so, for once, she stayed quiet.

Victoria pushed her sunglasses up to serve as a headband for her shoulder length blond, shiny hair that revealed just a few wisdom streaks of gray.

"It's just me in my cabin so I better go unpack and get settled in," She turned and took a step toward the building. "It's nice to meet you. Too bad it was under these circumstances. Are you sure you and your son are okay?"

"Yes," she reached down to Ben who joined her and whose arm went around her waist. "We're fine, right, Ben?"

The boy nodded and looked up at his Mom and then Victoria and smiled.

The gravely crunch of approaching footsteps made the trio turn. Kyra retrieved Barnaby from the well, and she met up with her father as he approached.

"This is my husband, Alex, and our daughter, Kyra." Kyra gave a small wave, and Alex extended his hand more out of ritual than warmth.

"Don't forget the friendliest Henderson, this is Barnaby." Ben added.

Victoria bent to pet the Labrador who wiggled in appreciation. "Mom, I think some ice cream would make my arm feel better." Bennett looked up with his big blue eyes.

"I bet the owner has ice cream, let's all see if we can find some." Victoria assured the boy.

"Otis seems like a nice man. A bit quiet and maybe a little sad, but nice." Nicola said.

"What makes you say that?" Victoria sounded surprised and shielded her eyes from the sun to study the man.

"I see a lot of hurt people in my line of work. When people experience trauma, it often shows on their face. I can just tell that man is living in a world of hurt."

Nicola watched as Otis McIntyre, the handsome, rugged, middle-aged, cowboy who owned Mountain Shadows Lodge, turned away from the young men and walked their direction. As he approached the family, Otis smiled. He towered over Ben, confirmed ice cream was on the way for anyone who wanted some, and told Bennett all about the fun he'd have this weekend.

Nicola watched closely. There was an attractive vulnerability about the owner.

Maybe she didn't need pool boys after all.

CHAPTER 3

Otis McIntyre was a handsome man with sandy blond hair streaked with gray and blue eyes the color of the nearby lake. He oozed aging Brad Pitt vibes, but as he stood in the middle of the stone archway at the entrance of his lodge watching his guests arrive, there was nothing inviting or attractive about the look on Otis's face. He walked past Nicola, Victoria, and Ben and approached the group of young men unloading the van.

Similar scenes of guest arrivals played out every weekend of the short, precious Canadian summer. From the Victoria Day long weekend in May to Labour Day each September, new guests arrived at the secluded resort nestled in the majestic Canadian Rocky Mountains. The property included land with challenging hiking trails that led to breathtaking views on the edge of cliffs with waterfalls. Near the lodge was a perfectly circular lake with water so clear, you could be in up to your nose and still see your toes. It was icy cold, as most mountain lakes are, but it was clear and refreshing, and guests loved all the fun the lake offered.

From mid-October to early May, winter programs were available, always with the caveat of weather risks and avalanche threat levels pending. Spectacular downhill and cross-country ski conditions brought visitors from around the world during winter months. Extreme snowmobiling enthusiasts flocked to the back country and risked everything for the thrill they sought. Snowshoeing and ice fishing were also among the activities offered. An exhilarating day outdoors was usually followed with hot chocolate, or hot toddies, around the massive fireplace that took up most of one wall in the main lodge. Many friendships, and more than a few love affairs, were kindled on those snowy evenings.

In every season, Mountain Shadows Lodge offered those who visited panoramic views, tranquility and rejuvenation, but with every interloper's arrival, Otis's resentment built. This was his sanctuary, but he was forced to welcome guests purely for financial reasons. Upkeep for historic buildings in a remote location was astronomical. The revenue was needed to off-set costs including upgraded plumbing and wiring and a long overdue roof replacement on both the main building and the handful of guest cabins adjacent to the lodge.

Otis bought the lodge ten years ago. He'd been a guest whose strong connection to the place made it impossible for him to leave. He loved it the moment he arrived, and he felt he was the best version of himself here. The mountain air, beautiful water, and dense forest all restored his soul, and his will to live, every morning.

The combination of mountains and waterfalls, nature at its most glorious, attracted all kinds of people for all kinds of reasons. Otis always found people were much different when they left his sanctuary. The tension etched on their faces when they arrived was erased. The dilemma for local people was striking a balance between promoting the natural beauty of the region to tourists while keeping the natural treasure a secret from most of the world. Mother Nature played a hand in limiting visitors to the brave few. Wicked thunderstorms and floods caused mudslides that shut off access roads throughout the spring and summer. Regular snow storms and treacherous, icy driving conditions in the winter served to isolate the region. Visiting this part of the world is not for the timid. Nature balanced the hazards with exquisite beauty including the spectacular aurora borealis phenomenon, more commonly known as the northern lights.

Soon after he purchased Mountain Shadows Lodge, Otis realized, begrudgingly, he had to share his sanctuary with strangers as he needed to pay his bills. His timing was good, and he capitalized on the increasing need for people to get away from it all. He found the concept funny as his experience was that most people brought all their stressors with them on vacation. Laptops, cell phones, children, parents, and, sometimes, so-called friends. He had witnessed a few friendships collapse over the years often fueled by the one-two punch of alcohol and bad weather. As for technology in the middle of mountains surrounded by a dense forest, it was unreliable at best. Otis also knew that guests sought out the lodge for many different reasons. Some truly wanted to run away and hide. Mountain Shadows was the perfect place to disappear.

Otis was blessed with a gift that had served him well. It helped him avoid problems as a school boy, as a young roughneck working on the oil rigs and later in life dodging overly enthusiastic middle-aged women looking for someone with whom to share the rest of their life. He married once, but the love they shared died many years ago. He gently, but firmly, declined all offers made by female guests. Otis's gift, or superpower as he thought of it, was his ability to spot trouble when he saw it and, as he walked toward the Jeep that just pulled up and almost hit a kid, he knew he was looking at it now.

After providing both Henderson kids with ice cream, Otis approached the three young men spilling out of a beat-up Jeep and onto the semi-circle driveway. He guessed they were in their early twenties, a demographic not always compatible with a peaceful mountain retreat experience. As duffle bags and cases of beer were stacked on the luggage trolley, two of the men started kicking an empty can at each other eventually sending it flying straight at the feet of Tyler Donahue, his summer student. Tyler bent down slowly and picked up the dented can and walked it to the recycle bin for beverage containers. Otis watched the three young men. No respect. That's what was wrong with the world, young people had no respect for other people, property or nature.

Otis extended his hand to the dishevelled young man, one of the passengers in the Jeep. The new arrival wore rumpled clothes and looked like a hippy from a bygone age, a trend that had made a resurgence lately in the hipster era. Otis approached and said, "Welcome to Mountain Shadows Lodge. That was a close call. See that it doesn't happen again." His tone caught the undivided attention of the young man.

"Sorry, man, it won't. I'm Logan. These are my buddies Carter and Ethan. Carter feels horrible about what happened."

A young Black man who was introduced as Ethan held up a makeshift cardboard sign that read *The Stagger Inn* with an arrow for directions. It was written in faint blue felt pen with ink long past its prime.

Otis said, "There's plenty of signage here. Hand it over, and I'll put it in the recycle bin." He confiscated the sign without resistance.

Otis wished he hadn't allowed these three college students access to his beloved Mountain Shadows. These entitled young men learned early that stylish clothes, a certain charm and perfect smiles would get them what they wanted. Women, jobs, a free ride. They were the kind of guests Otis hated. Binge drinking punks. Trouble. Otis knew it when he saw it, and it had just checked in for the long weekend.

Throughout the afternoon, Otis and Tyler welcomed a total of eleven guests comprising three groups and one single woman. Tyler thought it was weird and a bit sad to see someone check in on their own, but he understood the appeal of the place and hoped her stay was peaceful. The woman, Victoria, was the second to check in just after the family of four with a friendly dog.

Otis returned to the middle of the stone archway at the entrance of the lodge watching the last of the weekend guests arrive. A small purple hatchback filled with three young women, a blond, a brunette, and a red head, pulled up with music blaring Backstreet Boys hits from the nineties. The car was overloaded with luggage, some of it held together with duct tape.

"Are we late? Damn, we're always late." The young woman nodded to the man standing in front of her and checked her watch.

"Relax, Brooke, we're fine. Hello, I'm Jaclyn, and this is Brooke, the time police, and Cindy is over there, staring at those guys. Cindy! Hello, Cindy! Quit staring, they've noticed you."

"I don't believe it." Cindy whispered.

"Yeah, I know, we finally made it! Woo Hoo!" Brooke said, her eyes following Cindy's gaze to the other guests still outside, and she whispered, "Oh, hello, lover."

"Do you know them, Brooke?" Cindy asked.

The young woman labeled as the time police looked over at the men. She hoisted up her blue jeans that probably fit better a year or two ago. She lowered her sweatshirt to hide a multitude of unhealthy food choices. "Not yet, Cindy." A silly smile broke over her entire face.

"Can I help you with your luggage?" A young man approached introducing himself to the new arrivals as Tyler. He bent to lift one of the bags, but his hand was swatted away.

"Don't touch that," Cindy yelled.

"Whoa, sorry." Tyler jumped back, not used to being admonished for helping guests. "I was just trying to help you, it's my job. What have you got in there, a bag full of money? Must be something important." His laugh was nervous and shaky.

She shot him a dirty look. "I'll take this one," She extended the pull handle of the black case on wheels and pulled it bumping along the gravel onto the smooth concrete main entrance way of the impressive lodge. Stone pillars and glistening wood appeared throughout the structure. The natural smell of pine trees wafted through the entranceway.

The guests entered the building and, like others before them, made noises of appreciation.

"Wow," Logan looked around and nodded.

Brooke stood nearby and said, "It's beautiful, better than I hoped. Can you imagine what it looks like at Christmas time with all the snow and twinkling lights?"

Logan smiled at her, "It would be like a beautiful Christmas card."

"Are you two really talking about winter right now?" Jaclyn laughed. "I'm ready to change, put on a bikini, and dive in the lake. Okay, let's get our cabin keys, settle in, have the orientation they insist on, and get this weekend going."

Tyler began placing the remainder of the luggage on the trolley he provided. Otis helped, and soon the last arrivals made their way to the registration desk.

As the groups checked in, Otis slapped a smile on his face and went through the automatic process of receiving their required information, answered their many routine questions with information he had previously provided while silently counting to ten and biting the inside of his cheek. Otis waved his arms indicating directions to the pathways leading to the cabins and other amenities mentioning a full orientation would be provided within the hour. Soon, all of the expected weekend guests were checked in, excited to begin their vacations.

During registration, Tyler watched the guests closely. This study helped him decide how best to interact with them. Some liked the fun, familiar approach, while others wanted staff to remember their place. He learned the technique the hard way. Tyler mentally categorized the three groups as frat boys, wild girls, and what looked to him like a stressed-out family on the verge of falling apart. He saw tension behind the smiles of the parents, and their cute daughter looked anxious and annoyed at her little brother.

Tyler also saw before him a group of immature guys probably trying hard not to be grownups, fighting to recapture their fun high school days. Next, Tyler studied the young women and knew that this type of gathering could be a fun, wine-filled weekend or three days of built-up hostility, hard feelings, and regret. The family was interesting, the father looked like he wished he was part of the guys' weekend, and the mother watched her husband watching the guys. The kids will have a great time, but it was a toss-up about the parents. The lone middle-aged woman wasn't going to be a problem, and the family probably would behave, but Otis would want him to keep a close eye out for the younger guys. He could already tell they were rowdy, obnoxious and entitled, a bad combination. Tyler realized, he was likely more grown up and responsible than they were if first impressions were any indication. It was the guys' turn to approach the registration counter to provide their identification and put a credit card on file just in case of damage or leaving without paying their tab. Tyler wondered if he imagined that Otis hesitated as he handed over the cabin key.

Otis stated, "One key per group, please don't lose it."

Otis was about to turn away when he saw an expensive-looking, red leather wallet left on the front desk. He picked it up and waved it in the air.

"Is someone missing this?" he asked.

The guests turned in unrehearsed unison.

"That's mine." Her tone was accusatory, yet the mistake of leaving it behind was hers.

Cindy grabbed her wallet from Otis and followed the group past the stone fireplace with embers still glowing from the chill blasting fire of earlier that morning. The guests walked back through the high beamed foyer and semi-circle drive toward the path that led to the four cabins in a row.

The weekend had begun.

CHAPTER 4

In Cabin Four, the one farthest away from the main lodge, three women did their best to destroy the ozone layer directly overhead. Hairspray, bug spray, tanning spray, and perfume combined to create a noxious cloud.

They called themselves JUGS—Just Us GirlS—and changed into matching light pink tee-shirts with white lettering to announce their allegiance. JUGS membership consisted of Jaclyn Lee, Brooke Richards, and Cindy Elliott, secretly known as Cindy Yell-A-Lot, for obvious reasons. She was a complicated individual. Since high school, Cindy demanded an annual get together and, since she made all the arrangements, the other two found it was easier to just comply. One weekend a year seemed manageable. The gatherings were humble in the beginning, often gathering for pizza and beer, as no one had money. They eventually morphed into wine-tasting trips, beach vacations, and now a mountain retreat.

Cindy informed her friends that this trip had special meaning for her and that she had high expectations for the weekend. She didn't explain further and the others chose not to ask. The other girls kept their expectations low as Cindy was prone to exaggeration. She had the best meal, the worst cold, the sexiest boyfriend. Years ago, she wouldn't quit talking about her boyfriend, but Jaclyn and Brooke never met the mysterious man, never saw pictures, and eventually they began to wonder if he really existed.

Brooke and Jaclyn had their own plans for a fun-filled weekend, probably involving the couple of the guys they saw checking in ahead of them. Like always, they had a secret pact. They promised each other that Cindy would not get in their way of a good time.

The smell of coconut, mango, and vanilla wafted from the open patio door of their cabin onto the small deck facing the lake. A cluster of candles had been lit to get rid of stale air, and the combination was reminiscent of a perfume counter in a department store rather than a mountain getaway. While the modest kitchenette and living areas remained tidy, the small bathroom counter was stacked with makeup bags, blow dryers, and more hair products than an average salon.

"Hey, am I the only one who thinks that old dude is super cool?" Brooke asked.

"I think the exact same thing, sexy too," Jaclyn smiled. "What do you think, Cindy?"

Her friend was distracted, trying to find something in her over-stuffed, over-priced purse.

"Yeah, he's okay. You know, helpful, manly." Cindy agreed.

"I think it's his confidence. Being self-assured is extremely appealing." Jaclyn stated.

"I just know we are going to have a great time. The weather is gorgeous, those guys are hot, and I'm about to get the party started." Brooke opened a bottle of white wine and poured three portions into glasses she found in the well-stocked cupboard. She added what she hoped was fresh ice from the mini fridge freezer to the lukewarm beverage, gave it a swirl, and took a giant gulp.

The women maneuvered through three sets of brightly coloured carry-on sized suitcases with wheels to find a seat in the living room. The wheels were of no assistance on the uneven rustic pathways from the lodge to the row of cabins.

"Okay, who brought the Boner Award?" Brooke asked. The award which was actually a failed attempt at an abstract sculpture class during an earlier girls' weekend getaway. Intended to be a piece of art for Jaclyn's entrance table, it ended up looking like an impressive replica of male anatomy. From that trip onward, the idea morphed into making the accidental phallic symbol a coveted award for whoever did the most ridiculous thing on any of their trips. Each winner had to display it somewhere in their home for the entire year, explaining what it was and why it was on display to all who visited. Each of the women had won the prize more than once. Once Brooke forgot her passport and, thanks to her Mom bringing it to the airport, she just made the flight to Las Vegas. Another time, while on a very tame hike, Jaclyn, who has a poor sense of direction, got lost. Cindy got it for showing up an entire day early for a trip.

"I have it and I'm ready to go." Always the punctual one, Brooke placed the award on the fireplace mantle and joined the others on the deck.

"Well, we did it, ladies. Here we are at another JUGS reunion, Woo Hoo!" Jaclyn waved her friends over for a group hug, and they took a moment to acknowledge the individual and collective effort it took for them to get to where they were today. They met in college, each nervous and alone, and quickly recognized common interests in each other. Their friendship started when they were insecure students far away from home and strengthened as they evolved into strong, independent, career women.

"Thanks again, Cindy, for all the work you did." Jaclyn added.

"Well, if I didn't coordinate these trips, I'd never see you two." Brooke and Jaclyn had the most special bond, and Cindy was on the edge of the friendship embrace. It happens in groups of three, everyone is part of the trio, but one person is always gently nudged toward the outside. Cindy had always known it, always felt it, and genuinely didn't mind.

"You two go ahead." Cindy said pressing her fingers to her temples. She'd been uncharacteristically quiet since they arrived. She barely touched her wine.

"I'm trying to fight off a migraine, you know traveling days are always too much for me to handle. Maybe it's the altitude."

"That's awful. You did all the work to get us here, then a week ago you got a stomach flu and almost didn't make it. Now a migraine, poor you. Are you sure you can't come with us, Cin? Do you want us to check on you in a bit?"

"No, I'll probably sleep so it would be better if you just leave me alone. I'll be good in a little while. I'll join you later." She crawled into the big double bed in the room closest to the cabin's back door away from the lake. "It's so nice and quiet and shady in this room." She snuggled under the quilt and closed her eyes.

The twosome headed outside. They were used to their friend's whims and knew it was easier to go with the flow rather than fight Cindy's wishes. A litany of waiters, hairdressers, coffee baristas, and hard-working retail clerks could attest to the level of difficulty they experienced when they encountered the female nightmare with a curly, auburn ponytail. Classic good looks did not always equate with classy behavior, good manners, or even good intentions.

Brooke and Jaclyn headed toward the lodge. Cindy heard them talking, giggling, and then shrieking as a buzz of wasps swarmed them. Eventually, the only sound Cindy heard was that of two pairs of flip flops smacking in rhythm, fading away.

When she thought it was safe, Cindy got out of bed. She spit out the remnants of what used to be her fingernail. There was nothing she could do but wait.

CHAPTER 5

The Henderson family invaded the second cabin. They were like many busy families, overscheduled, sleep deprived, and in a constant, slow burning state of stress and anxiety. As parents, Alex and Nicola, did their best to ignore the symptoms of a family in crisis while in public, but, privately, the tension manifested in snide comments and sullen resentment. The kids felt the tension every day. They were unaware of the nature of the stalker's phone calls but were fully aware that something was wrong. This trip was for the kids, for their protection. The intent was for them to enjoy themselves in a beautiful setting where the only objective was to be safe and have fun.

    Nicola was warming to the setting and was determined to focus on what was most important to her—her family. She stood in the cozy bedroom of the cabin that would be their home for the next three days, at least. She unpacked their shared suitcase and put their clothes away, hers on the left and his on the right, just as she had done for fourteen years. Together they checked the locks on the windows and doors and determined they were adequate. She filled cupboards with packages of pretzels, nuts, and trail mix.

    Nicola dusted off her khaki shorts and put on a clean white V-necked tee-shirt and freshened what little make up she wore. With a splotch of sunscreen, a swipe of mascara, and a kiss of lip gloss she was ready for orientation. The extra effort was part of her life-long need to make a positive impression. She laughed at herself thinking the local grizzly bears weren't going to care if her hair was out of her eyes, but she secured it with a headband because she cared.

Nicola was exhausted from the lack of sleep since the note arrived in her mailbox, and it showed on her face. The hammock outside the cabin was calling her name, but she resisted the temptation. Instead, Nicola wiped the back of her neck with a cold, wet facecloth hoping it would jolt her enough to get through the afternoon without a nap. The hectic pace of last-minute organizing, packing, and other essential preparations for the unplanned escape made her wonder if it was worth it. She tucked the suitcase under the bed and joined her husband outside the kids' room. Some vacationers never bothered to unpack, just lived out of their suitcases, losing track of what was clean and what wasn't but, that was unimaginable to Nicola. She had a system for everything. Her mind didn't function otherwise.

"Why can't he sleep on the couch?" Kyra's whiny little girl voice always hit a shredded nerve with Nicola. "We'd both have more space, and it's highly inappropriate that I'm sharing a room with my little brother."

Alex looked at his wife, noticed the irritation on her face, and tried to lighten the situation. "Did you know it was highly inappropriate?"

"I had no idea." She played along.

Kyra continued. "The bunks are hideous, and there is no room for my stuff."

Her parents watched as she spread a white hand towel, brought from home, on the pine dresser and began the ritual of placing her toiletries from large to small, tall to short in an immaculate display. Creating order out of chaos was calming to the fourteen-year-old. Nicola knew where that trait originated.

Alex slung his arm around Nicola's shoulder. Together, they filled the doorway and watched their son on the top bunk line up his wilderness survival items on the wall shelf. He had a flashlight, a compass, a full reusable water bottle, a few granola bars, bug spray, sunscreen, and two action heroes.

Plus, he brought all his secret agent stuff like notebooks, a walkie-talkie set, and a mini recording device. There was lot to listen to in the forest. What his family didn't see was a box of wooden matches taken from their upstairs fireplace mantel along with a pocket knife, with a surprisingly long blade, which he found in the garage. Ben kept both items concealed in his backpack.

Ben had evolved from a super hero phase to an obsession with secret agents. His interest stemmed from a spy kit that a friend recently gave him for his eighth birthday. He examined everything with a magnifying glass, took copious notes on his family's conversations, and examined many discarded hand-written items he found in the trash. As well, he left clues for his parents to find, including their own toothbrushes. Alex and Nicola, and definitely Kyra, had had enough of the spy stuff. After this weekend, Nicola made a silent vow to somehow shut it down.

Nicola watched Ben and thought the activities hadn't even begun, and he was already having fun. How could her kids be so different? One basked in sunshine, the other had a perpetual storm cloud over her head that was ready to burst at any moment. Ben was a content soul, happy with whatever came his way. Kyra thought the world owed her everything and was behind on its payments. Nicola tried not to put a white hat on one child and black hat on the other, but it was a challenge.

Alex said, "Okay, guys, let's leave all this for now. Ben, grab Barnaby's leash and you and I'll take him for a nice, long walk."

"Cool," Ben jumped down.

Alex led the way, and Nicola warmed as she watched him. She knew she and her husband didn't match each other. She was sturdy, awkward, and intense. Even in the most expensive outfit she owned, she knew she resembled an unmade bed. He was strong, athletic, and casually sexy without even trying, but when he tried, he was something to behold. The faint hint of lines around his eyes only added to the appeal. It wasn't easy being married to a man so attractive.

She made a silent vow not to think of the stalker and to focus on everything right in front of her, all that really mattered. The advice she received was to disappear for a while, and, when the culprit was no longer able to get the reaction that fed his compulsive behavior, he or she would move on to the next target. She prayed that's what would happen. Nicola was okay most of the time, except when she thought about the Polaroid. Someone climbed a tree next her house, at considerable personal risk, in order to take a picture of her naked. It was impossible not to think about the kind of person who would go to such extremes.

Nicola knew they all needed this long weekend to reconnect instead of waving to each other in the driveway heading somewhere else. The kids didn't know about the danger, but she was sure Kyra sensed something was wrong. The next three days would be great for their family. They'd get to see each other without the barriers of technology and a calendar full of events separating them.

Nicola took a deep, refreshing breath and said, "Kyra, let's go for a quick swim."

"Sounds good, let's go." The smile on her face pleased her Mom.

A sharp trill sounded from the spruce trees overhead.

Kyra tilted her head, "Look at all the cute squirrels, Mom. Can I put some of my sunflower seed out for them?"

"I guess so. Use the plastic purple bowl that got melted in the dishwasher last week. I just brought it to build sand castles."

Kyra rolled her eyes and said, "Mom, we aren't four years old."

Nicola walked over to where she had unpacked their kitchen belongings. She wasn't sure what the cabin had that would allow her to make treats for her family. She over packed as everything she needed was in the cupboards and drawers of the small galley kitchenette.

Nicola handed the oddly shaped bowl to Kyra.

"Okay, listen, don't make a mess and keep it away from the sliding doors. I don't want any rodents to get in the cabin."

"Squirrels aren't rodents. They are too cute."

"Yes, Kyra, they are. Just ask anyone who has had them in their walls or damaged their roofs. They go into sheds and build their own homes, stockpiling acorns and using sticks and bits of tissue and whatever else they find to keep them warm each winter."

Kyra filled the bowl with sunflower seeds and sat down on the steps to see if there was any interest from the fuzzy, noisy, tree neighbours.

"Honey, they are probably full from eating everything Ben has dropped on the ground. I think it'll be a while before they come back. We'll check later. Why don't you leave a note telling Dad and Ben that we've gone for a quick swim? I already have my suit on underneath so I'll go ahead and take the beach towels and find us a good spot. I think I saw a small pad of paper on the nightstand in our room. Leave the note on the kitchen counter and let them know we'll meet them at the lodge for the orientation, okay?"

"Sounds good, Mom. I'll meet you down there in two minutes."

Kyra ran back to her shared room and shrugged out of her jeans and favorite gray hoodie to the bright blue bikini her Mom thought was a bit too mature for her. She pulled her blond hair into a ponytail, grabbed a water bottle, and searched for a pen. She scribbled a note on the pad that was on the nightstand her Mom mentioned and drew flower petals by her name. Kyra finished her note, making sure to include a heart with her signature, and then ripped the top page from the small pad of paper to place on the kitchen counter.

She froze.

Written underneath the top sheet of paper was a message in black, block letters.

DON'T LOOK UNDER THE BED

Kyra dropped her own note and watched as it fluttered behind the night table. She didn't know what to do, who to tell. Her Mom's been so stressed lately she couldn't worry her with this stupid, lame joke. It was a joke, she reassured herself. For her own peace of mind, she knelt down and quickly scanned under the bed. As she expected, there was nothing there. Not even dust. Kyra ripped the creepy note off the pad and put it in her backpack. She grabbed her towel and ran to the water as the cabin's screen door slammed behind her.

CHAPTER 6

In Cabin Three, the matching luggage was meticulously unpacked, and the luxurious toiletries were neatly arranged on the rustic bathroom counter. Just like in all the other cabins, there were two bedrooms but, in this cabin, the second one would remain untouched. Victoria stared at the glistening lake through the large living room window. The lake was like glass, perfect for water skiing or fishing or floating.

She almost didn't make it here. Half way into the journey, she wanted to turn around but the road was too narrow. There was no shoulder, no turn offs.

It was her own fault. How could she have thought this was a good idea?

She turned back from the view and looked at the empty cabin. She was here alone. A familiar ache gripped her and wouldn't let go. She shook herself and refused to give in to the dark thoughts that kept her company most days. She was here now, still unsure why. A mirror in the entrance captured her reflection. Older, but still her.

"Now what?" she asked herself.

CHAPTER 7

"Honestly, I thought that geezer was going to kick us out." Ethan laughed and, having just witnessed the destruction of his sign, was busy with its replacement. The guys were in Cabin One, by design, as it was closest to the lodge. It was also closest to where the staff stayed, in the addition next to the main building.

"This place is a disaster already, and we just arrived. How can it already smell like stale beer and ass?" Carter looked around the room with the key still in his hand and was amazed at the damage already done. The cabin living area was piled high with duffle bags, sports equipment, hiking boots, jackets, and two large coolers. Already the place was out of control.

Logan unpacked the grocery bags of snacks that contained a jumbo size bag of chips, peanuts in the shell, and beef jerky. Soon the kitchenette looked like his small apartment and already felt like home.

"Nice work finding this place, Carter." He grabbed a beer and opened the curtains to reveal an amazing view of forest, water, and mountains. The sliding patio door to the left, led out to a covered veranda. He slid the door open and with the cross breeze from the window on the opposite side, cool fresh air filled the room.

"Look, there's bunk beds, a double bed, and the couch." Logan observed. "Why don't we just rotate between the bunks and the couch and save the double bed in case Carter or I make friends with one of those lovely ladies checking in after us? Sorry, Ethan, I didn't see anyone who would capture your interest. The owner is too old, and already hates us, and the apprentice is too young."

Ethan shrugged, "Story of my life."

"Too bad, buddy. Grab another brewski before we go swimming. We need to make a toast to our adventure." Logan said as they each grabbed a frosty can of Molson's Canadian from the ice-filled cooler.

"I'll go first, to good friends." All three lifted dripping cans so cold they stung. One by one, they each contributed, the next was Ethan.

"To fantastic weather and a shit tonne of alcohol,"

It was Carter's turn.

"To an unforgettable, take no prisoners, balls to the wall, guys' weekend." He drained the can, belched and continued. "This trip is exactly what I needed. Work sucks. I may not go back."

"Yeah right, me either." Logan agreed, knowing it was bullshit. He grabbed the empties and threw them in the recycle bin provided. "Let's go hear all the rules and regulations, and then we can figure out how to break most of them. After the big lecture is finished, we can go do what we want, on our own. I don't plan to spend the weekend with seniors or kids or whiny, high maintenance women. We are going to do our own thing."

"Agreed," Ethan kicked off his footwear to change into sandals and threw his running shoe at Carter who ducked just in time.

"To a fantastic party-till-you-puke weekend," Ethan added and cracked another beer for each of them, and they raised the dripping cans in another toast.

"Let's go," he said.

CHAPTER 8

The covered deck off the main room of the lodge was spacious and inviting. During registration, guests learned of a welcome reception to provide a brief overview of the accommodations, activities, and general information that included a little bit of history of the lodge and a few comments on safety requirements specific to the area. Slowly, the guests appeared and took a seat on the deck facing the lake. The sunshine bounced little diamonds of light off the lake surface mesmerizing all who gazed upon it.

Before joining the others, Nicola was able to get a signal near the water and called into the police station for updates. She smiled when she heard Yvette's voice.

"Hillside Municipal Police Services, how may I direct your call?"

"Hey, Yvette, it's me."

"Nicola, I didn't know you were taking time off. I didn't see any paperwork." Yvette's comment was more of a teasing nature than an admonishment. Yvette often joked that it was she who ran the entire detachment, and they'd fall apart without her attention to detail, especially involving the necessary administrative requirements of modern life. Yvette was not included in the inner circle of those who knew of Nicola's stalker.

"I'm sorry, Yvette, it was a last-minute thing. Family time, you know." Nicola cringed. Yvette didn't know what family time was like as a middle-aged woman on her own. "Is the boss in, could you please put me through? I forgot to tell him something important before I left."

"Sure thing, Nicola, enjoy your time away."

Nicola smiled thinking of how Yvette was the one who always remembered staff birthdays and circulated a card and collected for a cake for all to enjoy. It was a wonderful day when Nicola surprised the receptionist by doing the same act of kindness for her and added a bouquet of flowers to celebrate Yvette's fiftieth birthday. The bewildered look on Yvette's face and her beaming smile was worth the extra effort.

"Lancaster here." Nicola jumped when the gruff voice of her boss answered.

"Hey, Glen, just checking in."

"Hi, Nicola. Nothing to report here. Surveillance, both in person and digital, is in place. Whenever possible, a patrol car cruises by your house. Nothing came from the names you provided. All deny having any contact with you recently. There's no evidence to the contrary. I know you're freaked out, but I'm hopeful the worst is over. We haven't caught him, yet. We will. Try to enjoy your getaway."

"I'm not sure that's possible, but I'll do my best."

As she ended the call, Nicola felt no relief. Stalkers chose their victims for a reason, however insane. A random smile in the grocery store, a slight or insult landing sharply, unrequited love, or obsession or jealousy. She knew stalkers were usually male by a four to one ratio. They often fall into three main groups: a former intimate partner, an acquaintance including a friend or relative, and, lastly, a stranger. Due to her expertise, she understood there were categories for each stalker including the rejected, the resentful, the intimacy-seeker, the incompetent personality, and, perhaps most frightening, the predator. Research indicated it is those who fall within the rejected and predator category who are most likely to harm their victim. What she didn't know was what category matched her stalker. She was terrified to think the picture appearing along with the note put her stalker in the predator category.

Unfortunately, even with all of her professional knowledge, Nicola now realized she may have unknowingly made countless mistakes dealing with her own situation. Something she said or did could have triggered feelings of obsession or rejection escalating to the point of stalking and increasing the potential for violence. She disregarded the anonymous phone calls at work and, eventually, disconnected her overnight answering machine knowing any victim could call 911 emergency services. The next day the first note arrived in the office.

With that note, Nicola knew the problem had escalated, and she took action following all the safety protocols. She told everyone in her inner circle. She informed those closest to her but only select members of senior management in the police detachment.

Her discussion with her children was a slightly sanitized version of the truth. Kyra was told there was an issue with somebody who was causing trouble, and it was related to her work. Kyra grasped the general essence of the situation when Nicola compared the situation to bullying without knowing who the bully was, and Kyra promised to be extra careful and not to talk to any strangers. Nicola then explained a little bit to Bennett, and, as a family, they established a safety code word that, if anyone approached either of them and didn't know the code word, they are to run away as fast as they can while screaming for help.

Ben picked the code word.

Barnaby.

Over the ensuing weeks, Nicola lost sleep, lost her appetite, and lost the feeling of safety she had taken for granted all her life. As a precaution, she changed up her routine and stopped going to her gym, stopped going for pampering appointments. Once, when she went to her regular hair stylist, she felt as though she was being watched through the huge salon windows the entire time.

"Everything okay?" A man's voice came up behind her.

Nicola jumped and almost dropped her phone in the sand by the shoreline.

"Hey, sorry, didn't mean to scare you." The handsome lodge owner backed up, took off his hat, and wiped his forehead with the back of his shirtsleeve.

"Hi, Otis, I was just lost in thought." They both walked up from the beach to the deck where people were gathering and Nicola caught sight of her son and their dog.

"Where's your father, Ben?" Nicola arrived on the deck and looked around for her husband.

"He told me to go ahead of him as he had to take a leak and headed into the trees. That was a while ago." Ben grinned when he heard other guests' chuckle.

"He left you alone?" Nicola could feel her temper rising.

"No, Mom, I was with Barnaby, and I knew how to get here. I have impressive navigational skills."

She smiled at her sweet boy and said, "So where is Dad now?"

"I'm right here, got a little lost." Alex appeared disheveled and out of breath. "One tree looks just like the other, go figure," Alex shrugged and climbed the steps to the deck while brushing pine needles off his golf shirt.

Logan stood up when he saw the family approaching.

"I apologize again for getting off to a bad start. It's great here, isn't it?" His smile was sincere, and Nicola decided to give him and his friends a second chance, but she wasn't over the near disaster.

"Looks like the bar is open. No one is driving for the rest of the weekend. Can I grab you a beer, wine?"

"It sure is great here, yes please, I'll have a beer and one for my wife too. Hey, I'm Alex, this is Nicola, Kyra, and Bennett. We're the Hendersons."

"I'm Logan Davenport, and that young, handsome man at the table over there is my friend Ethan Jordan. We're here on a guys' trip." The young men got up to shake hands and officially greet the newcomers.

"I enjoyed a few of those guys' trips in my younger years. They were fun, I barely remember what that's like." Alex laughed. No one else did. Logan handed out the beers, and Alex took a swig.

Nicola noticed the young driver she confronted earlier run up the staircase on the west side of the building.

"Sorry I'm late." He said, approaching the group and extending his hand. "Hey, I'm Carter. I had to run back to get some sunscreen. I burn like crazy. . . like melanoma crazy." Carter pointed to his white blond wavy hair.

He approached Ben and said, "Glad you are okay, buddy." He turned to Nicola and Alex.

"Again, I'm very sorry about what happened earlier." Carter reached down to pet the drooling dog and maneuver his cold nose away from his crotch.

"Hey, boundaries, dog, boundaries." Carter said, laughing and then asked. "So who is this creature?"

"That's Kyra, my sister." Ben replied and protected his ribs from Kyra's sharp elbow.

Carter did his best to choke back a laugh. "Uh. . . I meant the dog. What's his name?"

"He's Barnaby, he's my best friend. He won't bite you, unless I tell him to."

"Good to know. I love dogs. Hello, Barnaby." Carter crouched down and slowly presented his open hand upward in a gesture of friendship. The Labrador stepped forward, sniffed the hand presented, and could tell an ear rub was in his near future even if there was no treat offered. Barnaby accepted it and leaned against the man's leg.

"What's on your arm?" The little boy asked pointing to Carter's inner, left forearm.

"My tattoo? Oh, that's my good luck charm. It's my nickname Ace, like the Ace of Spades; it brings me good luck when I need it."

"How come the last letter looks crooked?"

"The guy was trying something new and kind of messed up but you can still read it, right?"

"Did you get mad at the guy because he messed up?"

"Nah, it's just a tattoo."

"Cool. Mom, can I get a . . ."

"No."

Carter smiled at Nicola and turned toward the young girl standing next to her beaming up at him.

"Are you as excited as your brother about all the fun things to do here?" Carter asked Kyra.

"Oh yeah, I can't wait." Kyra flipped her hair back and took a step toward Carter. Nicola looked at her wondering if that was a smile she saw on her face.

"I've never waterskied before, but I've always wanted to. I'm pretty athletic. I play volleyball, soccer, and basketball."

"You suck at basketball." Her brother said.

"Shut up, Ben. While we're out here, you do your thing and I'll do mine. Stay away from me."

"Okay, I don't care and I won't miss you."

To Carter, Kyra said, "I'm sure I'll be able to get up once I know a little more about it. Do you know how to waterski? Maybe you could teach me?"

Alex interrupted. "Whoa, kiddo. Carter doesn't work here, he's a guest too. I'll teach you." His offer was met with a scathing glare.

Carter looked at the girl and said, "We'll get you up on two skis at first, and then I'm sure you'll be able to slalom in no time." Kyra beamed, not exactly sure what that meant, but certain it would happen if this hot guy said it would.

"How about you folks?" Logan came over to stand beside the older Hendersons.

"I'm up for anything." Alex reached for a second beer from the bar set up on the outside deck.

Nicola answered for her husband. "Alex is always up for anything, the life of the party. The original Goodtime Charlie."

Alex, the life of the party, looked around and offered an awkward half-smile.

Nicola continued, "I, on the other hand, am looking forward to some fun, family time." There was a subtle warning to both men in the words delivered with a friendly smile. She kept the need to escape a psycho stalker to herself.

Nicola noticed two young women arrive from the lodge's deck entrance followed by the older woman named Victoria.

Ben held up a magnifying glass he pulled from his ever-present backpack and asked loudly from across the deck. "How come your shirts say JUGS?"

Everyone was silent.

The little boy walked his dog to where Brooke and Jaclyn stood slightly embarrassed but laughing along with the others.

Ethan added, "I was wondering the same thing, but I wasn't brave enough to ask." His smile lit up his face as he approached the women.

"It means this trip starts as Just Us GirlS but," Jaclyn added in a hushed tone as she leaned toward the young boy and said, "Between me and you, I'm glad boys are here too."

"Same here," Ethan said with a wink to the women as he stared at Alex.

Ben smiled, nodded, and walked away, oblivious to any undercurrents floating in the outside air.

Alex turned to Nicola and asked, "Is he pretending to be a scientist, a reporter, or a spy with that magnifying glass? I can't remember."

"It changes hourly. I can barely keep up with his imagination."

"I guess we should be happy that it keeps him busy and out of trouble."

"Yup, exactly."

Nicola shot a look at her daughter, all hormones and attitude. Then she looked back at her son and smiled. He was at the age where he thought his Mom had all the answers, could solve every problem, and could kiss every hurt away. If only that were true.

Logan walked over to Victoria and asked, "Can I get you something to drink? I think we are encouraged to help ourselves."

"That's right," Otis nodded. "Please make yourselves at home. If you need anything, let me know."

"I think I'll just have a coffee. I need a little boost of caffeine after my early start." Victoria said.

"I'll bring it over to you." Otis offered.

"Thanks."

Ethan approached Victoria, introduced himself, and sat down next to her. He took a large swig from a freshly poured can of beer and said, "Ah, heaven in a frosted glass mug."

Victoria saw him watching the young women. "They are all very beautiful, aren't they?"

Ethan paused, looked at the woman, and said, "As are you, madam. Now, shouldn't an elegant, sophisticated lady such as yourself be surrounded by champagne and caviar not beer and hot dogs?"

Victoria threw her head back and laughed. "You are too kind but, I'll have you know, I love beer and hot dogs. Also, I recognize a flirt when I see one." She stirred the cream in the cup of coffee Otis brought. "Sadly, I'm much too old for you."

Ethan's smile was almost as bright as the sun. "Oh honey, I have to be honest with you. I'm much more interested in Big Daddy over there." He nodded in Otis' direction.

Victoria's eyes widened as she followed his gaze and she smiled. "Well, best of luck to you, my new friend."

Nicola had also been watching Otis and couldn't help but stare at the man who looked as though he belonged on horseback at a cattle ranch, not in charge of a mountain resort. He had looks, swagger, and that intangible aura some men possess. Maybe her infatuation had to do with the fact that she and Alex hadn't connected on an intimate level in far too long. Nicola smiled to herself and thought Kyra might not be the only one with hormones out of control.

Nicola continued to watch the lodge owner move deftly behind the counter pouring hot coffee from a thermal carafe and adding just enough cream to make a silky, caramel-coloured beverage that Nicola wished she had ordered.

Ben turned to her and said, "Mom, do you think Barnaby will like it here?"

"Well, I think Barnaby will love being outside most of the day, and he'll love swimming in the lake. Remember, you promised to look after him if we brought him. That means feeding, walking and toweling him off so he doesn't bring sand and dirt into the cabin. Most importantly, cleaning up after him when he does his business." Nicola was grateful the lodge was pet friendly. Otis even suggested Barnaby could be tethered on a long leash to the wishing well so he could be outside if they went in the boat, or horseback riding or just needed a break. He could have both sun and shade from the nearby trees edging the entrance to the lodge. Otis already provided a metal bowl of water. It was obvious the man liked dogs. Nicola wondered why he didn't have one in this beautiful place. In that moment, she realized she hadn't thought about the stalker for quite a while. Maybe this place was the right destination for her and her family. Nicola noticed the orientation was about to begin and had her kids take a seat.

CHAPTER 9

Tyler Donahue skidded on the gravel as he rounded the corner from his bunkhouse that was attached to the opposite side of the main lodge. If he was late again, Otis would kill him. Tyler blamed his chronic lack of punctuality on the hard work, fresh air, and his life-long tendency to stay up way too late reading, online scrolling when possible, or doing nothing productive. At least he managed to throw on the navy tee-shirt with the lodge logo and the khaki shorts he was wearing that were only on day three. He hadn't showered and wished he had, as his unruly hair would not stay out of his eyes. A dip in the lake would soon solve both problems.

    Working at the lodge was Tyler's dream summer job. He grew up in the area and spent many summers fishing, hiking and exploring. He knew the location of all the ravines, the cliffs, and the caves. As kids, the area was a personal adventure-land for him and his friends. Now it was his workplace, one he needed in order to pay for any classes he hoped to register for in the fall. He was only sixteen but was already planning his future. He hoped he'd be able to work the next two summers at Mountain Shadows and then take a year to work full time prior to university. Some students chose to take a year off between high school and university. Many romanticized it, calling it a gap year, and often used the time for travel and debauchery. Not him.

Tyler had no choice but to work after he graduated and he hoped to make enough money each year to pay for as many courses as possible towards an education degree. He was great with kids, maybe he'd become a teacher. Tyler wasn't sure what he wanted to be when he grew up; he just knew he didn't want to worry about money and job security like his Mom and Dad. But that was before the drunk got into his car on a snowy night a few years ago, ending all his parents' worries and created all of Tyler's. With permission from his Grandma, whom he moved in with after the death of his parents, Otis took Tyler in for the summer, gave him room and board and a decent wage in exchange for his considerable hard work around the property. His Grandma ran a local horse stable and provided guided trail rides to interested guests of the lodge.

Now it was Tyler's job to remind the newcomers they were no longer in civilization. The mountains were spectacular, but the beautiful setting brought with it great risk. He would be sure to cover all the rules of Mountain Shadows Lodge but planned to take extra time explaining the truth about nature. Both the glorious and terrifying truth. Timid people should not visit this place; they should stay in their recliners with the remote control in one hand and a sugary drink in the other. Tyler knew this place could be terrifying.

He glanced over the group and did his own quick risk assessment of the new guests. The three guys would likely be more adventurous than the three girls and hoped he wasn't being gender biased. He was new to the job but not to the fact the guys could endanger themselves in the wilderness as easily as girls. He liked Victoria. She held his hand for an extra-long time when he greeted her, and he noticed she seemed sad. She was unlikely to venture too far away from the main area. He was particularly focussed on the family with young kids and planned to direct the safety part of his orientation to them. He needed to be super diligent keeping an extra close eye on the kids.

As he took a sip of water and cleared his throat, the summer student seemed slightly off balance and not all together organized as he referred to bullet point notes on a scrap of paper. The new guests were seated on patio chairs and seemed reluctant to pull their eyes away from the panoramic view of lake, forest, and mountains.

"Hi, everyone, I'm Tyler and, yes, I do have the best summer job in the world. Sure beats packing groceries or putting fries in paper bags or being paid to shovel anything."

Polite laughter trickled through the group.

"I've been asked to go over some of the basic information that we hope will make your time here extra special." He grinned and glanced toward Otis at the doorway leading inside the lodge, but there was no response.

"You should have received a package of material at check-in that will explain most things for you, and I'm available to answer any questions, just flag me down anytime." This offer was directed at the young women closest to him.

"I just want to highlight a couple of things, and then I'll let you get on with your weekend. You'll find it very peaceful here because it usually is peaceful. That's mainly due to the fact that cell phone and Internet access is intermittent at best, probably because of the trees. You may have noticed that already."

Tyler looked toward the young teenage girl scowling as she sat with her family and continued.

"But that's good, right? We have a landline in reception, but we ask that you only use it if you have an emergency. We encourage you to be offline this weekend. We have a basket in the lodge for you to store all your devices so that you can enjoy a technology detox.

"Breakfast is always buffet style with hot and cold choices. Lunch is casual and, if you would like, we can arrange a to-go brown bag meal as we want you out in nature enjoying a hike or a picnic. Tonight, dinner will be a barbecue style buffet with a couple of meat options, vegetarian options for you, and lots of side dishes and salad. If you provided any special dietary needs when you registered, we have made all the necessary arrangements. After dinner, we hope to have a campfire at the beach with a few tasty goodies provided. If you have any other dietary requests, we will do our best to meet your needs. Any questions?"

There were none.

Nicola noticed the slight shake in his hands as he held his notes and a bit of a quiver in his voice. Tyler was clearly trying really hard to look like he wasn't trying at all.

"I'll just mention one or two highlights of the area. One of my favourite things here is the outdoor shower." Tyler pointed down the hill toward the beach.

The guests got up to take a look and jostled for position. They all wanted to see where he was pointing and rested their eyes on the cedar wood of the outside solar shower. It looked like a little log cabin without a ceiling and included an extended cedar base. Next to it was a rain barrel to catch all the water. The enclosure was just big enough to turn around in, and there was a black bag hanging above with a nozzle pointing downward.

"Look at those blue eyes," Brooke whispered to Jaclyn indicating Carter as they hung back from the others.

"Quit it, he's too perfect. Too gorgeous, those types are a nightmare, always hogging the bathroom mirror." She laughed.

"Oh, like you'd know," Jaclyn said, "He's a step up from the last creep you dated."

Brooke lowered her sunglasses slightly and said, "I have to admit there is something wonderful about staring at hot men on a hot summer day."

Jaclyn shivered involuntarily. "Oh my God, you need a boyfriend. You can feel something in the air besides the scent of suntan lotion. I think it's the vibrations of sexual tension. It's going to be a good weekend." The two women collapsed in a giggle session.

The women watched as Carter listened intently to Tyler's comments and reached back to offer Victoria his hand as she navigated through the outdoor furniture to get a better view.

"Although you can heat water a variety of ways, we choose to do it old school. The bag you see up above is called a bladder," Tyler said pointing upward.

"Ewww, gross," Cindy said as she made an appearance and walked up the steps, while rubbing her temples, to join the group.

"Hello, again. Welcome. Yeah, not a very nice name, but the warmth it generates from the sun to heat the water creates the most heavenly shower you'll ever experience. Everyone is welcome to use the outdoor shower and, of course, you have a regular one in your cabin. We gather rainwater in the barrel over here next to the shower and fill the bladder with it. We have a screen lid on the barrel to keep out leaves and debris. You have to wait a little while for the sun to heat it up. In the summer time that takes an hour or two so it's best to plan ahead. Consider it a spa treatment that you book an appointment for, there's a list at reception to book your day and time, it is well worth the wait. Just never forget to fill it up after your shower or you will hear about it from the next guest in line. I'll monitor it as well. I mean, not you showering, I won't monitor that, just the water situation." Tyler's cheeks flushed and he stopped talking.

Nicola looked at the beautiful, tranquil oasis and wondered if she'd be able to enjoy an outdoor shower. She'd definitely need Alex to be nearby in order for her to feel safe.

"I'm thinking two of us could fit in there and I don't mean you," Jaclyn continued to whisper to her friend.

Brooke stifled a laughed and gave her friend a gentle push, "Keep dreaming and listen to the young guy. We might miss something important."

"Like you said, there are easier ways to heat the water, right?" Logan asked.

"Yes, of course, we could use propane or electricity but we're all about nature here."

"That's awesome." Logan nodded, thinking the kid seemed to be all about nature, and perhaps not so much about showering.

Tyler continued, "Don't worry about privacy as no one will see you. One more thing. We ask that you all be respectful of your surroundings. We provided refillable containers of biodegradable shampoo in your bathrooms so please be kind to the environment and use that shampoo."

"Oh wow." Jaclyn looked toward the water and put her hand to her face to shade her eyes. "I've always wanted to wash my hair outside with fresh, cool water while standing in the sunshine."

"Funny," Logan lowered his voice so the kids couldn't hear. "I've always wanted to watch a beautiful woman wash her hair outside with fresh, cool water while standing in the sunshine."

"Well now, this might be your lucky day." Jaclyn giggled and caught up with the group.

Nicola knew that shower was among the first on her activities list, and she didn't even care who saw her. She just wanted to look up at the trees and then blue sky and mountains, with their peaks covered in snow, even in summer. They seemed touchable. Treetops, mountain tops, and sky. Nicola felt her shoulders slowly sink downward from her ears. She felt safe here. Her tension lessened and she looked at her family. They looked happy.

Otis spoke up to add, "There is a waterfall not too far from the hiking path. I must make it clear, the waterfall and the area surrounding it, are completely out of bounds. Do not consider using the waterfall area as a shower option. The rocks are extremely slippery and the area is treacherous. If you go near the falls, it will be considered trespassing, and you will be asked to leave Mountain Shadows Lodge immediately."

The stern tone in his voice left no doubt that Otis would follow through on the threat if needed.

Tyler continued, "Just a reminder about the large basket behind the reception desk. It's for your cell phones and tablets and anything else you'd like to break free from in order to experience an authentic digital detox. I assure you the items will be locked up if no one is at the desk or in the office and, of course, this is strictly voluntary. Guests do find it adds to their relaxation and enjoyment of their time in the mountains. Trust me, all of the emails and demands will either have been handled by someone else or waiting for you after the weekend. It's your call."

Ethan leaned over to the three women and whispered, "A waterfall sounds like a perfect place for a photo op. I'll surrender my phone, but I'll keep my digital camera handy. Let me know if any of you gorgeous women care to have a photography session." Ethan shrugged when the women didn't respond.

"We recycle as much as we can, you'll see the receptacles throughout the area. You can put your beer cans in as well." He watched the young guys replace their beverages.

"Victoria, would you like some wine now?" Carter asked.

"No thanks, I'm good with coffee. It's a little early for me." She smiled up at him.

"Maybe I can get Otis one, I'm trying to get on his good side after our rocky start."

"He might decline as he's on duty right now. Maybe you can mend fences another way."

"You're probably right. Oh, well, I'll think of something."

Tyler took a deep breath and referred to his notes.

Ethan raised his hand and asked in his raspy voice, "Hey, Tyler, I heard some weird stuff has happened at this place."

"Yeah, I heard the same thing," Brooke added in a voice no stranger to late nights and cigarettes. "People have gotten lost, or hurt, or worse. We are kind of stuck out here on our own. I guess danger is part of the plan when the journey involves hairpin curves, with a wall of granite on one side and a gorge you can't even see the bottom of, on the other."

"Logan, have we ever met before?" Nicola approached the tall lanky man.

"Nope, not that I remember."

"Hmm, you look so familiar. I just can't place it." Nicola shook her head.

Alex was standing beside her. He leaned in grabbing her waist and murmured in her ear, "I think the reason he looks familiar to you is that he looks like Shaggy from Scooby Doo."

Nicola's jaw dropped and she looked at the lanky, scruffy, disheveled young man wearing clothes a bit too big for him and said, "That's it. That's where I know him from," Her shoulders started shaking as she and her husband fought back laughter trying not to interrupt Tyler.

Nicola looked at the woman who walked to the back of the group. She changed from her arrival outfit and was now dressed in black yoga pants and a pale yellow, V-necked tee-shirt. Her red hair was in a high pony tail, and Nicola thought she introduced herself as Cindy. She could ask her husband; he probably knew her name.

"Oh, I think you're referring to the folklore that's been passed down from generation to generation. It makes it more appealing if there is something not quite right about a place. I suggest you just ignore anything you've heard and apply common sense during your stay here. Again, everything is fine here. If you follow my instructions, you won't have any problems. Whatever you do though, don't go into the forest alone, and especially don't go in there at night. It gets really dark in the mountains."

"There is one more very important matter I must bring to your attention. Again, I'm sure nothing will happen, but I have to remind everyone that we are in the wild and there are animals everywhere. This is their turf; we are the intruders. There are mountain lions, mountain sheep and elk, and moose and bears. . . oh, we have lots of bears. . . brown bears, black bears, and the occasional grizzly bear. You'll likely smell them just before you see them. The best way to describe it is that bears often smell like hot garbage. You'll never forget the aroma. If you see a bear, don't make eye contact, don't go near them, don't feed them, and, whatever you do, don't get between a mama bear and her babies. Oh yeah, and don't run because they can run faster, and climb a tree quicker, than you can."

"Geez, that's a long list of things not to do. What is it that we should do?" The pretty Asian woman named Jaclyn asked.

"Play dead." Otis's booming authoritative voice from behind the group made everyone jump and turn his way. Both his arms were crossed and his slim, booted, blue jeaned legs were crossed at the ankle as he stood leaning on the doorframe. He nodded for his protégé to continue.

"Yes," Tyler continued, "Play dead if you are on the ground, but, if you are walking, back away slowly without making eye contact. No sudden moves. The goal is to remove yourself from the situation. If that doesn't work, then the opposite approach is recommended. Try making yourself appear as big as possible and make loud noises. That could save you. Or not."

Otis added, "Bears are primarily omnivores, they like berries and fish. I'm sure you've all seen videos of bears catching salmon as they swim upstream. Look, bears are intelligent, magnificent creatures. Black bears rarely attack without provocations. Grizzlies, however, can be a challenge on occasion. In my opinion, grizzly bears are just regular bears with anger issues. You can tell the difference as grizzlies have a hump on their back. Bears are in this region, it's their home." He pointed to the group. "You are the visitors. I ask that you respect that fact."

Seeing the fear on some of the faces, Tyler added, "Don't worry, like I said, I'm sure everything will be fine. This weekend is about being back to nature and that could include bugs, rough terrain, wildlife but also lots of fun with water activities and trail rides and nature hikes. You'll have a wonderful time; we just ask you be smart about it."

Victoria turned to Nicola and gently suggested, "I can see what a great Mom you are, but I feel I have to say to you, don't take your eyes off your kids, especially the young one. Like Tyler said, a lot can happen out here." Her brows were furrowed, and Nicola could see the orientation had worried this woman. That, along with the close call in the driveway. Nicola wasn't offended by the comment as she saw the genuine sign of concern, not judgment, on the older woman's face and heard real concern in her voice.

"No worries there, I watch them both like a hawk." She smiled reassuringly. "As far as Ben's concerned, he's a good boy really and listens to me, most of the time." She and her son shared a smile. Ben was leaning against his mother, trying not to squirm but obviously bored.

Victoria smiled back at both her and Ben.

As Nicola gave Ben's shoulders a squeeze, she watched Victoria and wondered why the woman was so interested in her family and, most of all, why she wasn't here with hers.

CHAPTER 10

"Well, that's my overview. Thanks for paying attention everyone," Tyler concluded as they returned to the deck. "I've posted an updated copy of, um, I don't want to call it a schedule because we are all over scheduled, but a list of activities and options of things to do here. It's on the bulletin board encased in the glass cabinet on the wall outside the main entrance. You may have seen it when you arrived. It's kind of like an old-fashioned version of social media. You can leave messages for each other and you might want to watch that space for any notices that come up. I might even throw in a joke of the day. Stay tuned.

"Alex, what activities do you think the kids would like?" Nicola steered her husband off to the side of the group.

"Kyra would love horseback riding and I think Ben would too."

Nicola let out a sigh, "Good, I agree. With all that's happening, my nerves couldn't handle them doing anything too risky."

"Any updates?"

She shook her head.

Nicola grabbed Alex's arm as they quietly discussed whether they'd let the kids go white water rafting or ride an all-terrain vehicle. The other option was the quiet trail ride on horses that were used to novice riders. Everything sounded dangerous to Nicola, but she no longer trusted her own judgment. They decided to talk about it with the kids later.

Tyler spoke, "Now, snacks and drinks have been set up on the buffet table at the far end of the deck," the rest of the sentence was lost in the sounds of scraping chairs and the excitement of seeing Otis setting up his special welcome cocktail, The Avalanche. A mini mountain of crushed ice was placed in tall glasses with a rum-based punch cascading downward filling it with a concoction that tasted refreshing and had been the undoing of many guests. A nonalcoholic version was provided to the kids. It was a hot afternoon and a cold drink was appreciated by all.

Logan filled a plate with cheese, grapes, and crackers from a plastic wrap covered charcuterie board before he joined his friends. He swatted the air with his free hand as though conducting an orchestra. Wasps and flies were also fans of exquisite mountain scenery, secluded resorts, and delicious happy hour snacks.

Brooke leaned over to Jaclyn and said, "Look at that beautiful wavy hair. He's a bit rough looking but still. . ."

"Stop it. Guys are a distraction," Jaclyn said.

They watched Logan as he wiped the condensation from his glass and then dried his hand on his jeans. Both women stared at the man across the deck from them until he looked their way and smiled, dimples clearly visible from a distance. They both took a sudden interest in the activities list just handed to them by Tyler.

At the edge of the deck, Otis surveyed Tyler as he answered a few questions and chatted with each guest. The kid had done well and had an easy charm about him and a good work ethic, a rare and admirable trait.

Tyler approached Victoria and took a moment to sit with her to ask what activities interested her.

"I'm not really a white-water rafting kind of gal. I don't ever go in the water; it terrifies me so I think I'll pass." She smiled.

"Oh, that's too bad. It really is fun. Is there anything that appeals to you?"

"Just being here is a major accomplishment for me, Tyler." She looked down and rubbed her hands together.

"Yeah, I hear you. Life is very busy, I'm glad you chose to take a break and spend the weekend. I look forward to talking to you again."

"I'm going to go white water rafting," Ben announced.

His mother raised her eyebrows at him and wasn't sure that would happen. Her son, ever the daredevil. Nicola repeated, "We'll see about that, Bennett. No promises."

Tyler continued with the last portion of the welcome orientation.

"As you see, how you spend your time here is up to you. It can be adventurous with white water rafting or it can be relaxing on the lake in a canoe or going for a trail ride. If you aren't used to horses, don't worry, my Grandma runs the trail ride program and has beautiful, calm horses who are very used to novice riders."

"Not I," Ethan announced formally, "If it doesn't have an ignition that I can turn on and off, I'm not riding it."

Tyler laughed. "That's okay, I'm sure we'll find something you like. I have one more item that requires your participation and then you'll be free to explore the property. I've developed an ice breaker game that helps us get to know each other a bit more and I ask for all of you to participate. It's informal. I'll ask a question, and we'll go around and you can answer any way you like, there are no wrong answers."

He looked up at the faces. One of the guys, Carter, cracked his knuckles and the guy named Ethan stretched his legs out. Cindy crossed her legs and was busy exerting her energy with an aggressive ankle bobbing exercise. The rest of the guests seemed calm and chill. No one stood up and left so Tyler took that as a good sign.

"Here we go. First question, what song best describes you?" It took a moment before the guests came up with their answers.

"Who is going to be the brave one to go first?"

One of the young women who was holding a glass of merlot, raised her hand.

Jaclyn started by saying, "*Red, Red, Wine*." Everyone laughed and Tyler could have kissed her for breaking the ice to start the ice breaker. He could kiss her for a number of reasons.

"*I Fought the Law and The Law Won*," Ethan declared and explained. "I tried to get out of a speeding ticket, didn't work."

How about "*Lying Eyes*?" Cindy said as she joined the group and sat by Jaclyn who leaned over and asked, "Feeling better?"

Cindy shrugged. There was no explanation provided.

Brooke offered, "Considering the amount of chips I just ate, I'm going with *Fat Bottomed Girl*s."

"*No Regrets*." The answer came from Carter. "That's how I try to live my life."

"Good one," Alex gave him the thumbs up. Nicola rolled her eyes behind his back.

"*Crazy*," Nicola smiled, "If you looked at the activity calendar on our fridge, you'd understand."

The remainder of guests offered up a few other songs, but it was clear everyone wanted to have some time on their own.

"Okay, we'll do one of these little exercises around meal time and before the weekend is over, you'll know your fellow guests very well. Thanks everyone. See you this evening for dinner. It's time for me to get back to my other duties. I'll meet you here for our evening meal. Any questions before I go?"

The next few minutes was spent covering minor questions about the facility and area. Soon the groups departed to their respective cabins and their afternoon plans.

CHAPTER 11

A short while later, Tyler returned to his spot at the edge of the deck by the wood railing with the majestic mountain range as his backdrop. The deck faced south and the sunshine warmed it, but, once the sun disappeared, the chill would be felt within minutes no matter how warm the temperature was during the day.

"I hope you all had a chance to settle in and look around." Murmurs were affirmative. "We offered the reception earlier as a chance for you to meet other guests, ask any questions, and, most importantly, for you to begin your peaceful transition into vacation mode. I have heard from a few of you who are not too happy that the cell phone reception and Internet access is virtually nonexistent. You can sometimes get a signal by the beach or if you make your way back to the main road, but that's a bit of a hike. Emergency calls can be made and received at the main lodge. As I suggested earlier, I encourage you to take advantage of no phones, no screens, and to just enjoy nature. Weather permitting, this outside area is where most of the meals will be served. Some will be buffet style; others will be plated services. Tonight is different. Tonight we are having a hot dog roast on the beach. Our experience is that the first night guests are tired from travel and just want a quick, relaxed meal, so please follow me, everyone. I've set it all up for you with a picnic style meal with all the trimmings. We are lucky we are still able to have a bonfire by the lake. It's been so dry here I thought there might be a fire ban issued but, not yet. Having the fire on the sand, near the water, makes it very safe. I hope you're all hungry. Each night after dinner, weather permitting, we'll be able to gather on the beach to make s'mores or mountain pies. I'll show you how to make those later tonight."

Logan spoke up. "I brought my guitar if anyone wants to lead a sing along. I'm not a great guitar player, but I can pluck my way through something you might recognize." His words were directed at Tyler, but Logan's smile was aimed solely at the young women.

Everyone followed Tyler and Otis down the curving, sloping path barely visible amid bush and branches that led to the beach. The air was cooler, typical of the mountains, and Nicola was glad she brought light jackets for herself and the kids. Alex never felt the cold, and it was well-known among their group of friends, the more beer Alex consumed, the less clothes he needed.

Tyler walked confidently down the slope and shouted over his shoulder, "Be careful the tree branches don't poke you in the eye and watch out for the tree roots. Many toenails have been lost due to those nasty tree roots."

"Too late," Nicola added and looked at her big toe nail that seemed to be lifting up from the nail bed and the surrounding skin. It continued to display a kaleidoscope of purple shades.

The others heeded his warning, holding the narrow branches back for the person behind them who then returned the favour for the next guest.

Tyler faced the group.

"It's time for our second ice breaker." He heard an anonymous groan but chose to ignore it. The group stopped brushing the leaves and sand from their feet and listened.

In a quiet, serious tone Tyler asked, "This question is one of my favourites. The answers it generates are so cool. Ready? What would you do if you weren't afraid?"

"Afraid of what? I don't get it." Kyra asked.

"Um, consequences, I guess. What would you do, in life, if there were no consequences?" Tyler responded.

No one answered.

"C'mon there's got to be something you've always wanted to do, to get away with, a big risk you want to take but won't allow yourself to." Tyler looked at each guest, but no one volunteered an answer. His eyes landed on Ben who broke out into a smile with the beginnings of new teeth that barely fit his mouth.

"I'd go bungie jumping. I saw a video of it online. I think it was from New Zealand. They do an indoor one at the mall by our house, but it doesn't look the same. I'd want to jump from a bridge and be upside down when my head touched the water."

Victoria gasped. The others turned to her but said nothing.

"That's a cool one, buddy, I think it sounds awesome." Tyler smiled at the eight-year-old, gave him a high five, and then glanced at the boy's parents who didn't seem to share the same level of enthusiasm.

"Well, my thing is kind of the same. I've always wanted to sky dive." Carter announced. "There's just something about taking a leap of faith into nothing but air that appeals to me."

"That sounds like exactly your kind of thing, Carter." Ethan said. To the others he added, "He's a bit of a risk taker. For me, I guess I'd go zip lining like they do in the rainforest areas of Costa Rica, going from one mountain, zipping over a valley, to the next mountain. The workers catch you on incredibly small, and slightly decrepit, stands nailed in the trees and standing on them looks as risky as the zip line ride itself. I think it would feel like I'd be sort of flying but with a cable attached. Yeah, that would be more my speed." Ethan added. "You have something to hang on to and you can see the finish line, most of the time. And, you can hang upside down on the jungle ones and that appeals to me. I guess I'm still a bit of a kid, like Ben." The group laughed at his easy charm.

"What about you, Alex? What would you do?" Tyler asked.

"I'd quit my job and sail around the world." Alex had a ready answer.

"Cool, Dad, can we come?" Bennett asked as Nicola wondered if the family would be invited along on the fantasy sailing trip. "Oh, of course, buddy." Alex responded. "We'd all go."

Tyler continued with his roundtable question. "Kyra, what would you do if you weren't afraid?"

"I'd be a rock star, but I have stage fright."

"Nicola?"

"Me too, a rock star sounds good."

"Mom, you're too old."

"Well then, Kyra, I'd be an old rock star, there's a few of them around, you know." Nicola looked over to the young woman standing next to her.

"I'd quit university. I'm your classic perpetual student not knowing what they want to be when they grow up. I'm taking summer classes and the workload is killing me." Brooke stated.

"I'm the opposite," Victoria smiled as it was her turn and added, "I'd go back to school and study everything."

Victoria smiled and turned to Cindy, the young red-haired woman on her left, and heard her whisper, "I'd tell the truth."

"Pardon. What did you say?" Tyler asked, but there was no response.

Cindy was silent for a moment. She took a big swig of wine from her own turquoise to-go beverage container that she hadn't set down since orientation. She looked around at all the guests.

"Well, you know how fake people can be, they call it little white lies when they give a compliment they don't mean, but I believe in speaking the truth. That's it. I'd be truthful."

Jaclyn and Brooke shared a perplexed look. They'd never known Cindy to hold back on what she thought, ever.

"I'd make a lot more bad decisions if I wasn't afraid." Logan started laughing and shook his head. "Bad decisions make for great stories."

"Cheers to that, my friend." Ethan clanked beer cans with him.

"We are all just one bad decision away from disaster." Cindy looked at the two men.

"If you say so, pretty lady." Carter shot a flirty smile in her direction. "On second thought, you're right. Trouble can show up anywhere, but I'm usually the guy who goes looking for it. I'll probably make a few bad decisions this weekend. Don't worry, people, nothing too crazy. And I'm counting on my guys to get me out of it." Carter guzzled what was left in the can.

Nicola felt a shiver run down her spine. These young men were reckless.

A low, guttural sound came from the nearby bushes, its volume growing louder. The guests looked at each other and then at Tyler. He looked back at them, his eyes wide.

Everyone remained still. No one made a sound.

Except Barnaby.

Alex tightened his grip on the dog as the lab barked, his teeth bared. He tugged on his leash to be free.

Nicola was terrified. She looked at Alex.

"It's him." Her anguished cry startled everyone.

"Who?" Kyra asked. She saw terror on her Mom's face and ran to her side.

Out of nowhere, a mangy haired, four-legged figure darted from behind a large rock, past Tyler, and disappeared into the forest.

"Holy shit!" Cindy slurred.

"Fuck me." Logan yelled. "Oops, sorry, I forgot the kids were here."

"Geez Louise! What the hell was that? It looked like a German shepherd, was it a stray dog?" Jaclyn stood up ready to run inside the lodge even though the animal was not near her.

"It's only a coyote. He smells the food." Otis said. "Yeah, they do look like dogs, and wolves, they're related. You'll hear them howling at night. They get pretty loud but don't worry. As long as you don't corner them or startle them, they'll leave you alone. They are more afraid of you than you are right now. Remember to not leave any garbage or food out at night. You may end up with a lot of visitors like coyotes, bears, raccoons, even skunks."

"Yikes, be careful, kids. Do not go out exploring on your own." Alex looked at his two offspring. His voice was unusually firm and both kids nodded.

"Right, that's enough of that. Food's ready. Who's hungry?" Tyler said, snapping a pair of barbecue tongs in the air. Nicola watched him and could tell by his fast talking and shuffling from one foot to the other that he remained nervous. Nicola wondered why.

A summer barbecue buffet of hot dogs, hamburgers, beans, corn on the cob along with both a potato salad and a tossed green salad greeted the guests. They were invited to line up with their plates and to pile on the food. Wine and beer were served by Otis behind a make shift picnic table serving as a bar and lively music played, encouraging impromptu dance moves and singing. The portable camp table was large enough for all the food. The casual ambiance encouraged people to move around to the canvas chairs with their plates balanced on their knees, and they mixed and mingled and soaked up the last of the sunshine as it set over the mountain range. Night was setting in, and the bonfire was ignited to combat the chill.

"C'mon, kids, let's take a bathroom break. Alex, we'll be right back, keep an eye out for us." Nicola said. Victoria followed them up the hill.

"Good idea, I have to pee." Cindy announced. Brook and Jaclyn accompanied their tipsy friend.

"So, Otis, tell us about yourself." Logan spoke up. "When did you first visit this beautiful part of the world?"

Otis paused long enough before answering that it made Logan wonder if he had said something wrong, maybe got too personal.

"I first visited Mountain Shadows many years ago and found that I just couldn't leave. I made arrangements to buy the place shortly afterward, and I've been here ever since."

"You married?" Ethan asked.

Otis turned to look him in the eye.

"I was, I'm on my own now. I've found I'm quite good at it."

"Any kids?"

"One. Sam." Otis turned his back and continued clearing up.

Ethan continued. "I just ask because that Victoria is a nice lady, and I think she's probably close to your age. She's a heck of a lot better looking than you and she's definitely out of your league. But you never know, she might take pity on you and you might have a shot."

Otis raised one eyebrow and glared at him in warning, but Ethan could tell it was lighthearted.

"Did you see that gorgeous vehicle she arrived in? She must have some bucks. I think she's single too, just saying."

Otis turned from cleaning the grill with the barbecue brush in his hand and said, "Look guys, I agree, Victoria is a good-looking woman, but I'm very content with my life. Besides, who would put up with me now, so that's enough of your lame attempt at matchmaking. Not another word. Got it?" The men nodded and Otis turned back to cleaning the grill. Alex stood nearby watching the path his family took up to the cabin. A few minutes later, the group returned from the cabins, joined by Tyler. As the others settled in at the campfire, Ben walked over to his mother and father and leaned in close.

"Dad, do you know a kid died here a long time ago? I bet a coyote ate them."

"Who told you that?" Alex frowned and faced his son.

"Nobody told me, I just heard it. It happened a long time ago."

Eavesdropping again, Alex thought. "Well, if it's true, that's really sad, buddy. That's why we tell you never to go exploring alone. Make sure you listen when we tell you to wear a lifejacket in the boat and never go near the lake unless Mom or I are with you. Absolutely no swimming on your own. Got it?"

"Yeah, yeah," Ben picked up a stick and drew another BB, for Bennett and Barnaby, in the sand at the edge of the lake.

"I mean it, Ben, and get away from the lake." Alex rarely used his stern voice.

"Okay, Dad, chill." Ben said as he returned to the campfire.

"Supper was great. What's for dessert?"

"Ben, your manners," Nicola raised her eyebrows at him. The wilderness was bringing out his inner animal, and it didn't need much convincing.

Tyler approached and said, "Actually, Ben, we have a special treat for dessert and guess what? You and everyone else can help make it. We are going to make a dessert called mountain pies so, if it's okay with your parents, why don't you follow me and we'll get it set up." Tyler carried a large tray with a loaf of bread, canned apple pie filling, butter, and cinnamon.

"Okay, but I hope they are a lot different than cow pies cause I know what they are, just saying." Ben hopped down and got both a nod of the head and a thumbs up from his parents to go with Tyler back to the lodge.

"Straight there and back, Ben. And don't be gone long." Alex shouted after his son.

"I'll go with him, Dad. Hey, Tyler, you have a lot to carry, I'll help you." Kyra set her pop down and slow jogged to catch up with Ben and Tyler before anyone could protest.

"Do you need help, Otis? I'm happy to help out. You seem to be doing everything. No extra staff around?" Victoria asked, hoping it didn't sound like a criticism.

"Oh no, you are a guest here. Tyler and I have it all under control, but thanks anyway. Why don't you join the others," he nodded to the campfire area and disappeared up the hill probably to fill the industrial dishwasher she'd seen earlier. She turned to look at the group gathered around the campfire. When she turned back to Otis, he was gone.

"Okay then," she said under her breath, to no one.

Victoria heard two of the women offer to help gather more wood for the fire. Brooke and Jaclyn approached the tall, wide display of chopped wood stacked against the side of the deck covered with a tarp. Without being asked, they each picked up an armful of logs. Victoria liked their initiative and willingness to help. Jaclyn, the smaller of the two, had a stack twice the size of the bigger girl, Brooke. She was deceptively strong.

The two women brushed the pieces of bark off their sweatshirts and joined the others around the stones. Dusk was settling in, and the cool air was filled with the crackling sound of dry kindling.

The three guys returned to their chairs and leaned in to each other.

Ethan nodded in Victoria's direction as she made her way down the slope. "I'm just wondering what the hell a woman like that is doing here in this place. It makes no sense. She looks as though her days should be filled with trips to fancy stores and getting her nails done, not swatting mosquitos and black flies at a rustic location."

Carter glanced over at Victoria and sighed, "Yeah, I get it, she doesn't fit in, not like the family. Those kids look like they are having fun."

Logan added, "I guess everyone needs a little break from their routine, even if it's a high class, rich lifestyle. Who cares? All that matters is that we have a blast."

He shook his head and said, "She just doesn't belong here."

Logan's eyes drifted back to Otis. He whispered. "He's being polite, but I think deep down he's still pissed off at us." Logan whispered the obvious and his buddies agreed.

"Just wait until later tonight. He'll really have something to be mad about." Ethan laughed and headed back to the picnic table for more potato chips.

CHAPTER 12

Tyler and the Henderson kids gathered the dessert ingredients from the kitchen. He paused to look through the window facing the lake at the bon fire scene below and said, "What I've been wondering about is the real reason everyone came here this weekend. I get the fact that it's a summer long weekend and a great escape into nature is the goal. I understand why a busy family like yours wants to get into the great outdoors. It's so good for people to be active and away from their screens. My Grandma's always talking about less screen time."

Kyra smiled, "We hear about that a lot too. I have no idea why we're here, but I'm glad we came. I didn't even know we had a vacation booked until my parents told me to pack."

Otis walked in to check on them, asked if they needed help, and, when his offer was declined, left. Otis picked up the shovel and Tyler heard him mumble something about going to fix up the loose gravel misplaced by the commotion earlier on the driveway before it got too dark.

When the young trio, followed by Otis, rejoined the group, the guests were standing, with their backs to the lodge, all facing west. The spectacular orange orb, sinking in the cradle of a pink, wispy sky, was mesmerizing. The setting of the sun behind dramatic mountain peaks was an ordinary miracle they were all fortunate to witness. The only sound was the crackling fire and the lake water gently, rhythmically lapping onto shore.

It didn't take long for the air to chill, and everyone pulled their camp chairs close to the roaring fire housed in a circular stone pit.

"Okay, anyone who wants our version of homemade hot apple pie join me over here," Tyler set out the food supplies on the nearby picnic table and several iron items that resembled fireplace pokers with a square, flat basket on the end. He opened the two sided, hinged square and placed buttered white bread with a few tablespoons of canned apple pie filling in the centre. He sprinkled cinnamon on each and topped it with another slice of buttered bread.

As predicted, both Ben and Kyra were fascinated by this fun way of outdoor cooking. The three frat boys along with Nicola, Kyra, and Ben made their mountain pies and had oven mitts on their hands while they cooked their concoctions in the flames. The air had cooled, and the smell of apples and cinnamon wafted over everyone. Within minutes, the mountain pies were ready to cut cross ways into triangles and shared with the group. Otis joined the group carrying two large thermoses, one filled with coffee and the other with hot chocolate.

Cindy stood up, struggled to remove the screw cap, and poured most of the wine bottle into her oversized container. She swayed slightly when she took a long drink and then made her way back with over exaggerated, careful movements and sat down hard in to her camp chair. The others watched her and were only able to look away once they were confident she wasn't going to fall into the campfire.

"Careful, the apples are scorching hot, kids." Nicola warned. "They'll burn your mouth."

Tyler cut mini triangles for everyone. Tentative tastes were taken, and moans of pleasure followed.

"Tomorrow I'll teach Ben and Kyra how to make mountain ice cream, but for now, how about a ghost story? I know a good one." Tyler offered.

"Sure, but not too scary, okay?" Jaclyn shivered.

"Yes, I agree," Nicola echoed. "Not too scary." The last thing she needed was a sleepless night due to her kids' nightmares. She thought of her stalker. She didn't need more reasons to lose sleep.

"Don't worry, I'll keep you all safe." Logan offered an extended hug but was ignored.

"My story happened in the late 1970s, long before we were born." When Otis and Victoria exchanged an amused look, he added. "Well, most of us."

Tyler continued, "A group, not unlike ourselves, was gathered at a bonfire on the beach having a great time. Out of nowhere, a guy approached the group dressed like a cowboy wearing jeans, boots, a cowboy hat, and sunglasses. The thing that caught everyone's attention was the sunglasses, because, get this, it was dark out."

"Oh, I don't like this story." Kyra whispered to her Mom.

"Don't worry, honey," Nicola whispered back. "It's not true."

Unconvinced, Kyra scooted her chair closer to her Mom. Ben, on the other hand, was mesmerized, hanging on Tyler's every word.

"The guy smiled and asked for directions to the local hospital which the group provided, and he tipped his hat and walked away. Moments later, they heard screeching tires and a crash at the top of the hill, not far from the lodge." Tyler spoke slowly and met the gaze of each of the guests around the circle.

"C'mon, Tyler. This story is lame." Carter shook his head. It was getting dark, and the only light was the glow of the campfire.

"Give him a chance, the kid's trying. Continue." Cindy slurred.

Tyler nodded, "When they heard the crash, all the teenagers ran toward it. They ran up the hill to the main road, but the crash site wasn't there. They then ran on the mountain road all the way to the bend, where the sound must of have come from, but there was no sign of the car or crash site."

Ben sat on the edge of his camp chair with his mouth wide open and, despite trying to look cool, Kyra leaned toward her Mom and grabbed her hand.

Tyler continued, "The group decided to report the incident. They contacted the police and, an hour or so later, were told a patrol car searched the road, but there was no sign or other reports of an accident. Later, they learned that a cowboy, looking like the one they described, had died in a crash years before, and every now and then, he wanders down to a campfire to come back for a visit. . . Just. . . like. . . NOW!"

Tyler shone a bright flashlight behind the group. Heads turned. There stood a man dressed exactly as described, cowboy hat and sunglasses included.

Everyone jumped. The kids screamed, Brooke ran away, Cindy fell over, even Ethan got up and yelled, "What the hell?"

The cowboy reached for his sunglasses and grinned.

"Alex!" Nicola screamed.

"That was awesome, Dad." Ben high fived his father.

"Dad, you scared me." Kyra yelled and stomped her foot.

"Sorry, honey. Tyler asked me to participate and I just couldn't resist."

Laughter filled the air, the nervous kind of laughter.

"Victoria, you don't seem scared." Nicola observed while trying to catch her breath. The last thing she needed in her life was more terror. Damn Alex.

"Oh, not much scares me anymore. I've heard a few ghost stories in my time. Enough to guess how they end." She laughed. "But I was impressed by your storytelling skills, Tyler. Well done, Alex, for slipping away without us noticing. You are very sneaky." Victoria's gaze stayed an extra beat on the attractive man.

"Thank you very much." He said, choosing to take Victoria's comment as a compliment. "My work is done." Alex grabbed another beer and joined his family.

Logan picked up his guitar and strummed a few familiar songs. Some sang along, including Kyra to her mother's surprise, others sat back and enjoyed the music. When a lively, familiar tune played, Carter got up and asked Brooke to dance. The others watched as they tried to two-step in the sand. The couple made their way closer to the water where the sand was packed making it a bit easier to dance. They were almost the same height and eventually moved in sync and spent as much time laughing as dancing.

Ben shivered and wrapped his blanket tighter.

"Time to call it a night, kids." Alex turned to Nicola, "I'll take them to the cabin, are you coming with us?"

"I'll finish my wine, and I'll be right up. Someone will help me find my way so I'm not alone." Alex understood her meaning.

The guys left, mumbling something about work to do, and they were followed shortly by Victoria. Otis and Tyler made their way up the hill, leaving Nicola and the three JUGS members with strict instructions to double douse the fire before leaving it, knowing they'd probably return to check later.

After she waved her family off, Nicola gathered closer to the dying campfire with the young women. "Mind if I stay with you for a while? I still am trying to unwind."

"Not at all." Jaclyn said, pulling a chair forward for her.

"Kids asleep?" Cindy slurred her words again and took a swig of her large container of white wine.

Nicola answered, "Well, you may have seen them just leave. They're heading to bed, probably still arguing about who gets the top bunk. I'm just glad Alex went with them. I convinced Alex to surrender his phone and be present for the evening. I think I married a workaholic."

"Is it really work?" Cindy's bleary-eyed face tried to focus on Nicola.

"Cindy, stop. You're just trying to cause trouble." Brooke admonished her friend.

Nicola gave a little laugh. "What do you mean, is it work? Yes, of course, it's work. He has a high-pressure job and a demanding boss."

"Who doesn't these days? But I noticed he's in good shape so you might want to answer his phone next time it rings or dings with a text when he's not around." Her head wobbled slightly as though her neck couldn't keep up with its movements.

Nicola leaned toward Brooke and said, "I think your friend may have enjoyed too many drinks and not enough food."

"Hey. . . hey, Nicola. . . do you ever have trouble reaching him? Does he tell you what he's been up to after the fact but never tells you ahead of time so you can't check up on him? Don't be mad at me, I just tell it like it is. Is he happier lately?"

Cindy's jabs were landing due to Nicola's chronic insecurity.

"Listen, listen, don't be mad at me. I like you and I just have seen one too many women get taken advantage of and . . . hey, if everything is good in your world, cheers to you." Cindy raised her tumbler with the lid removed and slopped half of her wine over the side without noticing.

"It's easy to find out if everything is okay, what's difficult is deciding if you want to find out. . . and what to do about it. . . just saying."

"Shut up, Cindy, leave Nicola alone." Jaclyn glared at the drunk woman.

Brooke asked, "What makes you the relationship expert, Cindy?"

"I'm no expert; I just know from personal experience what a crack in a relationship looks like, and when I look at you guys, I see a family falling apart."

"Okay, your evening is over. You are going to bed now." Jaclyn grabbed Cindy's arm and turned to Nicola to say, "Ignore everything she said."

"No, no, just one more thing." Cindy called back over her shoulder as Jaclyn dragged her up the hill. "I know this is none of my business, but you might want to check his phone next time you can, and, if it's password protected, chances are the simplest of password is the right one. Or, maybe you can put it up to his face when he's sleeping."

Nicola and Brooke watched Cindy successfully escape Jaclyn's grip. Cindy clumsily grabbed her chair and turned it to face the lake with her back to the women. She looked out at the dark lake still holding tight to her drink. Her legs splayed out in front of her and her upper body slumped.

Brooke picked up a stick and poked the embers of the campfire. "Typical. I apologize on her behalf. She's kind of like a kid we have to watch all the time. I'm getting tired of it."

Cindy shot up from her chair with surprising agility but still managed to spill the remainder of her drink, "Well, Nicola, what I'm seeing when I look at you and your hubby is what looks like two people heading for disaster." Even though her words were almost incoherent they wounded.

"Cindy! Stop! Sit down and shut your mouth." Brooke's anger was obvious to everyone. She turned to Nicola and said, "I'm sorry, ignore her, she's an ugly drunk. Don't pay any attention."

"Whadaya mean, ignore me? Don't ignore me. Don't ignore the warning signs. Classic cheater behavior. Always on the phone. Always walks away to take a call. Always looks a little bit guilty after every call. Classic. Good looking guy, boring life. Classic."

"Are you okay, Nicola?" Jaclyn asked.

"Cindy is verbally attacking my husband. Of course I'm not okay with it." She was disgusted with the rude behavior.

Nicola looked at the glow of the embers and thought about an old saying. . . something about the only ones who tell the truth were children and drunks. Something like that. She shook the sting of the words off and remained silent. She stirred the remaining bit of log sending sparks into the air.

"Hey, just tell me one thing," Cindy refused to quit talking. "Is what I just mentioned true? Are there times when you can't reach him? Does he tell you where he's going ahead of time or, does he tell you where he's been or what he's done only afterwards, so you can't check up on him, huh, huh. . . yeah, I thought so. Boom. Cheater."

Cindy's attention was focused on returning to a standing position. She managed to get up on one knee but collapsed backward. After three unsuccessful attempts, she lost strength and sat down and attempted to brush off the massive amount of beach she was wearing.

"Ugh. Why is this sand so sticky? I can't get the sand off. Gross."

Finally, on the fourth attempt, Cindy stood, unsteady but upright. With a look of pride on her face, and while swaying noticeably, she announced. "I'm tired of all of you, I'm sick of all the secrets and of all the pretending and I'm going to bed, 'night."

"Thank Christ! We've been trying to do that for the past ten minutes." Jaclyn mumbled.

The group waved her off and watched her half walk, half crawl up the embankment.

"She is not okay," Nicola ignored Cindy's hurtful words. She never liked seeing a woman drink too much. It was a bit gender biased but for good reason. It was dangerous to be so out of control, and Cindy was definitely out of control.

"This happens every time on the first night that we get together." Jaclyn snorted. "Watch, tomorrow morning she will vow to never drink again, and then she'll promptly order a Bloody Mary for breakfast."

"Yup," Brooke laughed, "I guess we've all done that. But, you're right, Nicola, I think I'll catch up with her, even though I'm not ready to sleep. I need to make sure she doesn't get lost or eaten by a woodland creature. That is unless I decide to feed her to some hungry wolf. I'm getting sick of being her babysitter. Again, sorry she was such a jerk. Good night, you two."

The two women watched Brooke link arms with Cindy as they climbed the path from the beach leading to the cabins.

"Let's put our bathing suits on and go for a night time swim," Cindy suggested.

"Not happening, Cindy." Brooke shook her head as she looked back at the beach to the two women who waved back.

"Nicola, go ahead if you would like to go to bed. I'm fine here for a while. I want to make sure the fire is out," Jaclyn looked around her surroundings as if looking for something or someone and then stared into the glow. Jaclyn smiled when she caught sight of a shadow of a male figure pacing on the deck.

Nicola had a feeling she may be messing up a potential romantic rendezvous.

"Okay, if you're sure. I don't want to leave you alone out here."

"You won't be." Her pretty smile confirmed Nicola's suspicions.

Nicola noticed the figure approaching. It was definitely male, but dusk had descended and she couldn't tell exactly who it was.

"Oh. . . okay then," she smiled. "Hey, I was young once. Honest. Goodnight."

"Goodnight." Jaclyn waved Nicola off with a little giggle.

CHAPTER 13

The sound of her children's rhythmic breathing greeted Nicola when she entered the cabin. Kyra's slight form, dressed in her beloved soccer jersey and sweat pants, was warm enough, no need to cover her. Ben was snuggled in a circle in the bed above wearing his moose-patterned pajamas, clutching his binoculars. Nicola's heart clenched. Her kids always looked so much younger when asleep. Nicola removed Ben's binoculars, placed them on his shelf, and pulled the comforter over his bare feet. She stepped on the edge of the bottom bunk to place a kiss on his forehead.

Nicola loved this time of day. She loved sunsets more than sunrises. She loved the time of the evening when the night draws in and when it's close-the-curtains time. It always felt cozy and safe. Shutting out the world had always been important to Nicola, even more so now, when her safety was threatened.

The kids were everything to her. She never felt that kind of love as a child, but she made sure Kyra and Ben felt it every day. The mama bear in her would fight anyone and anything who caused them any harm or robbed them of one second of happiness. Currently, the only person doing that was their father by his increasingly frequent absences. But that was going to have to change immediately. Nicola was tired of making excuses for him, sick of seeing disappointment and confusion on the faces of her beautiful kids. She had to admit Cindy's words struck a blow.

She went to her bedroom and Alex wasn't there. The bed covers had not been touched.

"Mom," Kyra's whisper startled Nicola, and she jumped. "Sorry, honey, did I wake you up? Where's your Dad?"

"Yes, you woke me up. Dad was here when I went to bed. I'll wait up with you until he's back, but I'd like to read for a while. I brought my book light, but I left my book in the lodge. Is it okay if I run and get it? I'll go straight there and back."

After Nicola's big lecture on less screen time, more outdoor time or reading time, it was impossible to say no.

"Okay, Kyra, but I'm going to watch you for as far as I can see you along the path until it bends right next to the building. No delay, got it? No looking for Tyler."

"Mom, you're being ridiculous." Kyra's red face and grimace told Nicola that her assumption was correct.

"Take a flash light."

"I know my way. I don't need one." Kyra yelled over her shoulder.

Snoring filled the air, but it was coming from Barnaby at the foot of her bed. The Labrador had as much fun the first day at Mountain Shadows Lodge as any other guest.

Barnaby woke up, scratched at the door, and Nicola decided to take him out as she watched Kyra leave. Ben was still sleeping, but she'd stay close to the cabin. Nicola grabbed Barnaby's collar, smiled as the dog did his happy dance, hooked on his leash, and out they went for his quick nature break. When Kyra returned, she'd go in search of her absent husband.

Kyra skipped along the path. Her Mom wasn't wrong, she did want to see Tyler just not right now. She wanted to get her book quickly and get back to the cabin before Tyler saw her in her lame soccer tee-shirt and sweats that she always wore to bed. Tyler wasn't lying when he said it got really dark at night in the mountains. She promised her Mom she'd hurry so she shifted to a fast walk, she just had to get her book that she remembered leaving by the end table near the big, stone fireplace in the main lodge.

Kyra smiled thinking about the cool JUGS girls who didn't treat her like a child. Earlier, they complimented her hair and her outfit even though she didn't like either. If she'd had more notice they were going on a trip, her clothes wouldn't be so hideous. The guys were friendly to her and helpful when she asked any questions. Maybe she would end up having a fun vacation, if that's what this sudden trip was supposed to be.

Another thing Kyra thought was weird was that her parents didn't want her to use her phone at all, no texting or posting on social media even though it was monitored by her parents.

Despite the new rule, Kyra thought she might take a picture of Tyler and post it if she could sneak one without him noticing. She knew her friends would think he's hot. Or maybe she'd take a selfie on the trail ride she was going on tomorrow. Her friends would be so jealous about her unexpected getaway.

Maybe she judged this place too quickly. Her parents were acting very weird back home, almost nervous before, but since arriving in the mountains, they seemed much happier.

Kyra squinted as she approached the bend on the path. Almost there. Something caught her eye in the dim light ahead. She squinted in the darkness. There was something laying at the edge of the path. She looked back toward her cabin, but she had rounded the slight bend in the path and couldn't see if her Mom was still there watching. The thing on the ground wasn't a fallen tree. The shape was thicker and lumpy. It looked like it was covered in dark material, like a big duffle bag. Maybe. She got closer. Could it be an animal? Maybe it's injured. She got closer. Kyra got closer until she could see.

The form was crumpled, but clearly human.

CHAPTER 14

The scream startled everyone who heard it but only Nicola, still inside her cabin, recognized it as her daughter's. Panic overtook her, and she dropped the leash.

Nicola flew out the door and down the steps with Barnaby barking at her side, his leash trailing on the ground behind him. Kyra was backtracking and running toward the cabin.

The sound of an air horn blasted through the night. If anyone managed to sleep through Kyra's scream, they certainly would have woken to the ear drum piercing sound of the air horn.

"Help! Help! Mom, someone fell and needs help." She was panting by the time she reached the bend in the path, more from adrenaline than exertion. Nicola met her and threw her arms around her girl.

"Mom, come with me." Kyra shook off the embrace and tugged on her Mom's arm. "I just ran away from there to get someone. Hurry, we have to go back."

"Okay, okay. I'm coming. Who was it?"

"I don't know who it was. It was a big lump all covered up. I could just see an outline of a person, I think."

"Okay, show me where." Noise in the bushes near the cabin caught their attention.

"Alex, is that you? Where were you? Get over here." She called for her husband over her shoulder as she saw him come up the hill that led to the lake.

"I went for a run."

"At this time of night? In the dark?" Cindy's earlier comments flooded her thoughts.

Alex held up his headband light as his daughter and wife took off running he yelled "Why all the noise? What the hell is going on?"

Alex caught up to them just past the bend on the path to the lodge.

"It's here, close by. I thought it was right here." Kyra pointed to the ground and looked around, confused.

"What are we looking for? What's happened?" Alex asked.

"I saw someone laying here covered up on the path. But there is nothing here now." She scraped her foot aggressively along the loose dirt, twigs, and leaves on the path. There was no indentation or noticeable markings. Alex shot his wife his best what-the-fuck look. Nicola ignored him.

Both Tyler and Otis came running out the back deck, lake side entrance from the lodge. Ethan arrived just before the staff members, his digital camera in his hand. He hastily detached the lens and hid each items in his jacket pockets. He didn't want his property confiscated by Otis.

"We heard a scream, is everyone okay?" Otis's hair was a mess, he'd obviously been sleeping.

"I saw a body out here." Kyra announced to Tyler, who put his arm around her shoulder.

Otis looked at Nicola and Alex for confirmation. They both shook their heads and shrugged.

Alex explained, "Kyra said she saw something at the edge of the path and thought it was a person in trouble. She ran to our cabin to get us, and when we got back here, there was nothing there. Absolutely nothing." There was no attempt by Alex to hide his annoyance.

Nicola understood the ups and downs of a teenage girls emotions and softly suggested, "Kyra, maybe it was a shadow or an animal just resting for a bit and then it took off when you screamed."

"No, no, it was someone."

"Girl or guy?" Tyler asked.

"I don't know. Whoever it was looked all curled up and covered with a tent or something canvas or a tarp. It was dark material. I couldn't really see."

"What's going on?" Carter appeared on the pathway, out of breath and sweating. "I ran toward the sound of the scream. Is everyone okay?"

"I saw someone injured on the path."

"Jesus, who was it? Where exactly? Should we call a doctor?"

Ignoring the young man, Alex softened his voice and approached his daughter.

"Honey, you said it yourself, you really couldn't see clearly and, whatever it was, it's gone now, and you don't have to worry about it." Alex was tired, his muscles ached, and it took all of his remaining fortitude to be patient with his daughter.

Otis stated. "It could be an injured animal, and we don't want it to suffer. Tyler and I will stay out here and have a look around, just to be sure."

Kyra was relieved that at least Otis was taking her claim seriously. Nicola put her arm around her daughter and led her back to their cabin.

"Is everything okay? I was getting ready for bed when I heard a scream and a blast. Is there an emergency?" Victoria, wrapped in a full length pink fluffy housecoat, wearing matching slippers with her hair wrapped up and covered in a towel, made her way carefully down the path from her cabin.

"We're fine, just a mix up," Nicola called to her concerned neighbor. "Nothing to worry about." Nicola's tone indicated that further details were not going to be shared.

"Oh, okay, good night then." The older woman was puzzled but didn't ask more questions.

"G'night, Victoria."

The Hendersons went inside.

"Why is everyone yelling?" Ben rubbed his eyes and blinked at the light in the cabin.

"It's nothing, sweetheart, go back to bed." Ben, a kid who was very grumpy without enough sleep, for once, turned around and did exactly what his Mom said.

"Just forget about it, honey." Alex hugged his daughter. "If it was someone who fell, maybe the person got up and carried on. Probably one of the party girls or one of the guys messing around."

"Yeah, maybe." Kyra replied, unconvinced. She crawled into her bunk bed and ignored the fact she didn't have a chance to get her book. Instead, she closed her eyes and thought how nice Tyler's arm felt around her shoulders.

CHAPTER 15

Moments before Kyra screamed, Ethan, Carter, and Logan gathered behind the lodge next to the lodge annex.

"Okay, guys, you know exactly what to do, right?" Logan looked at his friends who nodded. They formed a hidden huddle just outside the private residence at the back of the lodge.

"Yes, we've been over this a dozen times." Carter said and reached for his camouflage blanket and Ethan grabbed his power lens camera.

"We'll back into the bushes across from the Otis's door so we can get a great picture of his reaction. He'll really like us after this stunt. He might kick us out, you know." Logan said.

Ethan responded, "He'll have to prove it was us and we'll be back at our cabin when he comes looking."

The rooms that housed staff were on the opposite side of the lodge, farthest from the guest cabins. Checking the outside wall, the guys guessed Otis's room would be the one with the bigger window. Through a series of silent gestures, they solidified their actions. Dense bush surrounded that side of the building, perfect for their prank. Ethan and Carter dropped to their stomachs and shimmied backward into the bush covering themselves in nature's camouflage, settling on dark blankets they brought from the cabin. Ethan's nasal cavity filled with histamine, and he pinched his nose and prayed his seasonal allergies would calm down. Carter suddenly was overcome by a fit of giggles. A poke in his ribs managed to get them under control, but there was no guarantee he could keep his laughter in check.

"Carter, quit it, you sound like a school girl. We are going to get caught before we do anything. I heard Tyler mention that the wood narc goes to bed shortly after dark so that's around nine-thirty. It's way later than that now. Ethan, go hide yourself; get a clear view but make sure he can't see you."

"Okay, chill out, Logan. God, this is just a joke, not a military maneuver."

Quiet settled in. The two observers held their breath, and Ethan readied his camera, flash on.

Through peak holes between branches and brush, they watched Logan approach, stealth like, as though his life depended on not getting caught. Logan stopped. He turned around and observed his friends in the hiding spot.

Ethan whispered, "Wait. We need to set up the alibi."

"No, we don't." Logan hissed.

"Yeah," Carter said. "He's right we need to cover our tracks now so it looks like we were never here."

"How?"

Carter said, "I could go back to the cabin. Make it look like we were there all night. Like we were playing cards. I'll set everything up, and you and Ethan can come flying in and casually sit at the table."

"Okay, that makes sense." Ethan warmed to the idea. "Logan, you blast the air horn and take off. I run faster than both of you so I'll still get the shots as planned. Carter, go set up the cabin now to look like we're playing poker. I brought cards and poker chips, they're in my duffle bag. So set it up and put out beer and snacks. We'll need a beer after this."

Carter grinned, "This is going to be epic."

"I know." Logan smiled back. "Let's do it and get our asses out of here."

For a few seconds, the only sounds in the night were Carter's footsteps running away. Then, out of the silence of the night, a girl screamed. The sound pierced the tranquility and set everything in fast forward speed.

A nerve-shattering blast shook through the tranquil night. The air horn startled Logan and Ethan, and, even though they knew it was coming and were responsible, they froze for a moment, and then pandemonium broke loose.

The brief moment of silence was smashed by the commotion of Otis opening the back door and swearing. He appeared outside the back entrance quicker than they imagined. Logan started laughing. Nerves flooded Ethan, and he clicked the camera in a panic, temporarily blinding their subject. The guys had seconds to get to their feet and run through the bush abandoning the blanket. Ethan's finger remained on the button and an unplanned, night-time, panoramic photo shoot of the grounds of Mountain Shadows Lodge took place.

Otis kept blinking, trying to focus. Was he dreaming or did he hear a woman scream? What the hell was going on? Everyone should be asleep. He calmed his breath and tried to focus.

In the distance, Otis heard male laughter and branches whipping through the air and the sound of footsteps running on the packed down earth. No need to follow the sound, he knew the identity of the culprits. What surprised him was his lack of anger, and once he was sure he wasn't having a heart attack, he actually thought it was kind of funny. He remembered what it was like to be carefree and to have fun. It was a long, long time ago. Still, rules were rules, and he'd have to figure out what happened.

Tyler stumbled outside. "I heard a scream just before the blast."

"Yeah, I did too kid. Let's circle around back and find out what the hell is going on."

Logan and Ethan caught up to each other just as they reached the cabin. Hands on their knees bent forward trying to fill their lungs with air while tears of laughter rolled down their faces.

Ethan spoke through gasps. "Hey, which route did you take back? I couldn't see you."

Logan could hardly get the words out. "I went through the woods, can't you tell? I didn't want anyone to see me, I'm a mess." He looked down at his filthy clothes and asked, "Did you get the picture?"

"Yeah, man, I got about a million pictures. I panicked and forgot to release the button and my camera kept clicking away. Oh my God, this was great." Ethan's broad shoulders shook. He grabbed his right side and high fived his friend. "If Otis didn't have a heart attack, he, for sure, shit his pants. I know I almost did. At one point, I was running backward coming around the back of the lodge, still clicking pics. Let me catch my breath, and we'll see which shot is best."

"Otis is going to kill us." Tears of laughter were running down Logan's face.

"Not if we were never there, brother."

As soon as they could manage it, Ethan and Logan climbed the stairs into their cabin. And stopped in the entrance way.

Nothing was set up.

"That fucker. Where is he?" Logan asked.

"Hey, I'm right here." Carter was also panting. "Sorry, guys, I didn't have time to set anything up. I was running back and heard a scream. It was Kyra. I went to see if she was okay. She's fine, just some teenage drama. I'll set everything up now for our fake alibi."

A low, gruff voice behind them said, "Don't bother." The three men jumped and turned in unison to face Otis who shone a flashlight in their eyes. They blinked, put their hands up to protect their eyes.

"What are you doing out here at this time of night?"

Each offered a different explanation.

Carter said, "I heard a girl scream and went to see what was going on." Otis stared at him for a moment, shone the flashlight up and down his body. He noted the considerable sweat on his brow and dirt on his dark tee shirt.

It was obvious he had been part of the prank. The flashlight and Otis's attention moved on to Logan.

Logan hid the air horn behind his back and said, "I forgot something in the Jeep." Otis repeated the scrutiny and then turned toward Ethan.

Ethan added, "I thought I'd go for a nighttime swim." Otis's flashlight beam settled on the camera Ethan was holding. "After I put this away." Ethan added with a smile.

Otis looked from one to the other and in a voice several tones lower than his normal one, "Try again."

Carter confessed, "Okay, Okay, it was us. Sorry, Otis. Look, we thought it would be funny to play a prank. We're idiots. We sincerely apologize, right, guys?" His friends nodded like two toy Chihuahuas in the back window of an old El Dorado.

Logan said, "We were going to go to the girls' cabin to pretend to be a bear to scare them. They are being a bit ridiculous about grizzly bears. They are even afraid of all the harmless creatures in the forest so we came up with the plan to scratch on their windows and freak them out a bit."

Ethan added, "But then these two Romeos thought it might really piss the girls off and hurt their chances of hooking up with one or more of them, so that's when we changed the target to you. It's really their fault. I was all for pissing off the girls." Ethan's smile was contagious.

Otis could feel his annoyance lessen.

Carter said, "We were going to sit at the edge of the path and watch the show. You know, slightly frightened women in need of comforting hugs." He grinned and looked back at Logan. Otis saw the other genius smile in agreement.

Otis sighed deeply, shook his head, and said, "I think the only creatures these women should avoid are standing here outside, in front of me, at way past midnight. I suggest you go inside and stay there until morning." Everyone knew it wasn't just a suggestion.

"Okee dokee," With a salute, the trio turned to head inside their cabin.

"Wait," Otis looked at the air horn. "Did you bring this here or did you take it from my boat? Air horns are vital pieces of safety equipment, and, if you stole from me, you're out of here."

"No, no. It's mine, I brought it." Logan said.

"Hand it over, and hand over your camera, Ethan. Give me the items, and I'll let you stay. Refuse, and you can pack your bags and leave now."

The men reluctantly handed over the items.

"These items are now mine until you check out, which, if you keep up these shenanigans, maybe sooner than you planned. Understood."

The reply was in unison.

"Yes, sir."

CHAPTER 16

Otis made his way to the staff quarters heading to his room and scratched his head at the stupidity he just witnessed.

Tyler opened the door of his own room at the end of the hall. He had returned to his room after the discussion on the path with the Hendersons while Otis confronted the pranksters.

"Everything okay, boss?"

"Hey, Tyler." Otis' voice was weary.

"How did it go with the guys? Did you kick them out?"

"No, it's very late, and the roads are too dangerous for strangers to drive at night. They apologized, and there really was no harm done. Frankly, I need the cash from the rental, so I let them off the hook. I did confiscate an air horn and a digital camera." The owner put both items on a small table with plans to lock them in his desk drawer in his office the next morning.

Tyler yawned and stretched his arms above his head, "What was that other noise?"

"What do you mean?"

"I heard something a few minutes just after the blast and after Kyra's scream. I'm surprised you didn't hear it. I don't know what the hell it was, but it sounded like something crashed inside the lodge. I got up to check to see if something fell off the wall, but I didn't notice anything different. Then I saw movement through the big windows, something out front, by the main entrance. Whatever it was took off running past the front window, maybe a deer or a moose. I'm not sure, I was a little groggy. When you were talking to the guys, I went to check it out but didn't see anything. I turned the outside flood lights off earlier, to save money like you told me to, so it was almost pitch black out there. But, in the moonlight, I saw a shadow. I'm not sure what it was, probably an animal. It was just a flash of movement. When I opened the door, nothing was disturbed and nothing was there. I didn't know what the hell was going on so I went to find you and you were gone."

Otis said, "Maybe it was what Kyra saw on the path. Now what's important is the guests are back in their cabins, and the blast was a stupid attempt at a practical joke."

"So everything's fine? Am I off duty now, boss? I'm wiped out."

"Yeah. Good job today. G'night, Tyler. Get some sleep, tomorrow will be busy."

CHAPTER 17

Victoria returned to her cabin and stared at her reflection in the living room window. Her heart was still pounding from the earlier fright and she could see it in the eyes of the older woman in the reflection looking back at her.

She took deep breaths to try to calm the feelings of panic and dread. She shouldn't have come here, but it was too late now. Too late for a lot of things, including regret.

She tried to distract herself.

Think happy thoughts.

Thoughts of the good times.

Before.

CHAPTER 18

SATURDAY

It was the brightness in the room, along with the warmth of the sun on her face that woke Nicola early Saturday morning. She took a deep breath of the fresh air and a subtle scent of pine needles flowed from the open window above the bed. The morning, much like the others for the past few weeks, began peacefully until the moment a wave of panic washed over her as she remembered the threat she was under.

On her back staring at the bedroom ceiling, Nicola practiced her therapist's relaxation technique. She took a big breath in through her nose to the count of four, she held it for seven counts and breathed out through her mouth to the count of eight. The therapist suggested Nicola think of the word *calm* with the inhale and the word *down* with every exhale.

Calm down.

It worked, for a while.

Alex snored softly beside her, and she stretched as best she could, on her side of the bed that was crammed against the wall. They didn't talk about what happened last night. They just went to bed in silence.

Alex shifted his weight and turned toward her. In an unplanned, yet synchronized, move, she took advantage of the shift of weight on the well-worn mattress and climbed over Alex and got dressed.

It was the kind of summer day a person dreams of in the middle of a cold, gray January. Thoughts of winter reminded Nicola of images of brutal winds causing snow to drift across fields and highways. Images flashed in her mind of people bundled up, doing the penguin shuffle, trying not to slip on icy sidewalks. On those horrible days, motorists were unsure every time they applied the brakes if their vehicle would obey the command. Nicola hated the feeling that she never had full control of her vehicle on icy roads. Nicola hated the feeling of having no control, period. Since the notes began, she carried that disconcerting feeling everywhere.

But today, thoughts of ice and snow vanished. Today, the sun was up early and shone brightly throughout their rocky mountain sanctuary. There was no ice, no drifting snow, and no creepy pictures; only sunshine and a summertime feeling. Glimmers of refracted light sparkled on the lake. The shoreline's lapping waves erased all evidence of recent footsteps, providing guests of Mountain Shadows Lodge with a view of a fresh, sandy canvas.

She left the window cracked open last night. Nicola made sure it was not wide enough for anyone to crawl through. It was open just a bit, for a couple of reasons. First, to enjoy the mountain breeze. In order to sleep well, she needed her room to be cool. The second reason Nicola left the window open was so she could hear if there was any other commotion in the middle of the night. Something felt wrong about what Kyra said happened.

Her daughter was convinced she saw someone on the path, and Kyra was so disheartened when whatever she saw was gone. Kyra had always been complicated, and, when she was young, she sometimes played with the truth, but Nicola was certain her daughter was not lying about seeing something on the path. Nicola believed what Kyra said was true. She saw something in the dark that looked like a person lying on the ground. What exactly was on the path was unknown, but there was no doubt in Nicola's mind, Kyra saw something even if no one else, including her own father, believed it.

It's a terrible feeling not to be believed, and Nicola couldn't help but worry about how Kyra would process everything from the night before. It seemed as though worrying was all Nicola did these days, and a change of scenery was not going to lessen her anxiety when it came to her children's well-being.

Nicola grabbed her robe, a towel, and the biodegradable shampoo and body wash provided, and headed for the outdoor shower.

She placed her belongings on the bench just outside the cedar door and turned on the nozzle from the water vessel hanging above.

"Yikes!" Nicola yelped.

The water was colder than she expected, but she adapted and quickly washed her hair. She couldn't see much over the cubicle which she guessed was intended. The outdoor shower was as refreshing as Tyler described. Self-care always helped calm her nerves.

She wrapped herself in a large towel and made her way back to the cabin, got dressed, and, for the second time that morning, left her sleeping family and made her way to the deck on the main lodge. It was early, but she saw Otis had coffee ready, and she took an oversized mug down to the water and sat on one of the chairs near the long dead bonfire. The morning mist still hung over the lake, and steam rose from her mug. The only sound was of loons calling to each other with their haunting lilt.

Nicola inhaled a deep, calming breath. She wondered where Alex had been when he returned to the cabin at the moment Kyra screamed. How could he leave the kids in the cabin alone? She hadn't seen him for a while, long before she came up from the beach when she was talking to the JUGS girls. She rehearsed what she would say to him, but she drifted off before she could begin the conversation.

"Morning, Nicola," The hoarse-voiced Brooke called down to her from the deck.

"Morning, did you have a good rest?" Nicola saw Brooke reach into her pocket, and she hoped she wasn't going to light a cigarette. Fortunately, it was just a tissue that emerged.

"Slept like a log. I feel great. I understand there was some commotion last night."

Brooke's beautiful beach wave hairstyle was a little worse for wear today, and smeared mascara from the night had not yet met a washcloth. Brooke wasn't quite Instagram, photoshoot ready this early in the morning.

Alex appeared above the beach and was holding his phone over his head attempting to get a signal.

"Looks like he retrieved his phone from the digital detox box or drawer or wherever it was supposed to be secured. He's addicted to that thing." Nicola stated, before she stopped herself and remembered the awkward conversation from previous evening.

Nicola continued, "It's a fact of life for many people for whom work is more demanding than ever, and many people never get to completely shut off from their work life."

"Hmm. . . yeah."

"What?"

Brooke clearly wanted to say more.

"What Cindy said last night reminded me of an article I read. Tell me to stop if you don't want to hear about it."

Nicola took a deliberate sip of her coffee and winced when it scalded her mouth.

"It's okay, continue."

Brooke did as requested. "Apparently, there are telltale signs that should trigger some suspicion, and a spouse being attached to their phone is a major one." Brooke saw the alarm and flash of anger in Nicola's reactions and quickly added, "Not that I'm saying it's a problem for you two, I'm just saying what I read. Research suggests there are key indicators of infidelity, you know telltale signs. Are there times when you can't reach him, when you really don't know where he is? Cause that's another sign."

Nicola frowned, "No, he doesn't, you know, disappear, but there are times I have trouble reaching him." Her mind flashed to the night before. "To be fair, he doesn't always know where I am."

"Right, of course, and believe me, I don't want to repeat what Cindy was saying." Brooke backtracked. "I'm not judging, just reporting what I read."

Nicola wondered what the real motives of this young stranger were but curiosity won.

"Any other signs?" Nicola couldn't stop herself from asking.

"Two more major ones. Sudden different personal improvements, for example, working out more, dieting, improved, uh, personal grooming, if you get my drift."

Nicola understood but hadn't noticed any of these changes.

"And the other major one?"

"Well, it's a few new moves in the sack,"

"Oh," Nicola nodded but she didn't comment.

Brooke saw that she had crossed a line.

Nicola jumped up and said, "This is ridiculous. How did we get back on this topic anyway? None of you girls know us. Thank you for your concern, but I am happily married to a wonderful man."

"Understood." Brooke put her hands up as if to surrender and added, "I'm starving, let's go eat."

Nicola brushed the sand off her jeans not really sure where it came from and climbed the slope hurriedly. Her family appeared on the deck as she arrived, and she greeted her husband with an enthusiastic kiss and lined up to help Ben and Kyra with their plates.

One by one, other guests woke up and made their way to the deck where bacon, scrambled eggs with cheese and green onions, French toast, and fruit salad were being served. Juice, coffee, and tea were offered, and conversations flowed easily.

Nicola could see some of the faces around the large table looked tired. She knew she looked tired too. No wonder with all the noise, human and otherwise, she had heard outside her cabin's bedroom window.

"Otis, the food is amazing." Ethan turned to Logan and asked, "Hey, did you try the raspberry jam? It reminds me of my Grandma's, store-bought jam cannot compare. Did you make it?"

Otis laughed, "No, but it is locally made. I buy cases of it from the local farmers' market and put it in my cold storage area. I'll get some of the pickled cucumbers and pickled carrots later today. I try to buy enough each summer to last year round. I don't have the time, or the talent, to make preserves myself, but, I agree, there is nothing like homemade."

"This slow, home-style cooking is wonderful. I really appreciate it, Otis. I spend far too much time and money ordering drive thru fast food or delivery. I remember my Grandma's jams and jellies. It's very nostalgic for me, reminds me of my childhood." Logan said quietly.

"I agree," Ethan added. "Nothing compares. It must be the love that's put into it."

"Why does food always taste better when you eat it outside?" Jaclyn wondered.

"Also, when someone else prepares it," Victoria nodded. "This is delicious, Otis, thank you very much."

"You're welcome." Otis smiled his crooked smile and disappeared into the kitchen to retrieve a fresh tray as the young men had just finished the last of the eggs and bacon.

"Victoria, I think Otis likes you." Brooke announced with a smirk on her face.

"I think so, too. He's a good-looking older man." Jaclyn added.

"He's not that old," Nicola looked at Otis as he entered the lodge.

"Right, I didn't mean he's ancient. It's just, well, you are gorgeous, Victoria. I love your style; you're always so put together." Brooke said.

Jaclyn nodded. "You're on your own, he's single. C'mon let's make something happen here."

"Oh, girls." Victoria gave a little nervous giggle and brushed her hair back off her face and secured it into a gold butterfly clip that had loosened. "You just worry about your own love lives. Please don't waste your vacation time playing matchmaker. That ship has sailed for me, and I'm okay with that reality."

Tyler approached and Nicola asked, "What's up for today, Tyler?"

"Well, you know what time it is, right?

A joking, collective groan emerged from the group.

"Please, not another ice breaker," Alex stated.

"Right, you are. Let's all join the others."

"Actually, Tyler, let's do that a little later. Everyone is waking up at their own time. I don't think we're all here yet. We just need a little unscheduled morning. Is that okay with you?" Victoria suggested.

"Of course, it's fine. You are all in charge of what you do out here. However you want to spend your time, is up to you. Please let me know if you need anything. I do have some things I need to do, so I'll see you later." Tyler skipped down the path toward the water. Soon they saw him push a canoe out into the water, jump in, and start paddling away.

"I wonder what work involves a canoe ride. Is it my imagination, or did he seem happy to take off?" Victoria asked.

"No, you didn't imagine it. That kid couldn't get away from us fast enough." Brooke added.

CHAPTER 19

The groups separated after breakfast still deciding what to do with the day ahead.

"So, what's with Victoria?" Logan whispered as he and Ethan walked back to their cabin. Ethan picked bacon from his molars with a toothpick because the dental floss he carried in his pocket hadn't worked. Victoria was ahead of them. He motioned in Victoria's direction. "Have you noticed how much she stares at Tyler? It's not the paying attention to instructions type of staring. It's disconcerting, if you know what I mean."

"Uh, no Ethan, I rarely know what you mean." Logan quickened his steps away from the deck down the path toward the lake with a striped blue and white towel slung over his bare shoulder. "She's a nice lady. Why are you saying that about her? She's probably just concentrating when Tyler gives instructions. Maybe Victoria is here mistakenly thinking it was fancier and less adventure focused here. More spa like. Who knows? Who cares? All I know right now is why I'm here and that's to go for a swim."

"I planned to go swimming before I ate, do you think I should wait? Ah, forget it, I'm going back to the lodge to see what everyone has planned for the day. See you later." Ethan left.

"Hey, wait up, Logan," Carter yelled from their cabin deck. "I'm going for a swim too. He was already dressed in his swim trunks and ran down the path ahead of Logan into the ice-cold lake. He dove underwater and whipped his head when he resurfaced.

"You missed breakfast, Carter."

"No, I didn't, I grabbed some fruit and coffee when you were both still sleeping. I already went for an early run down the road. I scarfed more junk food than I should have when I got back. I thought I better undo some of the damage by going for a swim." He rubbed his washboard abs.

Hiding in the bushes, near the guys' cabin with a clear view of the lake, a pair of eyes watched as the young men ran down the hill and plunged into the frigid water.

CHAPTER 20

It was mid-morning by the time Tyler reappeared from his canoe trip. He and the guys dried off and returned to the patio deck where the remaining guests lingered. Tyler outlined the morning's activities. "Hey, I've got one more ice breaker and then we can go have fun. I'm not sure where Otis and Cindy are but thanks for agreeing to play along. Here's the question and your answer can be as serious or as light hearted as you want it to be: What is the worst thing you've ever survived?"

Brooke spoke up, "I'll go first. A bikini wax!"

Jaclyn followed, "Getting dumped by my first boyfriend. He was my world, but in hind sight, he was really a loser."

It was Victoria's turn, and Tyler smiled expectantly. She lowered her head and stared at the ground. The silence continued. Tyler looked at the other guests, some of whom shifted in their seats. Logan cleared his throat.

Finally, Victoria whispered, "I don't think I have survived." Silence descended and, to avoid further awkwardness, Nicola said, "We'll go next."

Alex and Nicola smiled at each other and answered simultaneously, "Marriage." Nicola shot a glance at the JUGS girls. "Just kidding, everyone." She added.

Carter continued around the circle, "Honestly, the worst thing I survived was the treacherous drive up here. That was a white knuckler." There were nods of agreement all around.

When it was her turn next, Kyra answered, "School, definitely school. It's the worst."

Bennett interrupted his sister, speaking quickly and loudly, as Kyra was about to explain further, "Losing my pet rabbit. He ran away. It was not my fault. I didn't forget to close the latch on his outside hutch." Bennett wiped his eyes with the back of his hand.

"Yeah, right." Kyra mumbled.

Seeing the beginning of a sibling battle percolating, Logan stood up in front of the group and lifted the front of his tee-shirt. He revealed a significant scar on his abdomen and said, "This. Skateboard accident years ago. Apparently, I wasn't as skilled as I thought I was."

Jaclyn smiled in his direction and said, "I wondered what that was from."

"Ethan, what about you?" Tyler asked.

"Well, as a proud gay, Black man, I could say that my entire life has been a battle to survive. It's not easy being constantly at the mercy of uneducated, Neanderthal bullies. But, that's not my answer. The worst thing I survived was never-ending ice breaker activities on my long weekend off." He laughed.

Tyler laughed and saluted Ethan, "Message received."

Otis appeared carrying armfuls of life jackets and asked, "Who wants to go for a boat ride?"

"Me, please. Mom, Dad, let's go for a boat ride."

"Okay, buddy, let's all go," Alex smiled at his son's excitement.

"Can Barnaby come?"

"Sure, he can ride up front. I even have a life jacket for a big dog." Otis smiled and called out to the young adults. "The water is like glass on the other side. Do any of you guys or gals want to water ski? The boat can seat six comfortably besides me."

"Are you joining us, Victoria?" Nicola asked.

"Oh no, I'm not a big fan of being in, or on, the water, but you all will have lots of fun I'm sure. I'm happy to stay here and read my book."

Kyra realized Tyler wasn't among the boating group and said, "You know, I think I'll stay back and read too if that's okay?"

Victoria looked at Kyra and said, "We'll keep each other company, if that's okay with your parents. We'll look after each other."

"Fine, Kyra, you can stay here. Keep close to the lodge and in sight of the other guests. I mean it, no wandering on your own. Listen to Victoria." Nicola said.

Brooke, Logan, and Carter all accepted the invitation and, along with Nicola, Alex, and Ben, they quickly changed into swimming gear. The others made their way down to the boathouse and helped haul the lifejackets and waterskies. Soon, most of the guests were racing across the lake in Otis' boat. Barnaby sat in the open bow with the other Hendersons, his jowls rippling in the wind.

They watched the boat wake, behind the motor, cut a path in the pristine water, and saw the lodge get smaller and smaller.

"Mom, I forgot to pee." Ben hollered over the noise.

"Oh, Ben," Nicola sighed.

Otis laughed. "Don't worry, out here nature calls often at the most inconvenient times. We'll just put you in the water and you'll figure out what to do. We're getting close now. Want to drive the boat, Ben?" Otis slowed down as they approached the opposite shore and let the boy grab the wheel but always maintaining complete control himself.

"This is awesome, look I'm driving." At that moment in time, Nicola thought, no one on earth was happier than her little boy.

Otis raised the outboard motor and was able to run the boat onto the sandy shore.

He provided some quick instruction, "For those of you who haven't skied before, here's what you need to remember. Keep your knees bent slightly and your feet parallel in the boots of your skis. Feel the tension as I idle the boat out and then, on your signal, I'll hit the engine and you'll be skiing. Remember not to jerk the ski rope and, if you fall, don't panic. Be sure to let go of the ski rope's handle as you don't want to be dragged through the water. The lifejacket will keep you afloat. If your skis have come off, try to swim to them, and I'll circle around to get you. Pat your head to indicate that you're okay. If you want to go faster, give me a thumbs up, and if you want to slow down, give me a thumbs down. You can take turns being my spotter, that's the person who watches the skier while I drive. Sound good?"

Heads nodded in unison.

The next hour was spent taking turns trying to get up on two pieces of fiberglass in order to skim the surface of the water. Carter, Logan, and Alex were quickly successful, each having varying degrees of experience, and eventually each deliberately dropped a ski to slalom on one.

"Show offs," Brooke said and rolled her eyes.

Nicola laughed and turned her face into the light spray from the boat and ran her fingers through her windblown hair. She loved being on the water, but she knew this reprieve from her worries was temporary. When she returned to the lodge, she'd call into the office for the latest update on the stalker and try to brainstorm a plan of action to catch the culprit. Slowly, she was shifting her mindset from fear and anger toward a strategy for resolution.

Brooke and Nicola, both slightly-out-of-shape women of different ages, made it up for quick spins, and even Ben got up briefly before falling as his legs parted. He had no fear and he was sputtering water and laughing when the boat came around to pick him up.

In between turns, and while ringing a precautionary bear bell, they picked blueberries from the nearby bushes to enjoy at lunch. Nicola, while loving the lightened sense of worry, it still remained, and she wondered if the decision to leave Kyra with Victoria at the lodge was tempting fate.

CHAPTER 21

Back at Mountain Shadows Lodge, Kyra was also having a wonderful morning. She finally got some time to herself, away from her parents' rules and far away from her annoying brother. She planned to make the most of her time.

"Victoria, I think I'll go for a little walk, I'm bored sitting around. Is that okay with you?"

Victoria took off her sunglasses and looked Kyra in the eyes. "It's okay with me, but remember you are supposed to stay close by. How about you take a quick walk around the property but not off the paths, deal?"

"Deal." Kyra bolted from her chair, hoping to catch up with Tyler at the main lodge, but she didn't see him. The area around the buildings was heavily wooded, and it was hard to see anyone if they stepped off the paths. Otis probably had him working on some difficult job. No wonder his arms were so muscular. Kyra smiled to herself as she pictured her crush in his sleeveless work shirt. Chopping firewood, clearing the pathway of debris, and hauling supplies was hard work. Kyra decided to reward Tyler for all of his efforts with a kiss the next time she saw him.

Deep in her thoughts of Tyler, Kyra came around the corner from the path. Due to the commotion the previous evening, she hadn't slept well and was softly singing one of the slow campfire songs from the night before. As she approached, she could see something glinting in the sunlight on the porch of their cabin. It was a small, silver dog food dish, similar to the one Otis set out for Barnaby but smaller, and beside it was an unopened package of sunflower seeds. Thinking it must be from Otis or Tyler to feed the squirrels, Kyra opened the bag, spilled a few seeds as she filled the bowl. She brought the remainder inside and placed it in a cupboard. Kyra grabbed her book that she finally retrieved from the lodge at breakfast.

Kyra returned to where Victoria was still sitting. "I'm going to read in my cabin and maybe take a quick nap. I promise I'll let you know if I am going swimming. If anyone is looking for me, that's where I'll be."

"Okay, Kyra. Thank you for telling me." Victoria smiled.

A short nap and an hour later, Kyra changed into her bathing suit and cover-up and found a beach towel. As an afterthought, Kyra grabbed her phone. What was the fun in being at such a cool place if you couldn't brag about it? Earlier in the day, once her parents left on the boat, she reclaimed her phone from the digital detox basket in the lodge. Kyra went outside and took a few pictures of the view of the lake from the cabin and managed to capture her own image in a couple of them. She quickly posted a couple of bikini shots on her social media accounts and then hid her phone under her pillow. Unbeknownst to her parents, she posted a couple of shots upon arrival the day before when she realized the place where they were staying wasn't hideous. The scenery was very cool, and the other guests treated her like a young adult not a child. And, of course, there was Tyler.

Kyra gathered her beach towel and set off. She loved to swim, but getting into a cold lake in the mountains was a challenge for even the heartiest of swimmers. She knew there was only one way to do it, you just had to go for it. She waved to Victoria and ran down the hill racing past the warning sign on the beach advising to never swim alone and that there was no lifeguard on duty. When the icy water hit her stomach, Kyra lost her breath so she decided to take the plunge to end the suffering. The frigid water shocked her system, but when she resurfaced, she felt fresh and alive. After a few quick intakes, she regained her rhythmic breathing pattern and swam to the closest buoy. She waved to Jaclyn and Ethan, who were in deep conversation, while they watched her progress from the comfort of the two Adirondack chairs near the end of the pier. She was a strong swimmer, and it was clear she was loving her time in the water.

A few minutes later, she pulled herself out of the water and onto the pier in front of Jaclyn and Ethan. She shook her wet hair all over them and ran away up the pier and back to the cabin. Their shrieks and laughter made her happy.

Kyra returned to her cabin to change, and when she stepped onto the deck, she saw seeds spilled outside the bowl, strewn all around it. There was no sign of animal life. She smiled, shook her head, and made a mental note to fill it upon her return, but from a distance across the deck, something inside it caught her eye.

There was something stuffed inside the bowl. It wasn't food. It was fur. She climbed the stairs slowly. She gulped and crossed the deck. Her wide eyes zoned in on what was in the bowl.

It was a dead squirrel . . . curled up inside the bowl.

She leapt backward, questions racing through Kyra's mind. Who would do this? Were the seeds poisonous? The seeds. Had anyone eaten any? Kyra ran to the cupboard. The bag of seeds was gone. Who took them? Kyra shook her head. She went back to the squirrel and stepped closer this time.

It wasn't real.

It was a realistic-looking toy squirrel. Who did this? And, the creepiest question of all, why would someone place a fake dead squirrel in a dog food bowl for her to find?

CHAPTER 22

The boat returned an hour later and its occupants scattered in different directions, all very happy with their adventure. Otis secured the vessel along the dock knowing more boat rides would be requested.

"Quit it, Ben, I mean it," Kyra's anger only enticed her younger brother to continue to splash water from his reusable bottle onto her carefully curled hair. Despite her earlier nap, she was cranky, tired, freaked out, and, definitely, in no mood for him.

Kyra couldn't quit thinking about what she saw on the path the night before and now, after finding the creepy fake squirrel in the dish, she was more upset. She didn't tell anyone and just left it for someone else to find and handle. Besides, who could she tell? If she told her Dad, he'd make them leave. If she told her Mom, she'd lose her mind, and she was already upset and nervous about something. She could tell Tyler. Maybe he'd know what to do. She'd have to get him alone first though, without Ben around.

She and Ben were waiting in the kitchen of the lodge. It was an ideal spot to encounter Tyler. Kyra shook her head as she watched Ben raid the cookie jar. The siblings were going on a trail ride all afternoon. Tyler's grandmother ran the local equestrian center and would soon be here to pick them up. Tyler gave them a quick lesson on how to be a good rider. He told them to hold the reigns gently as if holding an ice cream cone. He mentioned to let the horse know which way to go by steering with the reigns out in front and then to the right or left. Most importantly, he said, never let the horse eat the noxious weeds on either side of the trail as they are poisonous. It sounded so exciting to Kyra, and she couldn't wait to look grown up and skillful on a mighty stead just like in the movies. The activity had excited her when Tyler suggested it and her parents approved. Sadly, Tyler told her later he would not be joining them, and she would be spending the day on a smelly horse stuck with her idiot brother.

"Why did you do your hair and put on makeup? You look weird. Since when do you care what you look like when you're camping, give me a break. Oh, unless you are trying to impress someone. Do you have a crush on someone here? My guess is Logan."

"Shut up, Ben!"

Ben's stool was next to a basin of water where pans were soaking. He reached in and threw the sopping, soapy wash cloth right in her face and a considerable amount of smeared mascara appeared below each of her eyes. Quickly realizing his life was in danger, Ben tried to escape but slipped on the water he spilled. Kyra grabbed the basin and threw it with every ounce of strength her skinny arms possessed and hurled the dishwater toward her brother just as Otis and Tyler appeared. Ben ducked and Otis and Tyler were hit with dirty, greasy dishwater. Both soaking wet, covered in suds and food that had not been scraped off, they looked at one another then at Kyra and Ben.

"Out!" Otis yelled. "Both of you, out!"

Kyra and Ben scrambled to exit the kitchen, slipping on the slick floor like a deer on an icy lake.

"Tyler, grab a mop before someone falls and breaks a leg." Otis shouted.

Tyler looked at his clothes, shot an annoyed look at Kyra, and grabbed the mop.

Kyra felt her heart clench.

"Sorry."

It was all she could trust herself to say without bursting into tears of embarrassment. She glared at Ben, and both Henderson kids headed toward their cabin.

Within ten minutes, Tyler had the mess cleaned up and was wringing out clean water from the mop. He carefully carried the mop and bucket through the main hall. As he stepped on the massive carpet, something caught his eye. Although slightly worn, the carpet was woven with threads of navy blue, royal purple, and forest green on a light taupe background. At least that's what he was told the color was when Victoria was admiring it the previous day. The rug was okay because the busy, colorful design hid food and beverage spills fairly well. One color that wasn't in the rug was dark red. At least it wasn't supposed to be. Yet, when he looked down, placed perfectly beside his right shoe, so close he almost stepped on it, was a drop of what Tyler was sure was blood. A guest probably had a nosebleed or cut their finger. Otis would have a fit if he saw the blood stain, so in order to avoid Otis going on another tirade about the inconsideration guests had for his precious lodge, Tyler grabbed what he needed to clean the stain and wondered who was bleeding.

CHAPTER 23

Nicola just finished tidying up the cabin when Alex returned from a quick run. They enjoyed a very fun morning and could feel themselves relaxing. Alex wrapped his arms around her. He was shirtless.

"You're all sweaty, get off me," She smiled and shook her head. "Go for a shower."

"Nope, I'm going for a swim." He kicked off his running shoes and socks and ran barefoot toward the lake just as the kids returned looking wet and guilty about something, but Nicola decided not to ask questions.

"Tyler's grandmother will be here within an hour so stay close by, okay?"

"I'm going to read in the hammock." Kyra grabbed her book and left.

Ben grabbed an apple from the counter and took a giant bite. With a mouthful he said, "Guess what, Mom, I heard a big fight last night."

"Did you now? And what have I told you about eavesdropping on people's conversations. We talked about your spying game, it's rude. Chew with your mouth closed, please."

Ben wiped his mouth with the back of his hand and his Mom tore a piece of paper towel from the spindle and handed it to him.

"I wasn't trying to listen. It happened right outside my window. They were loud whispering."

"Oh, loud whispering. I didn't know that was a thing. So, who was loud whispering?" Nicola couldn't help herself.

"A boy and a girl, but I don't know who and, you know what else?"

Nicola semi tuned out and took a sip of coffee and wondered how her husband had so much energy to go for a run after being in and out of the boat waterskiing for an hour.

"Hmmm, what, Ben?"

"He said the F word and I don't mean fart. He said *F you* but you know he said the real word, but I didn't because I don't swear." The kid's eyes were wide. Possession of this big secret that he kept all morning had, no doubt, been a challenge for Bennett.

The infamous F word, Nicola thought. Did all kids have a fascination with the forbidden language of profanity? Nicola always worried about the normality of her children's behavior.

"Really? That's not very nice."

Ben shook his head. Pleased with his reporting skills and was not yet finished with his story.

Nicola put her coffee cup on the counter and gave her son her full attention.

"So, what did the girl say after that?" Perhaps it wasn't such a mystery, Nicola thought, where Ben inherited his nosy tendencies.

"She didn't say anything, Mom. She just started crying."

CHAPTER 24

It was early afternoon when Tyler knocked on the Henderson's cabin screen door causing sleeping Barnaby to bark. Tyler asked, "Hi, guys, I just heard from my Grandma's stable manager that your trail ride is delayed an hour or so. To fill the time, I wondered if Ben and Kyra want to learn how to make ice cream?"

"Sounds great, kids, do you want to go with Tyler and make ice cream?"

"I do." Kyra smiled at Tyler, quite pleased to be hanging out with him.

"Me too." Ben pushed his way between his sister and her new crush.

The Henderson family followed Tyler, with Nicola, Alex, and Barnaby making their way down to the water's edge. Kyra watched as the adults gravitated to the back side of the lodge near the water on what was shaping up to be a stellar summer day.

As they entered the kitchen through the door next to Otis's office, Tyler looked down at the little boy and asked, "Have you ever made ice cream?"

Ben rolled his eyes, "Why would we make it? We buy it at the grocery store or at the ice cream stand."

Kyra added, "Yeah, every Saturday in the summer, we'd all go for a walk to the local ice cream stand, and we could get whatever we wanted. It was kind of a reward for us each week. I guess it was for not killing each other, back when we were a normal family."

Tyler looked at her, "Aren't you a normal family now?"

"Not even close." Kyra shook her head. "I just have a feeling something weird is going on but maybe I'm imagining it."

Tyler decided to drop the subject. "At Mountain Shadows Lodge, we make ice cream without any equipment, just a few simple ingredients and a little effort on our part. No chemicals, no additives, no artificial flavoring. It's so good."

"Cool, let's do it." Ben licked his lips.

"Alright," Tyler turned and walked toward the kitchen, "We need some things from the back pantry. Follow me."

The three young people entered the sparse room with a large counter and appliances that had seen better days. Tyler gathered ice, rock sea salt, cream, sugar, and a small bottle of pure vanilla extract. Three small and three large, empty, plastic freezer bags were placed on the counter.

"Okay, we are each going to make a batch of ice cream, and we can get someone else to judge whose tastes the best, sound good?"

"I'm going to win." Ben announced.

"We'll see, Ben, maybe Kyra will." Tyler smiled and winked at her.

Kyra blushed.

"We need to put four cups of ice in a large plastic bag you can zip closed. In the large bag, we add a quarter cup of rock sea salt and mix it up. Set your small bag in a bowl and add a cup of cream, two tablespoons of sugar, and half a teaspoon of pure vanilla." Kyra helped her brother find the right measurements.

Tyler continued, "Now the fun part begins. Zip the small bag closed and put it inside the big one and seal it shut too. Make sure the ice and salt combination doesn't mix with the contents of the little bag. We shake it for ten minutes to create ice cream, not a little shake like you do with a juice box. We shake the closed bag until you think your arm is going to fall off. And then you shake it some more. I'll put the timer on. You are going to want to use oven mitts or a towel so your hands don't freeze. Ready, Go!"

After about a minute, Ben started to complain, made faces, and stopped shaking every few seconds. "This is no fun. It's not working. I just want to eat ice cream, not make it."

As the trio took a break from the ice cream making, a loud noise coming from the main lodge startled them. It was a thud but no other noise followed.

"What the heck was that?" Ben said, eager for a distraction.

Tyler shrugged. "I'm not sure, sounded like someone dropped something. If it was something important, we'd hear them asking for help. There's always some kind of weird noise coming from old buildings like the lodge. Keep shaking, look it's starting to morph from a liquid to a solid."

"No kidding, I heard lots of weird things last night." Ben announced. "First, there was this argument and then—"

"Shut up, Ben. You don't have to tell everyone what a little spy you are and that you eavesdrop on everyone's conversations. Mind your own business for a change."

Tyler looked at the boy and frowned.

"What did you hear last night, Ben?"

"Ignore him, Tyler, he's into being a spy. He listens to people talking; it's rude and he isn't supposed to do it." Kyra waved her arm in the hope to dismiss a conversation emerging about her brother's eavesdropping tendency.

"Okay, okay. Sheesh, my sister's such a grouch."

The shaking of ice cream continued in silence.

Kyra was in an equal amount of agony as her brother but just focused on Tyler and kept smiling in his direction. She was mesmerized by the movement of his tanned arm muscles. When she had lost feeling from her shoulder to her wrist, the timer dinged and there was sweet relief.

"All done, now grab a spoon and taste your creation. We'll get another clean spoon and go find someone to judge."

"Oh, it's so good." Kyra was proud of her thickened creation. She actually made vanilla ice cream.

They crossed from the kitchen in the main room of the lodge, on route to the deck, and saw two sofas at odd angles. Tyler looked around the main room and was puzzled. Something was different in the room other than the furniture out of place, he just couldn't figure out what. He glanced from kitchen to the sofas and back again but said nothing.

"I know what happened. I bet Logan and Jaclyn were kissing on the sofas. Or maybe they were wrestling. They like each other. I know because I heard them."

Ben noticed that Kyra's face looked like thunder and the young boy stopped mid-sentence. "Um, never mind." He dipped his spoon into his bag of ingredients that did not resemble ice cream.

"Yuck, mine tastes like salt, I think my little bag mixed in with the big one. Can I have yours, Tyler?" Ben made a face.

"Don't you want to make your own? Maybe you can fix it if you just added more sugar and shook it some more? You go get more sugar and your sister and I will wait here." The teens were smiling at each other as Tyler spoke.

Begrudgingly, Ben retraced his steps, found the bag of sugar, and proceeded to add six more scoops. He shook the bag trying not to think of how tired his arm was, and how the sugar wasn't disappearing. He now made sugar-covered salty ice cream. Yuck, he thought. He looked around the kitchen trying to come up with something that would fix it. His eyes lit up when they rested on an air horn tucked neatly behind the industrial sized coffee maker. If he had an air horn, he'd be cool like the older guys. His backpack was by his feet, and before he changed his mind, he quickly tossed the air horn in his backpack and put the backpack on over one shoulder. He ran with his awful ice cream and joined the other two in the main room of the lodge.

Tyler and Kyra were holding hands when he entered the room, and Tyler stepped back and said, "Let's take what we made to your parents and show them okay?"

When Tyler's back was turned, Bennett whispered to his sister, "Hey, Kyra, look what I found."

He opened the zipper of his backpack and showed his sister the air horn.

"You better not let Mom and Dad see it. I won't tell them if you promise never to scare me with it and to quit bugging me."

"Okay, I promise. But, Kyra, I have to tell you something else."

"Not now, Ben." Kyra turned and caught up with Tyler who was heading outside. Ben followed her.

The three ice cream makers went to present their creations to Nicola and Alex who, along with Logan, were relaxing on lounge chairs on the back deck facing the lake

Nicola took a scoop from the bag Kyra presented. She was still full from breakfast, but the kids were so proud, Nicola couldn't resist.

"You made this, honey?" she said, looking at her beaming, flushed-faced daughter. "It's delicious."

"Try mine, Dad," Ben presented Alex with the offering and watched his father scoop out a heaping spoonful from the freezer bag.

"Wow, kiddo, this is really something." Alex struggled to swallow the salty, sugar crystal-covered, frozen lump of milk.

"Hey! What's going on here?" Carter approached the Henderson family from the staircase leading from the cabins.

"We made ice cream. Tyler showed us how without a machine." Ben answered.

"Cool!"

"You are dripping wet, man. I'll bring you a towel." Tyler offered.

"Don't bother, buddy, I'm not cold. I was swimming in the cove just past the cabins, but if you guys are heading for a swim, I'll join you. I love being in the water on a day like this. We should race to the buoy out there."

"Challenge accepted." Logan darted down the slope ahead of Alex and Carter.

Carter shook his hair toward the kids and icy droplets flew everywhere causing Ben's giggles and Kyra's squeals of delight, her styled hair long forgotten, as she watched him run after the two already in the lake.

From the pathway to the cabins, Jaclyn saw Tyler and the Henderson children run toward the outer deck carrying something in plastic bags. Then she watched the guys splashing each other in the lake like kids. She shook her head and crossed through the main room on her way to patio in search of the sandals she kicked off earlier. In the middle of the room, her barefoot stepped on a spot on the carpet that was cold and damp.

"That damn dog probably peed in here." She muttered and hopped a few steps then hobbled with her heel on the ground and toes in the air. She felt dirty. Jaclyn made her way to the kitchen and grabbed a paper towel and poured an ample amount of dish soap on it. She scrubbed her foot harder than necessary while imagining what she would say to the fleabag's owners.

CHAPTER 25

"Have you seen Cindy? I can't find her." Brooke announced.

"Best news I've heard since I got here." Ethan's hangover was one of the worst he ever had, and he was struggling not to vomit. Consuming a big breakfast, which usually helped, did the opposite. Even a long, ice-cold cabin shower didn't refresh him. "No offence but your friend is a pain in the ass."

Brooke frowned and said, "When I walked Cindy back to our cabin last night, she was absolutely covered in sand. I remember telling her to leave her shoes and jeans outside, but she took off when I went inside ahead of her. I chased after her but didn't see any sign of her. I assumed she was heading back down to the campfire. She mumbled something about skinny dipping and I knew the others would stop her. I planned to go straight to bed, but I decided to go walk toward the road in case she went that direction but I soon gave up. I guess I drank more than I realized because I forgot to check on her when I got back. I assumed Cindy was still asleep when I got up for breakfast and, that she was still sleeping, when we took off in the boat.

"I just went to check on her and there's no sign of Cindy anywhere. Jaclyn hasn't seen her. I didn't notice it before, but there's no sand anywhere in the cabin. I don't think she was ever in our cabin last night and I'm starting to panic."

"Maybe she went home."

"No way. How could she? The car is still here and, besides, if she called for a ride service, it would cost a fortune. It's our collective rule that when we get into a vehicle with a stranger, we let each other know and screen shot and text the driver's picture and information. I'm trying not to think the worst, but all that talk of bears and wolves yesterday has me a little freaked out."

"Okay, let's not jump to conclusions. If she feels anything like I do, she probably just wants to crawl toward a shady spot and sleep until the world stops spinning." Ethan reached into his pocket and took out a small bottle of aspirin. He struggled with the child proof cap and finally was able to pop two tablets in his mouth and washed it down with cold coffee. He made a face and stated, "Okay, I'll help you look for her after I go for a swim. Maybe the shock of the ice-cold lake will fix my pounding head. I'm sure she's fine. Cindy is lucky to have a friend like you. Look, the guys are already in the water. I'll tell them you're worried, and we'll help you look for Cindy. Trust me, she's not far away."

Watching the young men swim, Victoria approached the Hendersons and Otis who joined them.

"Otis, you've worked very hard to ensure everyone gets what they need. Thank you." Victoria smiled and patted her slim stomach. "I better add a long walk to my itinerary. I've eaten much more than usual. When did the kids leave for the trail ride, Nicola?"

"They left just a few minutes ago. Ben was not himself this morning. He had fun waterskiing but something is bothering him. I know my little boy. Other than the commotion Kyra caused last night, Ben slept, but he seemed tired and grumpy this morning. He perked up making the ice cream with Tyler, and he was excited to get on a horse. I'm not so sure Kyra was as enthusiastic." Nicola turned to her husband. Alex was watching Carter, Ethan, and Logan in the water racing to the buoy, a considerable distance from shore. Their return trip back wasn't quite as fast, and Carter and Logan stumbled from the lake appearing exhausted by their race. Ethan remained floating face up in the water with his eyes closed.

"I wish I had that energy." Alex whispered and smiled at his wife.

"Says the man who went waterskiing and running this morning. Beside, you usually find the energy when it counts the most," Nicola leaned in close and whispered in his ear and watched the flush take over his face.

Alex whispered back, "The kids are gone, we have the cabin to ourselves. I'll put Barnaby on the leash in the shade by the wishing well."

"Let's go."

Before Alex and Nicola reached their destination, one of the guys called over to them from near the outdoor shower.

"Hey, did it rain last night?" Logan frowned and looked farther up the path.

"Nope, but I heard on the radio on the drive up here that it might this evening or tomorrow. Typical long weekend forecast, but there is still lots to do out here even if the weather doesn't cooperate," Alex answered while Nicola carried on to their cabin.

"That's weird." Logan said.

"What's weird?" Ethan caught up with the other two guys.

Logan squinted to see clearer. "The rain barrel, it's overflowing. See the puddle at the bottom, maybe it's leaking. I don't think the screen is on either. Oh boy, there will be hell to pay if Otis sees it."

"Great, someone must have filled it up, forgot to put the protective screen on, and now it's probably full of bugs." Alex was sure Nicola would want another outside shower later, after their quality time together. "Looks like a lot of water was added to the rain barrel."

Logan started to jog up the path. "Whoa, I thought I was in better shape." He half-heartedly broke into a slow jog. "My lungs are still burning from the swim."

Logan's foot landed on the deck of the cedar shower platform; he slipped, righted himself by grabbing the rim of the barrel and looked inside. His eyes widened and mouth tried to form words but no sound emerged.

Carter and Alex approached, followed by Ethan. The men looked from Logan's face to the rain barrel. Their heavy barefoot footsteps on the cedar plank base caused the water to jump and swirl. Strands of long red hair skimmed the surface.

A twisted arm appeared beside the floating torso in an impossibly contorted position.

Cindy Elliott was face up in the rain barrel.

Undeniably dead.

CHAPTER 26

The three men stumbled back, gazes fixed on the rain barrel. They froze. A moment passed in silence.

"What the hell? Did she fall in?" Logan asked. "She was hammered last night."

"Doubt it, it's too high. This is awful." Ethan said. "I think I'm going to puke."

"Stay here," Alex shook his head and added. "I have to get Otis and call the police. Don't touch anything."

Logan replied, "I'm not touching anything. Hell no." He held up his hands chest high, shook his head, and backed away.

"Me either," Carter took a few deep breaths. "Okay, we'll stay here."

Within a minute, Otis arrived pale and visibly upset. His hands trembled as he rubbed his temples. The other guests heard the commotion of Alex calling out for Otis, and one by one, the others followed, and the group formed a protective circle around the cedar outdoor shower. Otis regained his composure and instructed them all to remain at a distance and to not touch anything.

"Where are the kids?' Alex looked at Nicola fully aware that he should know the answer.

Nicola squeezed her eyes shut as if trying to erase the image before her. "Remember, they are on the trail ride at the stables. Nowhere near us."

"Right. Thank God" Alex's voice had a tremor.

"They'll be gone at least another hour. They can't see this." Nicola looked at Victoria who nodded.

"When it's time, I'll watch for them, Nicola. I'll make sure they don't come near here." Victoria left the group to sit on the bench at the entrance of the lodge. Nicola suspected she needed time alone as she grappled with the shock of what happened.

"Alex, come here," Nicola gestured frantically for him to separate from the others.

They walked toward the back of the lodge, away from Cindy's body, away from the others, but still in full view.

Alex spoke first. "That's it, we are packing all our stuff and getting out of here. It's not safe."

"Hold it, we can't leave. There is a dead woman right in front of us." Nicola pointed to the rain barrel. The police will soon be on their way; they'll think we had something to do with this if we run now."

"For Christ's sake, just when you think it can't get any worse." His shoulders slumped in defeat. "All I want is for you and the kids to be safe."

The shock of finding Cindy impacted each of the guests differently. Her close friends cried; the young men tried to offer inept comfort but soon gave up. Victoria and Otis, older and having experienced more of life's pain, remained silent, but their eyes reflected pure sorrow at the waste of a young life and also the knowledge that her death involved a truly sinister act.

A young healthy woman does not slip and fall into a rain barrel. She was placed there. What was more horrific was the slow realization, among the adults present, that the person responsible was likely among them. A wave of comprehension seemed to slowly flow over the group of adults as they made eye contact with each other while still processing their raw feelings at the discovery of Cindy's bent and broken body. The unspoken realization, the locked eye contact and dread of what was to come engulfed each as they stood silently.

The moment passed, and each person began their own method of dealing with the shock. Jaclyn and Brooke took priority, and Nicola coaxed them to sit down on the deck away from the view of the rain barrel. Others followed.

"We have to call the police." Tyler tried to hide the emotion in his voice.

Alex murmured, "The police are sort of represented here." He turned to his wife and said, "Nicola works in our local police detachment."

Every head turned to Nicola.

"You're a cop?" Logan's shocked expression betrayed his casual tone. "Wow, didn't see that coming."

"No... no, I'm not a law enforcement officer. I support people who are victims of crime."

Victoria took Tyler's hand. He let her. "Otis just went to call the police. You okay, sweetie?"

Tyler wiped his brow, looking much younger than his sixteen years. "Not really." Victoria gave him a motherly hug. He sat on the stairs leading up to the shower.

"How could this have happened?" Brooke's words were muffled by sobs. "We need to get her out of there."

"No, no one can leave and, again, don't touch anything." Nicola's orders sounded harsher than she intended. "Everything is evidence. Why don't you go inside the lodge, I'll stay with the body, I mean, I'll stay with Cindy. Victoria, will you take the girls inside, please?"

The older woman gathered Brooke and Jaclyn gently and ushered them inside while offering them both a Kleenex and a hug.

"I'm going to talk to everyone, and then I'll call into my detachment myself to give them an update. You know, just in case." Nicola said, more to her husband than the others. Alex knew exactly what she meant. Nicola's mind went instantly to her stalker.

"I'll phone the station right away, but I need you all to listen very carefully to me. You've all watched enough television crime shows and read enough books to know that the crime scene must be preserved. Guys, do not take one step closer to the rain barrel or the surrounding shower area. Period. And nobody leave. Understood?"

They all nodded and looked like obedient elementary school children listening to their stern teacher's instructions. Also, they all were in varying degrees of shock. There were nods all around, even from Alex.

"The staff and I will make the call and return immediately. Someone look after Jaclyn, she doesn't look well." Nicola looked over at the pale woman, and then to Tyler she said, "Let's join Otis."

Nicola clutched her chest. The familiar, rapid, boom, boom, boom made its rhythmic presence known. For the first time since her arrival at the lodge, Nicola's heart palpitations returned. Their first appearance coincided with the first message from the stalker. As she made her way to the lodge, she struggled to catch her breath and thought she might pass out.

"You okay?" Tyler looked over his shoulder at her.

"Yeah, I guess." Nicola calmed her body as best she could and recovered some sense of composure by the time they reached the lodge. They found Otis sitting at his desk, staring out the window.

"Otis, have you called the police?" He jumped, startled by her words, and shook his head.

Nicola picked up the land line telephone in Otis's office.

"911 state your emergency."

"We need the police. We found a dead body."

"Name and location."

"Nicola Henderson. I'm at Mountain Shadows Lodge." She knew her voice sounded cold, detached. She was in report mode. A brief matter-of-fact exchange of words followed, and the operator informed her the first available police officer was on the way. In silence, the trio returned to join the others.

Nicola, Otis, and Tyler left the office and decided to wait for the police arrival in the main lodge.

Ethan volunteered to stay near Cindy to ensure the crime scene was not contaminated. Carter volunteered to stay with Ethan after he took a quick break to relieve a call from nature. It was obvious to others, they both felt guilty for the cruel things they had said about the dead woman.

The others slowly made their way to the main building and gathered near the fireplace in the great room.

Logan announced, "Ethan's going to stay with Cindy's body."

"By himself?" Nicola asked.

"No, Carter's staying with him." Logan added. "I think they both feel bad for what they've said about Cindy."

Everyone found a seat in the main room and, for a while, no one spoke.

"Who could have done this?" Jaclyn's voice shook and she looked around as if expecting an answer.

"I don't know, Jac, but you should sit down over here with me." Brooke put her arm around the young woman's shoulders, and Logan joined her.

"I'm so sorry this happened to your friend." He said. Together, they had negotiated the stairs leading to the deck, and Logan managed to get both women to sit on the couch facing the fireplace. Brooke did her best to control her jagged breath but tears won out.

Jaclyn spoke softly, "She's so still. Cindy was always moving, always fidgeting. We'd go on walks and I could never keep up with her. We'd try to watch something on Netflix together, and she'd be up doing something every five minutes. It used to drive me nuts. Look at her now, she's finally still." She doubled over clutching her heart.

While Jaclyn wept, Brooke's fury spilled everywhere. Anger often followed in the footsteps of sadness.

"This is horrific. God damn it, how could this happen? Who could have done this? Is there no security in this place? Are we all in danger?" Her rant stopped as abruptly as it began.

Logan slowly approached her, "Jaclyn, I think you're in shock. Hot tea with lots of sugar is my Mom's solution for shock; please let me make you both a cup." Both women nodded, and Logan went to the kitchen.

Tyler and Otis made their way back to the nearby office.

In hushed tones, Tyler asked. "Boss, what do we do now?" He looked even younger than he had moments before. Otis, on the other hand, felt decades older.

"We wait." He leaned back in his swivel chair, the brown leather, cracked and scarred by years of use, molded to his slim form. The thought of someone murdered on his beloved property made him sick, and sad, but more than anything else, it made Otis angry to the point he had not reached in many years. A young life had brutally ended. Again.

As Otis sat staring out his office window, he was aware that Tyler watched him from across the desk. His young frame slouched forward with his arms resting on his knees. He looked lost, bewildered as the initial shock of seeing Cindy's body resonated with him. He had not yet recovered enough to realize the significance of what happened, but Otis, with years of experience and maturity, was far ahead of him. Otis was in the process of putting some ugly puzzle pieces together in his mind. He knew it would soon dawn on the others what was obvious to him. People didn't just randomly stumble onto Mountain Shadows Lodge. It was remote. So remote it required both written and verbal directions plus a map and, if preferred, a Google maps pin drop. The likelihood that someone stumbled upon this place and murdered a young woman was as remote as the lodge itself. Someone already staying here must have killed Cindy.

"The police will be here as soon as possible. We are all to remain here, and no one is to touch the body or nearby area," Otis said quietly. His hands shook as he placed the note he had scribbled with the police instructions down on the table. The loss of a young life in this beautiful setting seemed unimaginable to most but not to Otis. He felt sick, sad, and helpless, but more than anything else, he felt rage. There would be no coming back from this nightmare.

Within an hour, the tranquility of Mountain Shadows Lodge was violated by ear-piercing sirens, harsh, pulsating blue and red flashing lights and streams of yellow crime scene tape. Cindy's death was flagged as a major crime thereby allowing a full fleet of police resources to be allocated.

The Major Crimes Unit arrived with great fanfare followed shortly by Inspector Lancaster and another detective. This was a significant response from a small police force, and Nicola wondered if her presence was the reason.

Nicola watched Inspector Glen Lancaster exit his vehicle and saw his eyes dart around the area until they met her own and he nodded. He then walked slowly toward the owner of the lodge and extended his hand in greeting. Otis reciprocated. The men were of similar age and seemed to know each other well.

"Well, Otis, sorry to hear you have a bit of trouble on your property. It's been a while since I've been out this way. It must be years, I guess back when..."

"Hey, Glen, yeah, it's been awhile," Otis interrupted him. "I'll show you where to go."

Nicola watched the arrival from the front entrance and recognized all the faces including one she was surprised to see. Detective Dickenson known at the office, and out of his earshot, as Detective Dickhead. Cindy Yell-A-Lot wasn't the only difficult personality who had earned an unflattering nickname. He was a young, arrogant, know-it-all, and Nicola struggled to be polite on the few occasions their paths had crossed.

He approached with a slight smirk on his face that made Nicola clench her fists in an attempt to control her visceral reaction to him. She wondered why a negative first impression of some people could create an imprint that never goes away.

"Henderson, I heard you called this in, looks like you have a bit of mess on your family vacation. Trouble seems to follow you around, eh?" He shook his head and pulled out his notepad, then looked up, and stared at her, waiting for a response. Putrid wafts of his body odor intensified as he stepped closer and her nostrils couldn't escape the assault. He was her height and she met his gaze.

Nicola tried not to flinch at his words and wondered how much of her ordeal he knew about. No one, other than Inspector Lancaster and the female detective working the case, knew what she was going through. What did this asshole know? If he knew about her stalker, he didn't let on, and Nicola refused to give him the satisfaction of reacting. Shortly after she started work at the detachment, Yvette Tremblay confidentially told Nicola to tread carefully around Dickenson. She said the Inspector knew his detective could be a jerk, but he was a jerk who was good at his job. Although, personality-wise, Nicola was disgusted by Dickenson. It surprised her that, when she saw him arrive, she felt relief.

Before she could say anything to Dickenson, the forensic team arrived, and he went over to brief them. Nicola took the opportunity to be far away from him and, if she was honest with herself, also far away from Cindy's body.

Not long after the arrival of the police, the Henderson children returned with eyes and mouths wide opened upon seeing the police vehicles and the scene playing out before them. They ran from Tyler's grandmother's van calling for their parents. Ruth, owner of the horse-riding stables, who was pushing seventy years of age, was filled in by her grandson about what had happened. After an animated conversation between the two, Ruth looked past Tyler's shoulders and frowned as she saw Victoria greet the children. Victoria told the Henderson kids immediately that their parents were fine.

After a quick discussion, the police allowed Ruth to drive away. Victoria tried to smile as she waved the older woman off, in silent assurance she'd look after the kids, and she accompanied Kyra and Ben around to the entrance and witnessed the reunion. As Nicola and Alex wrapped their kids in extra-long hugs, Otis explained to Victoria the latest information she had missed by waiting out front for the kids to return. Seeing how upset she was, he placed his arm around her shoulder and suggested she come inside with the other guests.

"Hi, guys, I'm so glad you're back. Did you have fun? Wow, I see you got pretty dusty. Oh, well, we won't worry about that now." Nicola tried to keep her tone light.

"Mom, what happened? Why are the police here?" No nonsense Kyra was having none of her mother's attempt to soften the situation. Kyra sounded young and scared, not her usual prickly self. In the briefest of terms, Nicola told Kyra that something very bad had happened and she'd explain everything.

"Can I have a ride in the police car with the siren on?" Ben asked. "Hi, Barnaby, hi, buddy."

Ben ran to free his tethered dog, and, in the midst of overwhelming sadness, Nicola and Alex paused for a brief moment to appreciate a slobbering Labrador and a giggling little boy who had not yet registered the magnitude of tragedy that just occurred.

Kyra quietly watched her brother with a confused look on her face. She started to say something but stopped herself. Nicola watched her work through what she had just been told. Even with all the understanding, her daughter was still very young to have to be even remotely associated with a tragedy. Nicola hoped to keep the gruesome details as far away from her children as possible. She wished she could just tell them Cindy died in an accident, but she knew she had to be truthful for two reasons. Children always seem to sense when you are keeping something from them, and, more importantly, someone murdered Cindy and that someone could still be here. She vowed to not let her children out of her sight and to go back home as soon as possible.

Alex joined Nicola and together they ushered their children up the stairs and onto a bench on the deck away from the investigation.

Alex began. "Kids, something very sad has happened." He looked in their innocent eyes, and for once, they were not fighting or fidgeting when they sat next to each other. The tension in the air engulfed them and they listened patiently.

"Something terrible happened to Cindy Elliott, and, I'm very sorry to say, she died."

Kyra said. "But I just saw her last night. Oh my God, what I saw on the path, I bet that was her, was she dead when I saw her?"

"Well, we don't know if that's actually the case, Kyra. We can't be sure that what you saw was Cindy, but I know you believe it was, honey. We will need to tell the police about that but not right now. Okay?"

"Okay." Kyra's brows were deeply wrinkled, and she stared at her feet trying to make sense of everything she was being told.

"What happened, Dad?" Ben asked and Nicola wondered if it was her imagination or did Ben's voice sound even younger that before.

"We're not exactly sure."

"What happened to her? Did a bear get her?" Ben looked back and forth at his mom and dad for answers trying unsuccessfully to make sense of what he was hearing.

"Shut up, Ben." Kyra was overwhelmed by emotion and reached the point of either succumbing to tears or anger. Anger won.

The little boy picked up a stick and hopped down the stairs from the deck to the ground nearby, with Barnaby jumping behind him. He drew a BB in the dirt. Bennett and Barnaby. Nicola recognized it as his mechanism to reassure himself, a signal that he was still here and so was what he loved most in the world.

"Now stop, both of you, and listen," Alex looked at each of his offspring. "No, Ben, it's nothing like that. We aren't sure what exactly happened, but that's why the police are here. It's their job to find out. We are all fine so we are just going to stay out of their way and let them do their work. Understood?"

Nicola added, "That's right, kids, don't go near them. We will stay very close to each other but, right now, Dad and I need to talk. Victoria is going to take you inside and make you something to eat so you both go with her, okay? Remember to wash your hands."

Kyra agreed without any push back. She was old enough to understand the gravity of death, as much as a young person can, and Ben was hungry so there was no argument from him.

On his way inside, Ben turned and said, "I'm sad about Cindy, Mom. I could tell people didn't really like her, and she was a bit bossy, but she was nice to me, and she was really nice to Barnaby. I saw her yesterday petting him and talking to him when he was tied up on his long leash at the wishing well. Anyone who is nice to dogs can't be all bad, right?"

"I agree, honey." Nicola gave her son a warm embrace.

"Can we have nachos?" Ben looked up at Victoria who had joined the family on the deck.

"Of course we can. I make great nachos and I saw some avocados so maybe we can make some guacamole from scratch. I wonder if Otis has any salsa from the local farmers' market. Doesn't that sound delicious?"

"Yeah, awesome."

Nicola mouthed the words *thank you* to Victoria who nodded and opened the door into the kitchen. From a distance, and in the safety of her husband's arms, Nicola watched the crime scene investigation unfold and wondered who, among the people she had breakfast with that morning, had committed this gruesome crime. Another thought followed closely.

Nicola turned to her husband and asked. "Do you think this was him?" Fear could be heard in her hushed tone. She wanted confirmation that this wasn't the stalking psychopath and that he hadn't killed Cindy thinking it was Nicola.

"I don't know." She could tell he was thinking the same thing. Alex hugged her. She felt fear take over her body.

Perhaps it wasn't anyone staying at Mountain Shadows.

Maybe it *was* him.

Earlier in the evening, she and Cindy were both wearing jeans and a dark sweatshirt. Maybe her first reaction was correct. Maybe her stalker found out where she was staying and killed Cindy by mistake.

CHAPTER 27

Death had arrived at the Mountain Shadows Lodge, but no one told the gently lapping waves or the sunshine dancing on the lake water. The singing birds took no notice, nor did the swaying evergreen branches welcoming all and promising cool, shady respite. Nature didn't care that Cindy died, for death is part of every day and, for all left behind, life goes on.

Once the police took charge, Otis returned to his small office, and the other guests nodded encouragingly for Nicola to serve as main contact for the police officers. It was agreed that, as information emerged, she would relay it to the group.

"The police want to talk to us individually." Nicola reported back. "We are supposed to stay together in the lodge." The Medical Examiners van pulled up to the driveway shortly after the police arrived.

They turned and walked to the outside patio followed by the others. Carter joined his friends, looking as upset and confused as the others and not wanting to say something that would make things worse, if that was possible.

Nicola asked a question to no one in particular, "Why this location? There are much easier settings. Why Cindy? From what I saw, she had a significant head injury. Maybe that will come back as the cause of death, if she didn't drown. If so, the killer took her dead body and put it in the rain barrel. Why? Did the killer know her? Hate her? Was it random? Why did he hide Cindy's body? Was it to buy more time, to delay discovery, or was it to destroy evidence on her?"

Alex spoke, "You're not asking the most important question of all."

She looked at him expectantly.

Her husband responded, "Was it one of us?"

No one had any answers to share.

As the guests gathered in the lodge, Otis turned to his young summer student and decided Tyler needed to be busy while the questioning of guests took place. He needed to protect Tyler from what was to come, the removal of the body. If the police needed to talk to him, they could do it later. Tyler was going nowhere.

Otis checked with Nicola and Alex, and they agreed Kyra and Ben could help Tyler straighten up items on the beachfront. This would keep them away from the crime scene and the related police activities. The three headed toward the water to put beach toys and boat items away properly. Busy work. Otis suggested Tyler and the Henderson kids go into the kitchen and fill the cooler with cheese, crackers, and chips along with pepperoni, pickles, and pop. They all promised to remain within sight of the big window in the lodge. The adults knew a police officer was outside if the kids needed help for any reason.

Kyra bent to help Tyler get what they needed out of the cupboards and said, "You know the adults are just trying to get us away so that they can talk about what happened to Cindy."

"Yeah, I know. I kind of want to be away from that conversation. It's too awful." A memory of the sinister note she found on her parents nightstand flashed in Kyra's brain. It directed her not to look under the bed. There's no way it could be connected to Cindy. Kyra was sure it was just a joke probably left by Tyler, but now was not the time to ask him. If he did leave the note and Otis found out, Tyler could lose his job and she didn't want that to happen.

Kyra looked at her crush and thought she saw tears in his eyes. It made her love him more.

"I agree, Tyler." Kyra said trying to lighten the mood and be strong for him. "Ben, come with me and listen to everything Tyler tells us to do."

"Aye, Aye, Captain Bossy McBossy Pants." Ben saluted and ran ahead of the other two toward the shore.

Kyra rolled her eyes, and Tyler grabbed the heavy cooler while trying to stifle a laugh. He knew this was not the right time to laugh.

For the next several hours, the police went through all of their procedural requirements of gathering evidence and establishing a time line of Cindy's activities and interactions from the moment she arrived at Mountain Shadows Lodge to when she was found stuffed in the rain barrel of the outdoor shower. A forensics team had been there most of the day, collecting DNA samples from everyone, searching the premises including all cabins and removing all of Cindy's possessions in evidence bags.

It was now time for the guests to be interviewed individually. Over the course of the afternoon, each of the guests and staff members were questioned privately, and written statements were taken. Otis's office was a makeshift interview room as each person explained their whereabouts that morning and offered what they knew about Cindy Elliott. They were asked for their impression of what she was like, how she behaved.

Through the interviews, it was established the guys were setting up a harmless prank on Otis that also impacted Tyler. Each of the three young men and two staff verified each other's presence. Now it was Nicola's turn. Dickenson was behind the desk, and she took her seat across from him.

"What about you, Nicola," Detective Dickenson asked, "Where were you later on last night?"

Nicola took a deep breath. Her voice was shaky, "After the campfire gathering ended, I was with Jaclyn, Brooke, and, of course, also with Cindy still at the fire down by the shore. I left shortly after Brooke and Cindy went to their cabin. Kyra and I were outside when Alex returned from a run. I'm sure you heard about the prank. There was a lot of commotion, but eventually, everyone settled down for the night.

"Okay, that's all for now." Dickenson closed his notebook.

"Actually, there was something else, a bit weird that happened. Kyra thought she saw someone or something in distress on the pathway between the lodge and cabins. It caused quite a ruckus, but nothing was there when we went to check."

Dickenson nodded, added something to his notes, and asked Nicola to send in her children and her husband.

The Henderson children, accompanied by both of their parents, were quizzed outside about the last time they saw Cindy as was Tyler. The level of shock and confusion, and their ability to give useful information, varied with each individual, but eventually, all were questioned and told not to leave the lodge. A police officer would remain until the investigation concluded and would let them know when they were able to leave.

The lodge's great room served as a gathering place for the guests in the aftermath of the police questioning.

Dickenson approached Otis, "I need to see what you have regarding Cindy Elliott's registration here."

"Sure, follow me."

At the registration desk computer, Otis accessed Cindy's booking details she provided. "We always request emergency contact information given our remote location and that some activities include a certain level of risk."

Dickenson nodded from across the counter.

"Hmm," Otis said. "It looks like Cindy's emergency contact is her friend Brooke who is here at the lodge. Not a parent, not a boyfriend. Brooke, who was on vacation with her. Since she booked weeks ago, I didn't make the connection."

"Not helpful." The detective said and turned toward the two young women sitting on a sofa.

The detective approached both Brooke and Jaclyn for information.

"Do you know the names and addresses for your friend's parents or next of kin? We need to make formal notification, and we like to do this as soon as possible in these upsetting circumstances." He looked from one tear-streaked face to the other.

"Hmmm, I think her parents are both dead. She had no siblings. Maybe she has an emergency contact in her wallet?"

"Do you know where her wallet and any identification might be? Her purse was located in your shared cabin, but the wallet is missing."

"That's weird, she had it here for sure. I saw her put her credit card on file with Otis for incidentals, activities like a trail ride and drinks." Jaclyn said.

"Yes, she had it when we registered and got our cabin key. She was in such a hurry for some reason she left it on the counter and Otis gave it to her."

"Right, I remember."

"That's fine, we'll look for family contacts back at the office. Do you know if she was seeing anyone? Did she have a boyfriend?" Detective Dickenson tried to sound nonchalant, but both women knew the questions were anything but casual.

Brooke was first to speak. "No, I don't think she was in a relationship with anyone. In the past, there was someone around. Someone who always circled in her orbit, but I don't know who it was. She had a boyfriend on and off for years. You know that kind of couple that break up and get back together. Rinse and repeat. It always sounded a bit crazy, like an unhealthy situation. Like an addiction. It was weird, but I do think it was in the past, right, Jac?"

"That's right." Jaclyn added. "It was always on again and off again. I never asked because I didn't like hearing about it. I could never tell if they were together because she always seemed unhappy even the few times I knew they were together. The best indication Brooke and I had that they were seeing each other again was that she'd disappear. She'd become completely absorbed in another world, his world, that we knew nothing about. Then, a few months later, she'd emerge, swearing off men and announcing female friendship is the only relationship she needed in life and then she'd be gone again. Only, this time, she's gone for good." Jaclyn's voice quivered.

The detective reached for the box of Kleenex on the coffee table and offered it to her.

Jaclyn took one, blew her nose, and tried to compose herself.

"What's was your impression of the boyfriend? What's his name?" The detective took out his notebook.

Jaclyn shrugged and looked at Brooke who set her tea down and rubbed her forehead.

"Ah, I um, I'm trying to remember. She didn't talk about him much. I'm sorry I can't remember his name. The few times she talked about him I sort of tuned her out. I feel terrible."

"I never knew his name." Jaclyn said.

"We'll look into it further, but it's not much to go on. Is there anything else you want to tell me or think the police should know?"

"I don't think so." Jaclyn sounded unsure.

"No, nothing else." Brooke stated and turned to stare out the window.

"Look," Jaclyn said. "I know it sounds like maybe we weren't very good friends to her. I feel bad about that, but trust me, neither of us wanted anything bad to happen."

Detective Dickenson stared at the woman but said nothing. He knew guilt always played a role in grief regardless of the circumstances.

When the police officer didn't respond, Jaclyn continued. "Cindy was complicated, annoying, fun, smart, wonderful, and even horrible sometimes. She was all those things, but you've got to believe us, we didn't do this to her and we don't know who did. Tell him, Brooke, he thinks it was us. We're the ones who came with her, and we are the only ones who know her and now she's dead." Jaclyn's voice was loud and her breath irregular.

"Calm down now. Deep breath in and out. Slowly." The police officer recognized the hyperventilation associated with a panic attack. He approached the distraught woman and calmly, slowly said, "Breathe in and breath out. You're safe. Keep breathing slowly in and out. Think about the word calm when you inhale and the word down when you exhale. Calm. Down. There you go."

Brooke rushed to her side, "Jac, it's okay, it's going to be okay."

Jaclyn's shaken, jagged breath expelled, "Not. . . not okay. . . no. . . no. . . no. I feel so bad. I knew she was struggling. I could just tell. She needed professional help, counselling, but I just didn't know how to tell her that as she would have gone psycho on me. I didn't want to be around her and when I was around her. . . I just wanted to give her a shake and even slap her in the face. She was always whining and complaining, and I couldn't stand her." The crying bordered on hysteria, and after a few more notations, the detective stood and announced that the questioning was over for now and informed the women he'd be in touch with them if needed.

Brooke wrapped her arms around her friend and rocked gently side to side. "It will be okay, I promise. We'll be okay, we'll find out what happened, but right now you just need to sit here with me. That's all that needs to happen. You'll be okay, I'll make sure you're okay."

The police officers conferred with the Office of the Medical Examiner staff, and arrangements were made for an autopsy to determine the exact cause of death. The witnesses were asked to remain available for further questioning and to not discuss what they saw, or details related to the case, with each other.

Alex looked at the floor and spoke in a hushed voice making the others strain to hear him report, "They'll soon be taking Cindy away and will conduct an autopsy. They'll find out what caused her death."

"Stop. We aren't supposed to be discussing anything about this with each other." Nicola said.

"How can we *not* talk about it?" Brooke murmured.

"Christ, I'd say maybe floating in a tank of water with a bashed-in skull might have caused it." Logan snapped and turned away.

"Hey, buddy, calm down." Ethan put his arm on his shoulder. "Walk away, don't upset the girls more." He saw the devastation on Brooke and Jaclyn's faces. It occurred to Nicola that even in death, Cindy Elliott did not disappoint. She was the center of attention; everyone had gathered around her. Her auburn curls floated serenely in the water. The long dark lashes of her closed eyes rested above high cheekbones. Dead Cindy was finally still.

"She looked beautiful." Carter said. Though he spoke softly, his words jarred everyone.

"That's a creepy thing to say, even for you." Logan looked traumatized.

"He's right," Otis stated. Feeling the weight of the stares in his direction, he continued. "I mean she's not bloated or damaged."

"Not damaged," Jaclyn screamed. "My friend is dead. I'd call that damaged." She broke down in sobs and leaned against Logan's chest. He stroked her hair and offered quiet comfort.

Otis quietly explained, "I'm sorry. What I meant to say is that, even though there was discoloration, she could not have been in the rain barrel long. From what I could see, she had a broken arm and a gash on her head. It looked like she hurt her knee, but there's no other sign of a struggle. Her fingernails were not broken, if there had been anything under the nails, the water likely removed all evidence."

His matter-of-fact statement shook those around him. The realization set in that, if what Otis said was true, it meant everything happened when the rest of them were enjoying breakfast. As they planned their activities for the day, Cindy was killed, and her body was put in the rain barrel a short distance away from them.

"There is no way this happened while we were so close by, no way. It had to have happened earlier. Like last night." Logan refused to accept the proposed theory.

Otis spoke, "Well, she couldn't have been in water that long. She would be, um," He looked over at Cindy's friends. "Sorry, but she would be more bloated. From what little I know, submersion in water is not kind to a body." He walked away, regretting the further upset his words caused.

Logan took a deep breath and chose his words carefully, "Okay, wait. What he's saying is, if Cindy was killed last night on the pathway where Kyra saw something, then she had to have been put somewhere else before being placed in the rain barrel." Logan continued, trying to piece together the jigsaw of Cindy's death. "She wasn't in the rain barrel first thing as we were all near that area early this morning, and we would have noticed all the water around the base and the screen left off. And last night, you said there was nothing on the path when you went back to check. So where was she?"

"This is too much." Jaclyn shook her head. She brought her knees to her chest and slumped on the couch in a half-sitting fetal position.

"I know, this is difficult, just please hear me out." Logan took her hand in his. "We know Cindy was alive last night up until Nicola and Jaclyn saw Brooke walk her back to the cabin. Brooke said she took off slurring something about wanting to go skinny dipping. Brooke chased after her but couldn't catch up but knew, if she headed toward the water, the others were still on the beach to stop her. Brooke then walked a ways down the road just in case Cindy ran that direction, and, when she returned, she assumed everything was fine. Cindy's bedroom door was closed so Brooke went to sleep."

Logan looked at Brooke who nodded her confirmation.

Nicola stated, "I don't know when she went missing, but I know she wasn't in the rain barrel early this morning because I had a shower and refilled the bladder from the water in the barrel. I forgot to list my name on the schedule sheet. That lessens the time Cindy was in the barrel to just a few hours."

"God, this is gruesome." Brooke's anger had lessened, and her emotional strength was starting to collapse.

"Where could she have been during that time? It makes no sense. None. She wasn't in any of our cabins. She wasn't in the lodge. She wasn't in any of the vehicles. We searched all of those places more than once when we were looking for her. I don't have to tell you that she wasn't wandering around outside in the night because I think we can all figure out what would have happened to her if she was in the woods. She would have been dragged away by some wild animal and never seen again, or pieces of her would have been discovered." Carter's assessment was unemotional.

"Stop. I can't take this anymore." Jaclyn was shaking.

"Okay, I'll stop. Sorry, sorry, Jac." Carter's voice softened, and he knelt in front of Jaclyn. "I'm just trying to help. When Brooke said she couldn't find Cindy, Logan and I looked around. We weren't too worried about it, we just thought she'd turn up. I think it's important to figure these chronological details out as soon as possible, not just for the police investigation, but for your sake, and Brooke's and Cindy's."

Both Jaclyn and Brooke made a choking noise, half cry, half moan. Nicola saw the disbelief and distress escalating and realized she needed to gather information while it was still fresh in everyone's mind. She couldn't wait for Detective Dickhead. The shock of the death could easily erase miniscule details that could help the police with their investigation.

"I don't think we're supposed to do this, but I think we should share with each other everything we know." Nicola suggested. "When we noticed Cindy was missing, we searched everywhere. Our cabins, our vehicles, the property, and we searched the lodge."

"Well, wait a minute." Otis interrupted. A thought was clearly forming on his face but appeared to be not fully developed. "What you say is true. We searched the main room of the lodge, the registration area, the kitchen, my office, the fireplace, and living room area, and the entrance way, inside and out. There's one area we didn't search. I haven't been there in more than a month. Remember we talked about it this morning." Otis's voice was barely audible.

"Oh my God." Victoria covered her mouth.

"Where?" Nicola shouted.

Otis got up and dropped to his knees in the area between the sofa and chairs. He pushed the rectangular coffee table toward the fireplace. He threw back the oval-shaped braided rug to reveal a latch and a square shape cut into the hardwood wood flooring. The root cellar. Otis lifted the trap door, and the others quickly leapt to their feet and crowded around the small open space.

MOUNTAIN SHADOWS

A ray of sunlight entered the room revealing microscopic dust particles in the air, invisible until exposed by a sun beam. Along with the dust, an earthy, dank odor wafted from the space below. Those present stared into the square hole, some peering over the shoulders of those in the first circular row. What they saw was a set of steep wooden ladder type stairs and four walls of wooden shelves housing canned preserves of crabapples, plums, and other fruit difficult to identify. There were rows of neatly labeled canned tomatoes, assorted berry jams, dill pickles and pickled carrots, beans, and beets. Otis carefully half-stepped his way down to the middle of the stairs and leaned sideways to reach a string dangling from a naked light bulb. With one tug, Otis illuminated the entire cavern.

As the onlookers leaned forward, crowded shoulder to shoulder, not all able to see at once, Otis surveyed the area while remaining precariously balanced on the stairs. Nicola asserted her position to be able to see as much as possible. The center of the area was empty.

The surprisingly large space was undeveloped, remaining as rustic today as it must have been in bygone decades. The earth floor of the root cellar had clearly been disturbed, most noticeably near the bottom of the stairs and toward the back of the space.

But Nicola had reviewed enough crime scenes and photographic evidence in domestic violence cases to realize what appeared below.

Nicola knew what she was looking at.

Drag marks.

CHAPTER 28

"The blood," Tyler's statement got everyone's attention.

"What blood?" Otis asked as he climbed back up the ladder.

"Earlier today, I saw a drop of blood on the carpet right around here. It was just a drop. I thought it was from a nosebleed or somebody cut themselves. I thought it was from one of the guests so I just cleaned it up. Here, look." He went over to the flipped over carpet and flipped it back to show the correct side. A brown rust-colored mark remained. "I wasn't able to get all of it out, but I did get most. I didn't want to bug you about it, Otis."

"It's okay, Tyler. Go tell the police. Maybe they can still take a sample. Just tell me you didn't use bleach to clean it."

"No, just that environmentally friendly carpet cleaner and water. News flash, it didn't work very well."

"That's good. It's okay, Tyler, don't worry about the stain."

"I can't believe she was down there in the awful, dark cellar." Sobs emanated from Jaclyn, and both Brooke and Victoria held tissues to their eyes.

"Cindy must have been so frightened." Jaclyn turned to Logan.

"If she was alive." Brooke whispered.

The forensic team entered the room along with Tyler and Detective Dickenson. The group watched from a distance as the entire carpet was analyzed, and once a portion of the rug with the blood spot remnants was cut away and placed in an evidence bag, the entire rug was taken away.

"I have all of your individual statements now, thank you. I have just a few points I want to clarify and you can all remain in the room. Let's talk about the shower one more time." Detective Dickenson pulled a chair to the front of an impromptu semi-circle that had formed on the deck in the aftermath of the cellar discovery.

"What about it?" Alex asked as he looked at the beach area to check on Kyra and Ben. They remained out of earshot and seemed to be getting along. His kids knew the seriousness of the situation.

The police officer reached for a pen and his notepad from his jacket pocket and made eye contact with each member of the assembly. His face told them nothing about what he was thinking.

"Well, I want to establish who used it and when. I want to know who walked past it or glanced over at it. I want to know if one of you noticed anything different about it. After a quick examination, it appears the young woman was not killed in the rain barrel. Her body shows no typical signs of drowning, but forensics will be able to confirm if there is water in her lungs. My guess is she was killed somewhere else and placed there. The killer must have been in a hurry because I can quickly name a dozen ways to die in a setting like this place. But, placing her body in a barrel, where it is sure to be discovered within hours, tells me two things about this murder. The killer was in a hurry and, more telling, the killer was familiar with the lodge and its surroundings.

"I want to know everything about the crime scene before it became a crime scene. Or, I should say, one of the scenes of the crime. He paused and looked them over one more time, "The only thing that is clear to me, at this moment, is the fact that your fellow guest was not killed in the rain barrel and probably not in the cellar. There's just not enough blood. Investigators are currently looking for the original crime scene, the place Cindy Elliott was killed. Knowing that, I need to determine where she was prior to being placed in the barrel."

His words registered differently with each of the others. Jaclyn, Brooke, and Victoria were again close to tears. Logan, Carter, and Ethan were somber but quiet, as were Otis and Tyler. Nicola and Alex looked at each other and Nicola spoke.

"One of the first things I did here was enjoy the outdoor shower." Nicola shivered at the thought of it ever being used again. "Obviously, that was before Cindy was placed in the barrel because I moved the lid and the screen to refill the receptacle, bladder thing that warms the water.

"What time?"

"Early, about 7:30 this morning" Nicola said.

Alex added, "I showered there too. I don't know what time it was. I just stumbled out of bed and went straight there. The water was ice cold so I'm guessing it wasn't long after Nicola was there. No later than 8:00 am."

"Did you look in the barrel?"

"No, I forgot to refill the bag of water. Oh God, you don't think Cindy's body was there when I was showering. Oh God." Alex shivered involuntarily.

"Okay, slow down. Let's establish a timeline. I'll talk to you again individually, but for now, let's go over what is common knowledge."

Everyone repeated where they were the previous night and early morning and when they last saw Cindy. They discussed the orientation and her comments during the ice-breaker activities, the beach barbecue, the practical joke, and Kyra's discovery on the pathway. The conversation focused on the state of Cindy at the campfire and Brooke escorting her back to their cabin. The last known sighting of Cindy was by Brooke, and Cindy was fully dressed in her jeans and sweatshirt, sitting on the porch brushing off the sand stuck to her clothes promising to go straight to bed. Brooke clarified Cindy suddenly jumped up and mumbled something about going skinny dipping and took off. As there was no sand in the cabin, the consensus was Cindy never entered her cabin the previous night.

Jaclyn quietly mused, "It's obvious she didn't go to the beach and she didn't go to bed. Where did she go and who did she meet?" She looked around the room struggling to comprehend that someone providing her comfort could have been the one who hurt her friend.

It had been a long, exhausting day and finally, after considerable discussion, repeating minute details, it was established the guests could all go to their respective cabins. The two staff members, once their work was completed, were allowed to retire to their respective rooms in the lodge.

Dickenson stayed behind and reviewed his notes. His aim was to identify where everyone was late the night before and earlier that day. It was tedious but crucial work. He reviewed the time each person stated they were at a location, paying careful attention to who could verify the statement. Special note was taken of the drunken state Cindy Elliott was in when Brooke walked Cindy from the campfire to their shared accommodations. Jaclyn and Nicola confirmed the approximate time, and the lab would be able to confirm toxicology. Nicola recounted the circumstances when she left the campfire and that Jaclyn and someone else, possibly Logan, were by the beach. Nicola did not get a good look at the person hovering in the shadows.

While Dickenson carried on with his questioning, Bennett Henderson looked up at his Mom and tugged the sleeve of her sweatshirt.

"Ben, shh. The police officer is talking, and it's important that I hear what everyone says."

"I know, Mom. I gotta tell you something."

Between Cindy's death, her own lack of sleep, and the cumulative stress she'd been under, Nicola was ready to collapse.

"What is it?" she snapped.

She looked down at her son's wide eyes. He slowly shook his head, stood on his tip toes, and whispered three words in his mother's ear.

CHAPTER 29

"Everyone is lying."

"Why do you say they're lying, Ben?"

The investigation had wrapped up for the day. Detective Dickenson said his team would return in the morning and stated no one was to leave Mountain Shadows Lodge. Police officers would remain on site. Every guest, including both minors, were in possession of his card. His instructions were stern and clear. If anyone remembered anything new, they were to call the detachment immediately or tell one of the officers present, or both. The Hendersons returned to their cabin, and Alex, Kyra, and Nicola waited for Ben to respond.

"Well," the boy paused took a big breath and said, "I know for sure Logan and Jaclyn were not in their rooms because I saw them holding hands and walking down by the lake. And, I know Tyler wasn't in the lodge like he said he was because I saw him running on the path to the cabins, and I heard his panting because he was out of breath, probably because he was running."

"Right, so what else did you see?"

"That's it."

"You said everyone is lying."

"Well, everyone I saw is and the others probably are too. Not you guys. Oh yeah, I remember I saw Carter running. He was running the other way than he said he was. I saw Victoria walking to the main lodge, and the light in the office was on, but I don't think anyone was in there because you can kinda see in there, and I looked and no one was there."

Nicola threw her hands in the air, "Ben, you are not supposed to be snooping in anybody's windows. You know better than that. You were supposed to be in your bed out like a light. When was this?"

Ben's chin hit his chest. "Well, I guess it was when you were all running around with Kyra. You woke me up and I couldn't get back to sleep."

Nicola and Alex exchanged a worried look.

"Okay, listen to me, I'm only going to say this once." Alex knelt down in front of his son, took him by the shoulders, and said, "This information just stays in our family for now, understood? We don't know anything, really. We don't want to say something that could mislead the police. They have enough real work to do. Got it? Kyra, you too. Not a word for now."

The children both nodded.

"Did anyone else see you watching?"

"Nope, I don't think so."

"Good," Alex continued. "Look, Ben, I know you want to be a spy or a secret agent, but secret agents have to be very careful that the information they gather is correct. . . it has to be the truth."

"Right, Dad, it's called fact checking before you submit your report to head office."

"Wow, son, you really know a lot about this, but, listen to me, we are not going to be doing the fact checking. That's police work. I will be the one to inform them of this, if and when needed. We are going to let them do all the work for now, and you are going to stay out of their way. I mean it, Ben."

The little boy leaned back on the sofa. He put his hand behind his back out of sight and crossed his fingers.

"Okay, Dad." Ben was disappointed because he had so much more to tell them.

CHAPTER 30

"Why does murder happen?" Kyra looked at the adults seated around the table. It was approaching supper time, and Otis suggested Nicola and Tyler lead everyone back outside to the deck. No one was hungry, but the children needed a meal. The adults could compare information and to try help the police piece together a timeline of Cindy's last movements.

"It's a good question, Kyra." Carter said. "Anybody have an answer?" He sighed as others shook their heads.

"There are a handful of reasons for most murders, honey." Nicola's voice was gentle as she brushed her daughter's hair away from her face. She needed to navigate the situation carefully as Kyra would not be satisfied with a condescending answer. She thought of herself as more of a grown up than a child.

"What I've learned, through my work, is that there are a few common reasons such as revenge, jealousy, control, profit, greed, but sometimes it's just random."

"And sometimes there're serial killers, right? I saw a show about them."

Ethan gave a nervous laugh, "No need to worry. We are just in a perfect setting to film a horror movie, right?"

Alex gave Ethan his best shut-the-fuck-up look. "There's no serial killer. They are very rare despite what the entertainment industry would have you believe. No, murders are usually boring, I guess mundane would be a better word."

Brooke threw her hands up and asked, "Did you just hear yourself? My friend's death is not something that should be described as boring."

"Sorry, didn't mean anything by it." Alex hugged his daughter and whispered, "Try not to think about it."

Victoria said, "I feel badly saying this, but I just can't get past the fact that she was so disagreeable. I don't believe I've ever met such a rude individual. We were all victims of her drive by insults."

Jaclyn spoke, "She was one of those people who was fine until she was crossed and then God help you. You'd be on the receiving end of wrath like you have never experienced. There was a malicious side to Cindy where she'd find a way to use something shared in private against a person. It was either to embarrass them, to show superiority, or to get something she wanted. Her friendship came with conditions. Her name was Cindy, but it should have been Cinder because she burned everyone around her. She caused pain but she didn't deserve this."

Nicola chimed in, "It sounds like neither of you liked her very much. Why did you come on holiday with her?"

"I felt a sense of duty. I don't know, nostalgia or loyalty," Brooke shrugged.

"Guilt, definitely. Fear, maybe," Jaclyn added and looked around the table. "She didn't have anyone else."

"You were afraid of your so-called friend?" Logan looked directly at Jaclyn.

"For good reason, from where I'm sitting," Ethan stood and said, "She was so bitchy to all of us. Oops, language, sorry." He glanced at Ben who was focused on devouring his chicken fingers, fries, and coleslaw. Tyler prepared enough for everyone, but there were few takers. Only he and Ben were hungry; Kyra picked at the odd French fry.

"While she was alive, Cindy triggered something in me that brought out the worst. Now, Dead Cindy is doing the opposite. I feel sorry for her." Ethan admitted.

"Don't call her Dead Cindy." Jaclyn yelled.

"Sorry, my bad. I didn't mean to make you more upset. Geez, I'll just be quiet."

Logan moved his chair closer to Jaclyn and held her hand. "She did always seem to have a low simmering rage within her. I guess that's how certain people exist, always looking for something to criticize or looking for a fight. But, even though she was a challenging personality, she was still your friend, and you and Brooke have our sympathy, right, Ethan?"

"Of course, sorry," replied Ethan.

Brooke was more objective, "She used people, and she'd buddy up with someone to finagle an invitation or a new money-making opportunity or a new job. She was always on the look-out for something to benefit herself."

Otis took a sip of his coffee and spoke softly, "I just remembered something. Cindy offered to look over my finances to see if there were areas where I could save money. She said I could pay her off the books, like under the table. I politely declined, but what would a coffee barista know about accounting?"

"She was a university graduate with a degree in business. Knowing Cindy, she probably saw a few areas that needed attention from a business perspective. Maybe a tax deduction you are eligible to submit. She always gave us good advice. She knew a lot about book keeping, especially forensic accounting. She was fascinated by numbers. She always said they told the truth." Jaclyn choked out the words and started crying again.

Brooke hugged her and added, "You're probably wondering why she didn't work in her field. The simple answer is, she couldn't. She had a criminal record. I told the detectives about it."

The others looked surprised. Not Otis.

"What for?" he asked.

"Fraud. Something to do with fake documents and a loan she co-signed and then defaulted on, it was big. For a while, she was afraid she might go to jail. She didn't, but she was still making restitution on both the loan and the penalty. I think someone else was involved, but I never was told all of the details."

"That explains a few things." Otis didn't elaborate further.

"There was a scandal about a year ago when she worked as an accountant for a museum. Nothing was proven, but funds went missing and suspicion fell on her. She denied any wrong doing but lost her job, her reputation, and her certification based on the evidence available. She disappeared. We hadn't heard much of her since then, until she came up with the idea for the JUGs trip here."

Carter added, "Wow, she was complicated. Not to speak badly of her, but God she was loud. I think her voice scared the wildlife. Was she hard of hearing? She must not have realized what a loud talker she was. Most loud talkers don't know it." Some of the others chuckled, then caught themselves.

"You don't think she said something that someone overheard and killed her for it. No way." Ethan shook his head.

"Yeah, she was loud, but she did have some good qualities. She was always great at figuring people out." Brooke said.

"How so?" Victoria asked. She took a sip from the oversized coffee cup Otis placed in front of her. She knew this conversation was cathartic for the girls. They needed to talk about what happened and about their friend. Good or bad, didn't matter. Talking was a release of the shock, guilt, and, eventually, the true grieving process that was yet to set in.

"Well, she could tell what was important to people and either work to help them get it for themselves or. . ."

"Or what?" Victoria nodded and encouraged her to continue.

"Or make sure they didn't."

Everyone was quiet. The emerging picture of Cindy, by those closest to her, was far from flattering.

"Look, Cindy didn't have an easy life. Her dad left when she was young, and her mom turned into Menopausal Barbie with fake boobs, fake teeth, and looking for love through a series of bad boyfriends. The mom was a train wreck and, frankly, so was the daughter. As we said before, both of her parents have been dead for years." Brooke caught the disapproving looks of the guests assembled and continued.

"Look, I hate to speak poorly of her now, but Cindy was complicated, she could be petty, jealous, and really mean. She'd sulk over imaginary slights and then make you homemade chicken soup when she found out you were sick. You never knew which Cindy you'd encounter. She was difficult to predict and, just plain difficult."

"Brooke's right. We knew her better than anyone and still, we really didn't know her. Does that make any sense to you? She was private." Jaclyn shrugged and walked toward the edge of the dock to look at the sun setting behind the mountains.

"Is there anything else you know about her that might help the police? Nicola asked.

"I remember her saying she had a boyfriend. No one we knew ever met him." Brooke grabbed a blanket and put it around her shoulders while she rubbed her hands together trying to warm up. It would soon be dark.

She continued, "Like we said, there was a gap in time, a year or so ago, when she kind of disappeared from us and from everything. The guy she was seeing had her complete attention, and she didn't have time for anything else. She said her relationship was exciting, but I thought it sounded unhealthy. She looked exhausted when she finally agreed to meet me for a quick lunch. I forgot to tell you about that, Jac. It seemed to me her boyfriend didn't want her to go out without him or do things she used to love. It was a classic controlling situation. I didn't like it and I told her so. The result was I didn't see her again until this trip." Brooke's eyes filled with tears, but she blinked and they were gone. Like Cindy.

Jaclyn held her mug of tea to her chest and looked at her friend. "We never met him. We wondered if she was lying about him, made him up to impress us."

Brooke shook her head. "I don't know. We used to joke that he was imaginary, but I think he was real. It was strange how she didn't want to discuss details about him, and she told me it ended badly. I got the feeling he ripped her off somehow, I can't remember the details. I don't think she shared all of the story. Whatever happened really upset her at the time, and I don't think she ever got over it."

The guests were quiet, each lost in their own thoughts, memories, worries, and questions.

Victoria took advantage of the chance to say something she wanted to share all day. Her quiet, dignified presence captured everyone's attention. "I think it's necessary for us to all acknowledge what the police told us adults. We are all persons of interest. But I would like to state clearly that I don't think what happened to Cindy involves any of us. I don't know, I'm just struggling with it all. I believe someone must have made their way here, ran into Cindy in her drunken state, and tragically. . . somehow. . . she died."

Brooke was the first to break the following silence. "I was the last person to see her alive. Well, other than whoever killed her. The young woman's voice broke, and Carter crossed over to her chair, knelt in front of her, and wrapped his arms around her.

"Don't think about that right now, Brooke. Just try to remember how much fun she was having and how happy she was to have brought your group together for the weekend. Her last memories were happy ones, honest."

"No, they weren't," Brooke broke out of the hug and stared at Carter. "She was very worried about something. She kept saying things that didn't make any sense."

"Really, like what?" Carter asked as he returned to his seat.

"Like, she said, *'it can't be'* – *'there's no way'* and *'now what am I going to do?'* She didn't know I heard her muttering to herself."

"Any idea what she meant by that?" Ethan was interested.

"Nope." Brooke was shutting down.

"Cindy was a bit unusual, no offence intended." Logan spoke carefully. "Could she have been just talking nonsense to herself like we all do from time to time?"

"Maybe." Jaclyn was willing to consider all options.

Ethan continued, "She was intense, no disrespect to her. She really didn't seem relaxed at any time here. When we were playing a game, or the ice breakers, she was always saying things that were just a little odd." He held up his hands to indicate that it was just his observation.

Nicola approached the group carrying pens and pieces of paper from Otis's office. She sighed and said, "It's getting chilly, let's go back inside. Tyler, would you mind taking my kids to the kitchen to make hot chocolate for them? The rest of us need to be productive. All this talk is just making us feel terrible. I think we'll all feel better if we can come up with something that assists with the investigation. It would be helpful, I think, if we each list chronologically where we were, and what we were doing, from the last moment you, personally, set eyes on Cindy to the moment when she was discovered in the rain barrel. This is just for us, away from the stress of the police questions."

Each person took a pen and piece of paper Nicola handed to them.

"I know a lot of you saw her last at the campfire, drunk, but she went somewhere else after that, after Brooke took her up to the girls' cabin. We know she didn't go inside as there was no sand in the cabin. We need to find out where she went and who she encountered."

Reluctantly, the others complied.

CHAPTER 31

Kyra asked, "Is there, um, like a prison nearby where someone could have escaped and done this?" Her bottom lip trembled.

Alex hugged his daughter close. "No, honey. We really don't know what happened, but Kyra, look at me, you are safe here now. I'm not letting you or your brother or your Mom be alone. For now we will stay in the main lodge together with the rest of the guests. Safety in numbers, okay? Remember, police officers are staying on site all night. Go have some hot chocolate, we'll be right here."

She nodded and joined Ben and Tyler as they made their way to the kitchen. All she could think about was the strange note in the cabin warning her not to look under the bed and, now, the dead fake squirrel. She wondered if she should say something. It didn't seem very important compared to what happened to Cindy. It would just freak her mom out, so Kyra decided to say nothing.

Tyler returned quickly with a previously made charcuterie board and plates. The adults filled their plates, the young guys each grabbed a beer, and they all gathered in the main room of the lodge. While the kids were in the kitchen, Otis built a fire that crackled and snapped from the dry wood igniting. The occasional ember tried to escape, but the black screen placed strategically on the hearth saved the now bare hardwood floor where there used to be a carpet.

Victoria brought Otis a plate of crackers, cheese, salami, and grapes, and when she returned to her chair, Nicola stood and faced the group making eye contact with each of them.

In a quiet voice, so the kids couldn't hear her, she said, "A killer came here, to paradise, to this special, healing place and took the life of a beautiful young woman. Why? He, or she, took the time to place her in a spot where Cindy would be found at some point this weekend. Why? All the killer had to do was drag her a little distance from the pathways and she wouldn't have been found for quite a while, maybe never, if the wildlife got to her."

"Stop, I can't hear any more." Jaclyn pleaded with Nicola.

"I'm sorry, Jaclyn, I know this is difficult but I have to ask these questions. Why place her in the rain barrel? It makes no sense. I can't handle things that don't make sense." Nicola's voice cracked.

Carter shrugged and suggested, "Maybe the killer panicked, maybe he didn't mean to hurt her and just needed to hide her until he could think of what to do next."

Logan took up the latest theory and added, "Okay, so if that's true, then the rain barrel is like a storage facility. . . a temporary place."

Brooke looked at the two men trying to piece together what happened. "You guys think the killer wanted to go back and do something with the body later but it was discovered sooner than expected?"

Logan took Brooke's hand and gently said, "That kind of makes sense. . . if you can say that about any of this craziness. Maybe the idea was to take Cindy out of the barrel at some point and hide her in the woods, just as Nicola described, only they didn't get the chance."

"Maybe the reason she was put in the rain barrel was to destroy evidence on Cindy's body," Ethan stated. "Water can do that, right?"

Nicola spoke, "Okay. That's plausible. So, we know Cindy was hit on the back of the skull. At some point, she ended up on the edge of the pathway near the cabins, was probably in the cellar, and later placed in the barrel. What we don't know is if she was alive when any of that happened. The Medical Examiner's Office will make that determination based on whether there is water in her lungs. From the brief glimpse I got of Cindy's head, it looked like a nasty injury to me. Placing Cindy in the rain barrel would have been challenging. It would have taken considerable strength, and the person responsible would have been soaking wet afterwards."

The group looked around at each other, silently trying to remember who was wet when and who had changed clothes.

Otis spoke, "Unfortunately, between cabin showers, the water fight at breakfast, the activities in the lake plus the water sports, the answer was everyone was wet at some point earlier today, and we all changed our clothes."

Carter looked at him in disbelief and said, "You still think it was one of us?"

Logan held up his hand like a school boy and asked, "Is it possible that Cindy did all this herself?" All eyes were on him, none of them friendly.

Logan continued, "Look, could she have fallen, accidently hit her head, and, not realizing the seriousness of her injury, collapsed on the pathway? That is a realistic scenario. Could Kyra's scream have woken her up and, in her drunken and possibly concussed stupor, could she have made her way to have a shower and, instead, fell forward into the barrel? Maybe those marks in the cellar, or the blood drop, have nothing to do with Cindy. C'mon, I know it's ludicrous but anything is possible." Logan continued looking around the room for an ally. When he saw the disapproving looks on the others faces, he held up his hands and in a loud voice said. "I mean no disrespect, but she was absolutely bat shit crazy and very drunk."

Brooke responded, "You're an idiot."

"I agree," Victoria stood up and warmed her hands by the fire. She was chilled though the room was warm. Shock had that effect on her. "Pardon me, Logan. I do understand what you are saying. Cindy seemed on the verge of a mental breakdown, and I was exhausted after each encounter with her. She was what I call a one upper, whatever you did, she did more often or in a better way. She was overly competitive during games. She didn't seem content here, even though we know that this JUGS trip was her idea. She struck me as a very unhappy soul."

Ethan shook his head, "She struck me as just plain awful. I got a glimpse of how she treated Tyler. She ordered him around like he was her personal servant. He, of course, complied. As if she gave him a choice."

Jaclyn took a tissue from her pocket, blew her nose, and said, "We are getting off track but, it's true, Cindy has always been a control freak. We chose to ignore that part of her because I believed she had good intentions and a good heart. Brooke and I always felt a little sorry for her." Tears welled up, and she backhanded them away and sat up straighter.

Nicola spoke with authority and said, "Okay, enough of rehashing all of this. Let's get back to our main purpose. We have three questions to answer regarding the timeline between Cindy leaving the campfire and her discovery in the barrel: where were each of you, what were you doing?"

Ethan interrupted, "Is the last question what the hell happened here? Because that's what I want to know."

Nicola ignored him and said, "The last question will probably give us the answers to everything. The last question is. . . why. . . why was Cindy killed?"

No one answered.

Logan stood up and yelled. "Alibi. You want us all to provide an alibi? Okay, Nicola, I'll give you one. I was enjoying a weekend away with my buddies. I wasn't running around the property killing someone and moving their dead body around. Last night, when all this was going on, I was with my friends pulling a lame prank on Otis, and then I was down by the lake with my pants around my ankles. And, I wasn't the only one undressed."

No one spoke.

Moments passed.

Logan's eyes scanned the room until he found who he was looking for and met her gaze. "Sorry, Jaclyn, we have to tell the truth. We are each other's alibi."

Nicola continued to stand in front of the group. "Look, here's what I know. Alex went for a run, once he thought our kids were sleeping, and returned just as Kyra screamed. Brooke went for a walk to try to sober up. Carter and Ethan were together, after the prank in their cabin, playing cards. Otis and Tyler went back to their rooms after the incident with Kyra. Victoria came out of her cabin when Kyra screamed and returned shortly thereafter. Jaclyn and Logan were together as we just learned. Logan walked Jaclyn back to her cabin. They met up with Brooke returning from her walk. The women assumed Cindy was asleep inside as her bedroom door was closed. When Logan returned to the guys' cabin, he joined a card game with Ethan and Carter until the wee hours of the morning. I was with my family once I returned from the campfire and after the commotion on the path. The next morning Tyler and Otis were up early making breakfast for all of us. One by one, other than Cindy, we made our way to the lodge to enjoy our day."

Blank stares met her gaze.

Ethan was the first to speak. "Agreed. That's everything and we've accomplished nothing. I think we need a distraction. Hey, Tyler, come in here, buddy."

Tyler answered the call immediately with a questioning look on his face. Kyra and Ben followed and sat on the floor by their parents.

Ethan asked, "Do you have any more ice breakers for us? We could use a break."

Tyler shot a glance at Otis who nodded, "Yeah, I have a few. Are you sure you want to do this?"

Ethan said, "Yes, let's hear one. C'mon, you guys, we need to think about something else, even if it's just for a few minutes."

Nicola agreed. "You're right. Let's do this."

"Okay," Tyler rubbed his face and tried to remember one of the ice breakers from his notes. "Oh yeah, this is a good one. Do you have a phobia and, if so, what is it?"

"What's a phobia?" Ben asked.

His father answered, "It's something you dislike, something you can't stand."

Bennett looked at Kyra.

Kyra looked right back at him.

Ethan rubbed his hands together and said, "Actually, a phobia is an irrational fear. Okay, Tyler. I'll go first. I hate snakes, actually I hate all reptiles. They are creepy, prehistoric looking, nasty creatures."

"Aw, I feel sorry for reptiles. They get a bad reputation. They are more afraid of you than you are of them." Brooke stated.

"Yeah, yeah," Ethan put up his hand. "I've heard it all before, but it doesn't change my mind."

Tyler looked around the room. "How about you, Nicola?"

"I'm not a fan of heights." She said it casually, trying not to let on how serious her problem was with heights. Dizziness, dry mouth, heart palpitations, and shortness of breath. . . she hid all of these symptoms as best she could during the treacherous drive up to Mountain Shadows Lodge.

Carter said, "You know what I don't like? Dark, confined spaces, like back alleys. Bad things happen in back alleys, and I'm man enough to admit I don't like them." The look on Carter's face defied anyone to challenge him.

Jaclyn joined in, "I don't like fairground operators. Carnies. I know it's a stereotype. I'm sure some are great people. Just not the ones I've met at the fairground."

Logan added, "Oh yeah, that reminds me. I didn't think I had a phobia but I do. Clowns. I've hated them since childhood."

Brooke spoke, "Freeways. Everyone drives too fast, and they are far too casual. Some are on their phones and texting and they should be arrested.

And merging. Don't even get me started on merging, there's always a giant semi-truck in my way every time I need to merge or change lanes." The others nodded in agreement.

Tyler smiled, "Who is next?"

Victoria spoke softly, "Bodies of water and waterfalls, everyone thinks they are so beautiful. Not me, I find them terrifying. What about you, Alex?"

Alex looked at Nicola and said, "Elevators. I try to take the stairs whenever I can. It has been brought to my attention, I may be mildly claustrophobic."

Tyler looked at his boss, "Otis, I think you're the only adult who hasn't answered."

"Kid, nothing scares me anymore," was his response.

Everyone was quiet, lost in their own thoughts.

Nicola looked at the others and threw up her hands. "This is getting us nowhere. We're all exhausted, it's time to call it a night. Alex, kids, let's go back to our cabin. I suggest you all do the same.

"Be careful, it's so dark outside. I've never seen darkness like this." Carter said.

Tyler answered, "It's because we are in a dark sky preserve area."

"A... what now?" Carter turned to the young man.

"Dark sky preserves exist all over the world and are intended to combat light pollution. It's a real thing, and an important thing. Artificial light messes with humans, but, most of all, it messes with nocturnal animals like owls, bats, and many more creatures. Dark skies also allow us humans to protect our circadian rhythms, especially those involving our sleep-wake cycle. The dark skies also allow us to properly enjoy the specular blanket of stars and aurora borealis."

No one said it out loud, but some guests made the correlation between a dark sky and a myriad of opportunities, none of them good.

Carter watched most of the others leave. When it was just Victoria and the two staff remaining, he stood, stretched, and said, "Victoria, I'll walk you back to your cabin if you want me to."

"Well, it's been a while since a handsome young man offered to walk me to my door. Thank you, Carter. That would be great. Good night, Otis. Good night, Tyler."

"Good night." Tyler said.

Otis waved to his guests. They waved back.

Victoria turned back and added, "I hope we are all able to get some rest tonight."

They all heard the fatigue in Victoria's voice.

Ethan and Logan were entering their cabin located next to the lodge when they saw Carter and Victoria pass by with their heads together in earnest conversation. Ethan shook his head.

"What?" Logan asked.

"I still can't figure Victoria out. She appears extra disorganized and a bit silly. I think she's anything but. I think she's faking it. Look at her appearance, it's spectacular. Not a hair out of place, stunningly put together yet she comes across all flustered and out of sorts. I don't buy it. Something is up with that one. She pretends to be forgetful yet she sees everything and reminded me of a couple of safety things Tyler said that I had forgotten. I caught a glimpse inside her cabin. It's like she hasn't unpacked. There's nothing there. No food, clothes, make up, jewelry."

"Just because our cabin looks like a bomb went off doesn't mean everyone's looks like that." Logan remarked.

"No, I know, I get it. But why is she even staying here?"

Logan groaned, too tired to listen to any more of Ethan's ramblings.

CHAPTER 32

The Henderson family exited their cabin together. The parents were worried and the kids were grouchy. Everyone was nervous despite having police guards throughout the property. The closest one was stationed just outside their cabin.

Bennett approached the tall police officer who gazed down at the child. The boy looked at the walkie-talkie and the gun and then the face of the officer. The others watched in silence. Ben sighed, and his slim narrow shoulders slumped. He looked up with big round eyes of a young child and said, "Hello, officer. I have something to report."

The officer tilted his head, impatiently. "What is it?"

"Everyone is lying."

"Ben!" Nicola and Alex yelled at the same time. "We already talked about this."

"Sorry," Alex stood up and moved toward the officer whose eyebrows slammed together as he scanned the family. "My son is upset, and he's been playing a spy game. Please disregard what he said, he's confused."

"It's not a spy game, Dad. It's true. I told Mom but she didn't believe me. I took lots of notes, and I followed everyone and I listened, and I'm a good detective."

Alex laughed. The sound was forced and too loud, and he stopped midway making the noise sound even more inappropriate. He grabbed his son's arm. "Now listen, you know Mom and I were on the deck together watching what was happening in the lake, and Kyra was with you and Tyler making ice cream. Otis spent a lot of time with Victoria. It is none of your business where anyone else was at any point during our stay here. From now on, you better mind your own business. I mean it, Ben."

Detective Dickenson slammed his car door and joined the discussion as the Hendersons approached the lodge. The junior officer informed his superior what the little boy just told him. He pulled up his pant legs in order to squat down to Ben's eye level. "You know, young man, eavesdropping and spying on people is not only rude but also illegal and, sometimes, it can be very dangerous. Now, I'm going to ask your parents to join us because we are going inside for a little talk." He nodded to the Hendersons who followed him to the front entrance past several police vehicles parked throughout the circular driveway.

Prior to leaving, Dickenson gathered the guests and staff in the main room of the lodge. As he made eye contact with each of them, his voice was clear and loud in the otherwise silent room.

"I'm going to recap all that we know so far. If anything I say is incorrect tell me. If I miss anything important, tell me. If you suddenly remember something, no matter how small or seemingly insignificant it is, tell me. This is your opportunity, if something comes to light later on that you could have, or should have said, it may reflect poorly on you."

The detective took his time.

"Cindy Elliott was last seen leaving the campfire area accompanied by Brooke Richards who helped her to the deck of their shared cabin where Ms. Richards said good night to her after the victim refused to enter the cabin. Ms. Richards assumed she returned to the campfire area."

Brooke nodded.

"The next day, Ms. Richards and Ms. Jaclyn Lee woke mid-morning to find that Ms. Elliott was not in her room, and there was no sign of her having entered the cabin, namely, there was no evidence of sand in the cabin entrance or any of the rooms. This fact is significant because Ms. Elliott's clothing was apparently covered in sand from the previous evening, and there was no evidence of her changing clothes. She was found in the rain barrel with the same clothes from the previous night as some of you have identified. Having questioned the others, Ms. Richards and Ms. Lee assumed Ms. Elliott passed out from excessive alcohol consumption in her closed door room in their shared cabin."

Brooke and Jaclyn looked remorseful. Not checking on their drunk friend did not paint either of them in a good light. The room was silent as scenarios of exactly where Cindy was later Friday evening and early Saturday morning filled their thoughts.

"Late last night, two significant events occurred almost simultaneously. One, a practical joke and, the other, a sighting of a mysterious bulky item covered in some kind of tarp on a pathway seen only by Ms. Kyra Henderson." Detective Dickenson's voice changed to a softer tone, and he gently smiled at the young girl.

Nicola put her arm around her daughter's shoulder as they sat side by side on the couch.

"The question I have is, was that bulky item the body of Cindy Elliott? If so, had she fallen and injured herself and got up when she heard young Kyra scream. Or," he paused. "Was she dead already and deliberately moved by the perpetrator?"

Soft crying came from Jaclyn who said, "Brooke, you should have stayed with her."

Brooke squared off across from her friend. "Listen, it's not my fault she's dead. You did nothing to help me deal with her and I'd had enough of her bullshit. I needed to get away from her. I just went for a walk down the road we drove in on. I wanted to get away from everybody. At least I helped her up the hill, that's more than you did, Jaclyn, and we all know why."

The room was silent.

Detective Dickenson turned to Carter, Logan, and Ethan. "You three were involved in the air horn prank behind the lodge." It wasn't a question.

Carter spoke, "Yes, sir, we were all behind the lodge being idiots. Then we all ran back to our cabin. I was just ahead of the others trying to set up our cover up." He laughed nervously and continued. "But I heard Kyra scream and got distracted, and then the guys came running and then Otis arrived."

Ethan added, "Hey, wait. We can prove it, I took pictures. I think they're digitally time stamped to show you where we were."

"Oh yeah, you did. Great, where's your camera?" Carter asked.

"Otis confiscated it, remember." Ethan sounded like a kid in junior high caught with contraband. "These pictures will show where we all were. Even Otis and Tyler are probably in the shots. I didn't have a chance to look. Nobody did."

Otis spoke up. "I'll get the camera for you when you're done here, Detective."

Dickenson nodded and flipped a few pages of his small, worn notebook and then took a sip of the coffee Otis provided.

"Mr. McIntyre and Mr. Donahue, you were inside the lodge, each in your own room, and you both heard the scream and the air horn, correct?" Otis and Tyler nodded in agreement.

"Ms. Shea, you told me earlier you were in your cabin."

Victoria stared down at the lake and didn't answer right away. The quiet in the room made her look up, somewhat startled to find everyone looking at her. She said, "That's right, I came outside when I heard all the commotion."

"Mr. Henderson," Dickenson turned his attention to Alex. "Your wife and children were together but you weren't there. Where were you?"

All eyes turned to Alex who stood at the fireplace.

"I went for a run."

"At night? In the wilderness?" Dickenson asked.

"Yes. I had bear spray with me, and a bell so I didn't startle any ferocious animals. I wore a head lamp."

Dickenson paused and jotted something in his notebook. "Thank you for your cooperation. We now have a better understanding of where everyone was and a sequence of events that, while incomplete, is helpful nonetheless."

"I've spoken to each of you and I have your official statements. I'll review your accounts of Cindy's last interactions and last known movements."

The heaviness of silence filled the room.

"Before I leave, I want to share something with you that I've learned over the many years I've worked in homicide investigation. Murder often involves secrets and, always, very strong emotions. Often the root of the secret centres on jealousy, envy, resentment, or rage. Sometimes it's the desire for revenge or the need to control. I also know one more thing."

Collectively, the group held their breath.

They stared at the police officer.

Captivated.

After what seemed like an eternity, while meeting each stare, he spoke.

"What I know for sure is, secrets are like water in nature, difficult to contain and always seeking to be free. If any of you have a secret related to this murder, tell me now, because it will come to light. Secrets always do."

Detective Dickenson's words were met with more silence.

CHAPTER 33

At the large coffee urn, Nicola refilled her cup having lost count of the amount of coffee she had consumed. Brooke was making a cup of tea and as she repeatedly dunked the tea bag she spoke softly.

"I think her snooping finally got her into trouble." Brooke's tone was unemotional.

"What do you mean?" Nicola asked.

"She'd visit us, and we knew she'd go through all our stuff. She'd see our mail on the counter, pick it up, and read it. She searched our bulletin board for juicy items that didn't exist. She'd go into our bathrooms and sample our lotions and perfume. We wouldn't mind if she asked first. She felt anything that belonged to us, was also hers. Bizarre, right? It really pissed me off."

Nicola could see the remnants of anger on Brooke's face. Then a smile emerged.

"One time, when I knew she was coming over, I put ping pong balls, probably twenty of them, in our medicine chest. It took ages to do as they kept falling. Finally, I got them all to stay while I quickly closed the door. Sure enough, she went into the bathroom, and all Jaclyn and I heard was the sound of ping pong balls hitting the counter and the floor. She was busted. Served her right, the snoopy cow."

"What did she say about it?"

"She brushed it off, typical Cindy. She said something like, *ha-ha very funny. I was looking for a Band-Aid.* It was all bullshit." Brooke chuckled at the memory and then looked sad.

"That's definitely rude behavior. I did notice her manners weren't great. She was very blunt." Nicola was briefly lost in thought remembering what Cindy had said about Alex's behavior. Eventually she asked, "What's the situation with her family?"

"I'm not sure, she was always a little sketchy with the details. I don't think her childhood was happy; her Dad left when she was young, and her Mom was very self-involved. I'm not sure either one is alive, at least she doesn't see them. Cindy was smart and got a full university scholarship and that's when we met her. She met a guy at school and was crazy about him. Like we said before, it was strange we could never meet him. Jaclyn and I thought she was making him up. Then suddenly he was no longer in the picture. She still arranged our reunion trips once a year, but the last few were like a chore for us to attend. I know I sound like a bitch, but we really didn't have much in common except the so-called glory days."

The woman took a sip of her tea and winced when it burned her lips. She placed the mug on a coaster on the end table beside one of the comfortable, overstuffed chairs in the main room.

Brooke continued, "I think this all comes down to the kind of person Cindy was and that's what got her in trouble. Cindy was always crossing boundaries, she always wanted to know everyone's business. Sometimes, when people are snoopy, they find out things they wish they hadn't found out. I think she discovered something that was dangerous, and it cost her everything."

"So you think it was someone who knew her. What could she have possibly discovered here that would cause someone to murder her?" Nicola felt she was taking Cindy's death harder than this young woman, someone who knew Cindy for years.

"Isn't that what the police are here to find out?" Brooke stated. She took her tea and walked away.

Nicola's eyes followed Brooke as she took her tea and rejoined the others in the main room. She'd learned two things from the conversation. First, Cindy's curiosity may have exposed something that led to her death and, second, Brooke could be vindictive.

CHAPTER 34

Dickenson pulled Nicola aside and gestured for her to join him on the bench at the front of the lodge. A sense of dread seeped through her skin and into her bones.

He took out a cigarette, cupped his hands, and lit it. The smoke violated her nostrils. She waved the smoke away from her face but said nothing.

After a few puffs, Dickenson spoke, "This is a busy place. For people seeking solitude and respite, there was a lot happening Friday evening and Saturday morning. From campfire sing-alongs to pranks to ice cream making to water skiing. And, when everyone's attention was elsewhere, murder. It would be challenging, but I can see that it is possible. But, of course, no one I spoke to knows anything about what happened to Cindy Elliott."

He took a long drag.

Nicola looked out toward the tree line, and up to the steep hiking paths on the surrounding mountain. "People aren't always truthful during a police investigation."

"No shit," She flinched at his condescending tone.

"I mean, innocent people. Just because someone wasn't exactly where they said they were, doesn't mean that person is guilty. Look, I'm not sure what Ben said is helpful, but what if it is? I know he is prone to exaggeration."

Dickenson interrupted her. "You mean lying."

"No, I mean storytelling for attention. But even if he made up what he saw, couldn't it be helpful to unpack some of it? I'm able to help out in that way. For example, my children didn't murder Cindy, but they may have seen something that they didn't tell you. Same with the other guests here. Let me have a few conversations with the others. I've built up some good early friendships here and that might prove helpful for your investigation."

The twosome returned to the lodge in silence. Detective Dickenson smashed the cigarette into the stone paving blocks of the entrance and turned to face Nicola.

"Okay, Henderson, knock yourself out. I won't stop you. You can talk to all your camp-get-away buddies but, remember, officially you are on the lists of suspects too."

Dickenson walked toward the officer assigned to stay at the lodge, and Nicola returned to the registration area.

Inside, a heated conversation was underway between two so-called friends.

"Brooke, you were with Cindy. You walked her to our cabin." Jaclyn stated. There was a note of accusation in her voice.

"I didn't stay. I just went over all of this with Nicola," was the quiet response.

"For God's sake, Brooke. She was plastered, defenseless."

"I didn't know anything would happen to her. I was sure she was heading back to you."

"Then, where were you? I know you said you went for a walk on the road, but how do I know that's the truth? How could you have left Cindy?"

"Okay, calm down."

"Never tell me to calm down."

"Whoa, sorry. Okay, let's take a breath."

They were quiet a moment.

"How many times do I have to say it? She was drunk, out of control, shit faced."

"Cindy was also exhausted. So, why would I even consider the possibility that she'd disappear?"

"I guess we'll never know that answer."

Nicola heard every word from her secluded spot near the reception desk. It was only a matter time before people who were backed into a corner started turning on each other.

CHAPTER 35

Dickenson asked to speak to Nicola again, this time in the privacy of the lodge's office. He closed the door and sat behind Otis's desk. Nicola sat across the old desk piled high with what looked like ignored paperwork and unopened utility bills.

Dickenson flipped his notebook open and squinted at his scribbled notes made with a blue ballpoint pen that was running out of ink.

He looked up from his notes and said, "Quite the group of guests you're surrounded by. From what I see, it's a group of immature guys trying hard not to be grownups. They are still seeking thrills from an attempt to recapture their lost youth. That's a nightmare in the making. Next, we have a girls' getaway weekend that sure didn't go as planned. From what I've gathered, it began as a wine-filled evening punctuated with moments of blame, resentment, and regret. Then we have the older woman, Victoria. I haven't put my finger on it yet, but there is something odd about her. There's your family, of course, and finally, the staff, two men. One old, one young. Seems like a lean number of staff to run a place like this, don't you agree?"

Nicola nodded. "Yeah, I think the lodge may be in some financial difficulty. I don't have proof of that, just a feeling. Otis and Tyler are very careful about conserving electricity. They make sure to only cook just enough food.

Staff eats whatever is left. I'm not complaining. It hasn't been a problem. I've just noticed a few things."

Detective Dickenson paused and looked as though he was wrestling with a decision. Eventually he said, "I'm going to tell you something from the initial forensic observations. These items are not yet in any formal report, and I need you to treat this conversation as completely confidential."

Nicola nodded her agreement.

"I'm not sharing these details with the group, Henderson. I'm just telling you out of, I guess, professional courtesy. Also, you need to be informed in case this matter is connected to your stalker."

Suddenly, Dickenson was not being a jerk, not such a dickhead, which escalated Nicola's sense of fear.

"I didn't know you were told about the stalker. Do you. . . do you think it's related?" Alarm bells went off in Nicola's brain, and a familiar putrid taste rose in the back of her throat.

What had he learned that she didn't know?

"I'm not sure it's connected, but here's what we know as of now," Dickenson offered no comfort. He cleared his throat and began, "Preliminary findings confirm what you already saw. The body of a woman was found in a partial supine position, face up and legs bent to fit, floating in a rain barrel. Overall, her appearance matches the friend's identification of Cindy Elliott, a twenty-eight-year-old woman. Red hair, green eyes. No scars. No tattoos. Her height and weight have yet to be confirmed. The body was clad in what appears to be a dark hooded sweatshirt and jeans. She was wearing running shoes and no jewelry."

Nicola heard the words rattled off with no emotion. They were discussing a human being yet the descriptions sounded like they were discussing features of a vehicle for sale. Nicola's chest tightened and she tried to slow her breath.

"Shall I continue?" He looked up from his notebook.

"Yes," Nicola needed to know everything.

"There are numerous minor abrasions to her body including a surface injury to her left knee. There are numerous lacerations on the skin of the palms of both hands. Significant injuries appear in two other areas of her body." He paused.

Nicola held her breath.

"There is a depressed skull fracture consistent with an injury to the top and front of her skull. It appears to be caused by a blow to the head originating from a heavy object descending from in front, and above, her. This is likely the cause of death, blunt force trauma fracturing the skull and causing the resulting indentation. The other injury is a broken right arm. It appears all injuries took place prior to death. The water did not remove all the traces of the dried blood on the body. Again, these details are not official and have yet to be confirmed by the final report from the Medical Examiner."

"She suffered." It was a statement from Nicola, not a question.

"Looks like it." Dickenson said, shook his head, and closed his notebook.

They stared at each other a moment. Nicola fidgeted with a Kleenex in her hand. There were no tears, just sadness, and fear.

A thought occurred to Nicola and she stood and threw the shredded tissue in the garbage and asked, "Why are you telling me all this if it's not official? Why are you sticking your neck out for me? Seriously, you could be reprimanded for your actions." Nicola needed to make sense of this conversation.

Dickenson leaned back in Otis's worn leather chair and spoke first, "Yeah, you're right. I could be in a lot of trouble, but I won't tell if you don't."

Ah, there he was, the smug asshole persona had returned.

Dickenson continued. "Look, I have no reason to believe this death is connected to your situation. However, I would be remiss if I didn't warn you that it is very disconcerting to me that the victim of a stalker flees to a place where a murder occurs. I don't like the odds of that happening. If I were you, I'd be extremely concerned for my safety."

Nicola nodded but did not speak.

"I think, once the investigation is over, you and your family should return home immediately. I know you'll have better security there, in a more manageable setting. Remember, share none of what I told you with anyone else. This murder may have nothing to do with you and, again, these findings are not official. You are correct. My ass is on the line here, Henderson. I'm telling you all this as a courtesy. I just think for you, in your situation, forewarned is forearmed."

Nicola nodded again, not trusting herself to speak.

CHAPTER 36

After Nicola left, Detective Dickenson motioned for Otis to join him in the office.

"It's a hell of thing that's happened, eh Mr. McIntyre?"

Otis studied the police officer and responded quietly, "Yes."

Dickenson continued, "I understand this is not the first time a dead body has been found on this property, but you weren't the owner back then, were you?"

Dickenson waited for a response that didn't come.

"My staff are close to wrapping up their investigation out here and will return to our station as soon as possible. I'll continue to have constables on site for security purposes. While I won't prohibit anyone from leaving, I've requested you all remain at the lodge until our investigation is complete."

"Understood." Otis said and sat in his chair behind the desk just vacated by Dickenson. He pulled out the top left-hand drawer and frowned. He then began pulling out other drawers and searched his desktop covered in paper.

"It's gone. Ethan's digital camera with the pictures from Friday night on it. The camera is gone."

Dickenson frowned. "Who has access to your office?"

Otis ran his hand threw his hair. "Everyone. I didn't lock the drawer, and I never lock my office. That jackass probably took his digital camera back, that's my guess anyway."

Otis continued speaking, "There is one other thing you should hear. My summer student saw something last night that he has only mentioned to me. It may be nothing, but he can't get it off his mind, and he thinks you should know about it."

"Okay, bring him to me." Dickenson said with no enthusiasm.

Within minutes, Tyler knocked tentatively on the open doorframe, a worried look on his face.

Dickenson looked up from his notes, ran his hand through his hair, and said, "Your boss tells me you may have some information."

"Yeah, I'm not sure it's anything important, but I can't quit thinking about it, and it doesn't make any sense."

"What doesn't make sense?" It was clear Dickenson was out of patience.

"Friday night, when all hell broke loose, I saw something run past the front windows of the lodge coming from the direction of the cabins. But it looked odd, unusual" Tyler hesitated, not sure his words were enough to describe what he saw.

"Continue." Dickenson gestured for more information.

"It didn't look normal, and it was misshapen and all shadowy."

"Okay. This isn't much help to me. Was it human or was it an animal?"

Tyler put one hand on his hip and rubbed his furrowed brow with the other, "Look, man, I'm trying to help the best way I can. I legitimately saw something running past the lodge front window around the time everything went down. I was quite far away. We were heading out the back door toward the sound of the screaming so I just saw it for a split second. It could have been a very big animal. Moose, elk. It could have been a funny-shaped human. Hell, for all I know, it could have been a fucking Sasquatch. I just wanted to let you know about it."

The young man stormed past Otis who was listening outside the door. Tyler, with a face like thunder, rushed past his boss and ran outside.

CHAPTER 37

Ethan's voice was simmering on the verge of anger, a switch had been flipped inside him, but the people he was with were unaware. "I didn't take my camera." Ethan's voice was low and his words deliberate. He met Detective Dickenson's gaze directly and the law enforcement officer believed him.

"If not you, who?"

"I don't know who took it, but I want it back, ASAP. This is bullshit, Otis. I've had enough of your confiscations of our electronic contraband. We aren't in high school. Give us all of our property back now, Otis."

The detective walked over to a nearby constable and quietly ordered another search of all guest cabins. He then turned to Otis and Ethan and said, "It's clear to me there might be something on that camera someone here doesn't want made public. It may be nothing related to the murder, but my instincts are tingling in a way that tells me it's important."

Back at the guys' cabin, Logan held the screen of Ethan's camera away from the sunlight. He hit the arrow button scrolling through photos until he found what he was seeking. The images, recorded Friday night, were dark and blurry. Ethan must have been running from the scene of the air horn prank when he hit record. The video was shaky. The sound was muffled and distorted by heavy breathing and a crescendo of crunching footsteps on the decorative gravel. The runner, holding the camera, was on the lake side of the lodge. The footsteps stopped. The audio captured the sound of breaths. The camera view swept 180 degrees. The focus zeroed in on the main building's open back door and through the large windows at the front of the lodge.

The images showed the inside of the dark main room through to the softly lit front entrance in the distance and out to the surrounding grounds, illuminated with landscape solar lights.

The running resumed but not before Logan saw what Ethan's digital camera captured.

A blurry image.

Human.

Carrying a body over their shoulder.

CHAPTER 38

It was late Saturday afternoon by the time the police interviews ended, and all the police vehicles cleared the driveway.

"No one feels like eating."

"It may not be polite, but I do," Ethan admitted. "Sorry, I'm hungry."

"Typical." Carter shot a disapproving look at his self-focused friend.

"Okay, we planned a barbeque so we'll get on it." Otis and Tyler left to prepare steaks for the grill once the baked potatoes were ready. A tossed green salad and garlic bread completed the menu.

The meal was served inside, in the dining room. It was a more formal setting than necessary, but the consensus of the guests suggested it felt safer and, somehow, more respectful.

As the two staff members left, a few of the guests helped themselves to drinks. The guys were discussing the events of the day then the conversation drifted to sports. Cindy's two girlfriends were playing a board game with Kyra and Ben trying to think of anything but the events of the day.

Nicola poured two glasses of Pinot Grigio and joined Victoria outside in the Adirondack chairs on the deck. Nicola felt a new friendship building as she bonded with the older woman the moment they met.

"Are you okay, Victoria?"

"Not really." A shocking incident sometimes opens people up in surprising ways. Eventually, the conversation drifted toward the senselessness of Cindy's death. Gently, seamlessly, it drifted to the subject of Victoria's family.

Victoria paused, met Nicola's kind blue eyes, and softly said, "I lost my daughter and my husband ten years ago."

She saw the look of sympathy in the young woman's eyes. "I'm so sorry."

"I really can't talk about it very much." Victoria took a shaky sip of wine.

"Forgive me, I don't mean to pry."

"Forgiveness. Such a strange concept. You asking, I can manage, I just don't want to discuss this with the group. Sometimes, it brings me comfort to talk about Shelley Anne. Most times it just brings pain. When our daughter was little, she was fearless and independent. She made herself an ice cream cone when she was two years old by pushing a kitchen chair to the cupboard and to the fridge and helping herself. She was always so determined, so happy. Bennett reminds me of her. Or do you prefer to call him Ben? I've heard you use both."

"It seems it doesn't matter what you call your kids, they end up with nicknames anyway."

Victoria let out a little laugh, "Yes, my family always nicknamed everyone. My husband had a friend Brian who moved to Honolulu so he became Hawaiian Brian."

"You live alone, Victoria?"

"Yes. A lot of time has passed, and now, it's just me in our big house. I've thought of downsizing, but there are a million precious memories at home, and I don't think they would move along with me, so I stay."

Time passed, topics changed, and still Nicola hadn't heard Victoria's full story, but she stopped asking questions. Eventually, the guests gathered for a makeshift evening meal. The meal included forced small talk, compliments to the cooks but the empty spot where Cindy sat overshadowed any attempt of normalcy.

"I need my notepad, Mom, I left it on our cabin deck." Ben said.

"Okay, I'll come with you." Nicola said.

"I'll go with him. I need to get my antihistamine. My allergies are out of control." Brooke offered and then sneezed.

"Okay, if you don't mind. Ben, take Barnaby with you and come straight back. I'll watch you from the edge of the deck. Stay on the path where I can see you and hurry." Nicola was barking orders but she didn't care. Even though it was still light out, she just wouldn't let either of her children out of her sight.

It was Victoria's turn to bring Nicola refreshments. Nicola turned to take a steaming cup of tea from Victoria's hand and was jarred by an ear-piercing scream.

"Help, Help! Oh my God. . ." Brooke sounded frantic.

The entire group flew from the dining room and off the deck, the guys leaping into the air, not bothering to use the stairs. All ran toward the screams. Alex was the first to reach Brooke with Ben standing next to her, clutching his dog's leash, both his eyes and mouth wide open.

Brooke was standing outside the girls' cabin. Shaking, she pointed inside.

A sense of dread hit Nicola. No, not again. No, it couldn't be. No one was missing.

She hugged Ben, looked behind her, and saw Alex's arm around Kyra. Nicola looked inside. Before her was a scene of destruction. The chairs and coffee table were turned over. The items once on the countertops were scattered everywhere. Even the small fridge door, tilted and off kilter, displayed damaged food packages and broken wine bottles.

A quick glance in the bathroom revealed more damage. Makeup and personal items everywhere.

"Who could have done this?" Brooke asked.

"More like what? Probably a bear, right, Otis?" Tyler looked at his mentor who shrugged and continued to examine the outside door.

"That's going to take a while to repair. I'll help you" Tyler offered.

"That's a lot of damage for one bear." Nicola said.

"I'm sure I shut the door tight. I thought I locked it. It's an automatic reflex, city habits are hard to break. Maybe I forgot, I don't know." Brooke had stopped shaking and was trying to piece together her movements when she left, still in shock over her friend's death.

"Bears are smart," Tyler said in his camp ranger voice. "They can paw repeatedly in one direction at a cabin door or a fridge or food cooler, and they can squeeze into impossible spaces. They are surprisingly agile. They are very fast and climb just about anything. Tourists are to blame in most bear encounters. No offence. You often see people in the mountain parks on the side of the road feeding wildlife just to get the perfect Instagram photo. Once an animal gets a taste of human food, they want more. Judging by the empty packages here, it looks like this guy succeeded."

Without saying anything, each member of the group starting picking up items. Otis went to the kitchen area and examined the lid and bowl of a plastic Tupperware container that had a few grapes left in it and turned it over.

"I'm not sleeping here tonight," Jaclyn announced. "I'll sleep on a couch in the lodge."

"Me too," Brooke went to grab their pillows and duvets.

Otis put the container on the counter and said, "We have cots. I'll set up one up for each of you. Tyler, come with me." It was an order, not a request.

As the two men walked along the path back to the lodge Otis turned to his protégé and said, "Keep this between us."

Tyler nodded. He knew when Otis was serious.

"There were no teeth marks in the food containers. The scratch marks on the door were not animal, more like knife marks scratched to make us think an animal was responsible. That was no bear. The intruder was human."

"What the fuck?" Tyler was stunned. He stopped and looked directly into the worried face of his mentor.

"Yeah, kid. My thoughts exactly."

CHAPTER 39

S U N D A Y

Kyra was the first member of her family to wake up early Sunday morning. For all her complaining upon arrival and, despite the tragedy, Kyra loved the cabin and had slept soundly. She snuggled for a while in her warm quilt and could hear Ben's gentle breathing. She stretched her arms above her head baring her stomach and then lengthened her lean legs as far as she could. She felt surprisingly rested and ready to take on the day.

Kyra climbed out of the bottom bunk bed and quietly closed the bedroom door behind her. No sound was coming from her parents' room so she tip-toed through the cabin, slowly unlocking and opening the sliding door. She wasn't going anywhere after what happened the day before. She just wanted some fresh air.

As she stepped onto the cold deck, an involuntary shiver ran through her. She felt the morning chill on the back of her neck which was exposed by her messy top knot bun. The early morning fog was thick, and a disconcerting feeling grew deep inside her. As cold as she was, Kyra stayed outside mesmerized by the beauty of the mist on the lake. The eeriness was enhanced by the melancholy sound of loons calling out, in search of each other, through the thick atmospheric blanket. The sound was haunting. Lonely. Then the call was returned. Another response, softer now.

The air felt wet, and Kyra could feel a slight restriction in her lungs. Pressure. It was a familiar restriction caused by a skyrocketing humidex. What was unexpected to Kyra was her sudden feeling of intense anxiety. Still barefoot, and in her pyjamas, she made her way to the edge of the deck. From her vantage point above, she could see into the hammock situated below as the hill sloped downward.

In the hammock, Kyra noticed a small cluster of debris and leaned forward on the edge of the deck for a better look. Laying inside the hammock was a small stick figure made from twigs. Leaves were used to style a dress and a clump of grass substituted for hair. Kyra assumed Ben must have discovered another project out in the woods. She always knew her little brother was a weirdo. Now he's making stick people. Freak.

Kyra's stomach growled. She went back inside to grab a granola bar from the bowl her Mom set out on the counter and quickly returned to the deck.

The hammock was swaying.

It wasn't windy.

Puzzled, Kyra climbed down from the deck exposing her bare feet to sharp pine needles and fallen acorns to figure out what was happening.

The stick figure was replaced by four figures lined up in a row.

Two large. Two small.

All with their heads separated from their bodies.

Their daughter's scream jolted Nicola and woke up Alex. They stumbled and ran in the direction of the sound. Bennett stumbled after them. There, collapsed on her knees with tears pouring down her cheeks, Kyra with a shaking finger pointed to the hammock. Kyra's stomach lurched and a putrid taste rose in the back of her throat.

Alex bent down and looked carefully at the structure.

"Kyra, Kyra. It's not real. It's a bunch of twigs. Why are you so upset?" Alex gently hugged his daughter to calm her.

"It's our family. Their heads are cut off. It wasn't there a minute ago. I saw one stick figure and then went inside to get a granola bar. When I came back outside, the hammock was swaying and this was in it."

"Okay," Alex said, "This is getting out of hand. I can take a practical joke, but we are bordering on disturbing behavior here. Back inside, everybody. Whoever thinks this is funny could still be out here."

A half an hour later, showered and dressed for the day, the Hendersons walked together to the main lodge to get breakfast. Victoria, Ethan, Carter, and Logan were drinking coffee outside just as the sun burst through the earlier morning fog.

Victoria, seeing their worried looks, asked, "Are you all okay?"

Nicola explained the situation to the group who made puzzled faces and shook their heads upon hearing about the twig family display.

"Creepy." Logan said.

Victoria whispered to Nicola and Alex, "Could Ben be playing a trick on his sister?"

Ben heard her and said, "No way, I didn't do it."

"Look, Ben was sleeping and has denied any involvement and I believe him," Alex's voice was stern as he looked at his son. "Besides, these pranks involve a level of sophistication that my boy does not possess."

"Exactly." Kyra added in defence of her little brother. "Ben's not smart enough to pull this off. He still spends most of his days here trying to light his farts on fire."

"Yeah, it almost worked yesterday." He giggled.

Carter, Logan, and Ethan all stifled laughs to varying levels of success. Carter offered Ben a fist bump.

"What did you say?" Nicola yelled. "Ben, do you have matches? Give them to me right now."

The boy reached into his jeans pocket and handed over a small box.

His mother took them and said, "We will talk about this later."

Victoria stood up and approached Nicola, "I have a feeling I may know who it is that's responsible for the practical jokes." Victoria's calm, quiet voice held all of their attention in a way that Alex's rant had not accomplished.

"I've noticed that Tyler has a little crush on your daughter, and this may be a way to spend a little bit more time with her. I don't know this for a fact but, before everyone overreacts, perhaps we could have a private conversation with Tyler to see if this is true."

"He's in big trouble if it is." Alex said.

Kyra looked alarmed, "Dad, don't do anything to get him fired. Promise me you won't say anything to him. I like him."

"Well, that's just great."

CHAPTER 40

The shock of the previous day resulted in a slow, tentative start to Sunday morning for the guests, other than the Henderson family. Sleep had eluded most, some choosing to stay in their rooms or grab a quick coffee and return to their cabin. The morning calm was fractured momentarily by the hammock incident. Some were bothered by the antics, and others chalked it up to youthful dramatics.

It was almost noon before the guests gathered at the outdoor dining table as a group to share a meal the day after the discovery of Cindy's murder. The table had been previously set for lunch prior to the tragedy. It was covered with a white cotton table cloth to protect the plates and condiments from insects. Nicola removed the cloth and saw there was a place setting that would remain empty. Tyler quickly grabbed the bowl, glass, and cutlery and returned to the kitchen. Kyra readjusted the spacing of the chairs and table settings to fill in the disconcerting gap. Nicola smiled at her daughter in appreciation but fully aware Kyra did the rearranging more for her own compulsive needs than out of thoughtfulness.

Lunch was always intended to be casual, a whenever-the-guests-want-to-eat kind of meal. This worked out perfectly under the tragic circumstances. Tyler placed fresh buns and butter on the table. Wearing a sparkling white chef's apron and hat, he ladled chili from a slow cooker. Each guest mumbled their appreciation and passed their bowls for Tyler to fill, none of them very hungry. The young man went into staff mode and assumed responsibility for meeting the needs of the guests. He tried to entertain with small talk and offered his chili recipe for anyone wanting it. Sitting next to where Tyler stood, only Nicola saw his hands shake ever so slightly as he served the steaming culinary creation, one by one into the ceramic bowls. He was very good at covering how he was truly feeling.

Nicola tried to eat, but she felt a dreadful weight had settled on her family. Looking at them seated around the table, she could tell the carefree feeling her family enjoyed earlier in the weekend had vanished the moment the murder was discovered.

Hungrier than everyone else, Ben shovelled a spoonful of hot chili into his mouth just as his dad warned him that it was hot. Ben hung his mouth open in an effort to cool his food and, once he was able to swallow, he started up a barrage of uncomfortable questions.

"I've been thinking and I don't get it. Why would this happen? Why would Cindy jump into a rain barrel if she was so hurt?" Ben shook his head.

The other guests cringed and looked down at their plates.

"She wouldn't, you idiot, and chew with your mouth closed," Kyra's voice startled everyone. "Someone killed her."

Ben's eyes widened and looked from Nicola to Alex and then to everyone else. "What?"

Then his eyes started to fill up with tears, and he slumped against Alex.

"It is okay, Ben." He put his arm around his son.

"No, it's not," was his sad reply.

Eventually, the group separated, each member lost in their own thoughts trying to piece together their interaction with Cindy. They were weary of each other, having been forced together for hours. Each sought solace in different areas of the resort.

Jaclyn and Brooke returned to their cabin, still in shambles, in an attempt to gather Cindy's belongings, at least the ones that hadn't been taken away to be entered into evidence. They continued to search for her missing phone and wallet.

The Henderson family took Barnaby for a walk but remained nearby. No one felt it was a good idea to wander far.

Logan and Ethan headed to the beach, and Carter returned to the guys' cabin for a nap.

Victoria, Otis, and Tyler remained seated around the table. Not eating and not speaking. Eventually, the silence was broken when Victoria began gathering the bowls and cutlery.

"Victoria, you are a guest here," Tyler stated. "I'll get those." He took the dishes from her hand.

"It would help me to keep busy, if you don't mind." She looked at Otis, who smiled and said, "That's very kind of you, thank you."

Victoria could tell they appreciated her gesture. Both Otis and Tyler worked hard to cover it up, but it was obvious to her, Mountain Shadows Lodge was struggling.

When the industrial dishwasher was filled and activated and the table cleared of the lunch remnants, Otis sent Tyler on his way to see if anyone needed lifejackets or towels. Victoria glanced as the young man ran down the hill and then returned her gaze to Otis. He reached into a cupboard and pulled out a box of camomile tea. He tilted it toward Victoria and raised his eyebrows questioning her interest in joining him.

"Yes, please." She nodded and reached for a clean cup.

Back at the girls' cabin, the cleanup from the previous evening's unknown intruder was almost finished, and the search for Cindy's missing phone and wallet continued.

Brooke stopped sorting through the clothes strewn across the shared bedroom and said, "I knew something was wrong. I should have sat down with her and made her tell me what it was, but really, all I wanted to do was slap her across the face. She was such a bitch. I feel so guilty about it but she was being a jerk. This trip was the worst she's ever been. Her behavior changed the minute we arrived. It's like she had jet lag without flying. She had a migraine, she wanted to sleep, she snapped at everything we suggested. When she did say something, it didn't make any sense. She was so fucking annoying I couldn't take it anymore. I walked away from her last night and I'll regret that forever." Brooke broke down, and Jaclyn put her arm around her shoulder.

"Look, her wallet isn't here. I'm hot and sweaty and I need a break. I know you're frustrated too. Let's go for a swim."

Soon, both women were on their way to enjoy the cool water and sunshine as a figure hid in bushes waiting for the chance to enter their cabin for a second time.

CHAPTER 41

Nicola and Alex were laying on their bed while their kids played Jenga, the tower block game, in the front room. It was one of the few activities that was appropriate for both of their ages and one they both liked. Every once in a while, the quiet was pierced with shouts of laughter followed shortly by arguing.

Nicola lay nestled in her husband's arms and inhaled the smell of his aftershave. She needed his thoughts on what Ben told her. She needed to go over what she knew. "Bennett remains adamant that he knew some of the guests were not telling the truth about where they were the night Cindy died. He later clarified that it was only some people who lied, not everyone."

Alex rubbed her arm the way she loved and said, "Go on."

"The guys say they were swimming, but they were near the lodge plotting a practical joke. Jaclyn says she went to bed shortly after everyone left, but I know she was still at the campsite waiting for Logan. Carter says he was checking on Kyra's scream, but I didn't see Carter there until much later. He wasn't with us when Kyra said she saw something at the side of the pathway. It was me, Kyra, and then you joined us. Ben was sleeping. Otis and Tyler came running from the lodge, as did Ethan, and then Victoria came from her cabin. The other two girls and other two guys were nowhere in sight. I just assumed they were partying together. But now I wonder, was Cindy already dead and was it really her who Kyra saw on the path."

"So why did Carter say he went to check out the scream. He was supposed to be setting up a card game cover up to get them all out of trouble about the air horn prank. So, where the hell did he really go? Was he with one of the girls? A secret rendezvous perhaps?"

They both were quiet, neither had any answers.

Nicola went over all the circumstances again in her troubled mind. Brooke went for a walk and Cindy never entered the cabin. Jaclyn and Logan had sex on the beach. Alex was out for a run in the dark with a head lamp. Nicola was about to go looking for him with Barnaby when Kyra screamed. Carter and Ethan eventually showed up at the pathway. Tyler told Otis he forgot to secure the canoes so he went to do that which her son later disputed as he could see the canoes were still tied up.

And all the while Ben was spying on everyone.

The game playing in the living room ended abruptly, and her son appeared at their doorway.

"What does extortion mean?"

"Pardon me?" Alex said.

"Extortion. I want to know what that word means."

"Well, Ben, that's a pretty grown-up word. What do you usually do when you don't know what a word means?"

"I would usually Google it. But at school, I have to look it up in the dictionary, but I can't do either of those things here. So, Mom, what does it mean?"

"Umm, well, it's like when you force someone to do something or give you something, I think? Money maybe. Why, where did you hear that word?"

"Oh, I can't remember, probably on a show I watched."

Nicola rose from the hope of a lovely nap, stood on her tip toes, and looked out the small bedroom window and said, "Let's keep questions about things like extortion to ourselves for now, Ben. There is enough going on." She looked into her little boy's blue eyes. "People are tired, upset, and confused and will probably correct their stories in the morning when the details are clear. I know I'm exhausted and I think you are too. How about you lay down and try to have a rest.

"No, Mom, I can't rest. I have to find out who hurt Cindy."

"That's not your job, sweetie. That's for the police to work on and for us adults to help them." Ben was pleading to be involved in something she never wanted to touch his existence, the murder of someone he knew.

"That's enough, Ben. I mean it. You stay inside with Dad and Kyra in the cabin." Nicola kissed the top of his head. "I'll make you and your sister some hot chocolate, and you can have some of those oatmeal cookies I brought, okay."

"Okay."

Well done, Nicola thought. Bribing my kids with food. Epic parenting failure.

Once Ben was happily stuffing his face with cookies while playing with his spy gear, Nicola caught a glimpse of Jaclyn and Brooke sitting on the deck of their cabin. She quickly told Alex she was going next door and he'd be able to see them through the cabin window. Knowing Alex was likely to dose off, she gave Ben strict orders not to go anywhere.

As she approached the next-door cabin, Nicola heard Brooke ask her friend, "What was with all her pacing and packing and unpacking?"

Jaclyn responded, "She always told us organizing her things calmed her down and gave her mental clarity which is debatable. She was slightly compulsive. I feel guilty talking about her like this."

Nicola wanted to know as much as she could about Cindy and about this unusual, triangular friendship, so she said, "In the very short amount of time I knew her, I noticed Cindy kept making random, weird, cryptic statements." Nicola said.

"For example?" Jaclyn asked.

"Well, out of the blue, she said, 'You know, very few of us are who, and what, we seem,' and then stared at the ground, lost in her thoughts."

"What the hell did that mean?" Brooke asked.

"I questioned her but she didn't answer me. She was a very strange person."

"You know, that reminds me, something odd happened when we first arrived at Mountain Shadows. It's been bugging me. I don't know if it's important or not." Jaclyn scrunched a soggy Kleenex in her hand.

Jaclyn continued, "We were laughing and bending over trying to sort out our bags and admitting we brought too much on a trip, yet again. I mentioned this was our fifth anniversary of these annual college graduation anniversary trips. Cindy shot up tall, looked straight ahead and then at me, and said, 'It can't be.' I then said that yes, it was, and that I was surprised she lost track as she is crazy about details and sentimental about our friendship. But, when I looked at her, she was shaking her head which you usually don't do when you feel the first signs of an oncoming migraine. Why did she say that? I wonder if what she said was about something else. Anyway, Tyler offered to help with the bags and Cindy yelled at him. We grabbed our stuff and entered the lodge to register."

"I think she recognized someone." Brooke said.

"Someone here? Why do you think that?" Nicola asked.

"Well, after Tyler's orientation, back at our cabin, she said she had her own ice breaker question just for the three of us. She asked us what we'd do if we had the chance to confront someone who had destroyed our future and betrayed our trust. We both said we'd annihilate them and she said that sounded like a good answer. She didn't say anything more. I don't have a clue if her question was theoretical or real and, if real, I have no idea who she was talking about. Maybe it was someone from her workplace but I don't think so. There was something about the look in her eye made me. . ." Brooke paused.

"Made you what?" Nicola asked.

"Made me think she was talking about someone here, at the lodge."

"Who could it be?"

The young women shrugged in unison.

"Why would they choose to encounter her, if they knew Cindy still held a grudge and would recognize them?"

"Maybe to right a wrong or try to attempt to fix things?" Brooke suggested.

"Could be, but why bother, it wouldn't work with someone as unforgiving as Cindy. The person was probably someone who didn't like her and knew the feeling was mutual."

"That's a long list of people." Jaclyn said with a deep sigh.

"Okay, so someone who didn't like her came here, where she was vacationing. Coincidence?" Brooke asked.

Nicola shook her head, "I don't believe in coincidences. Not in my line of work. I think behavior is deliberate, it might be subconscious, but it is usually purposeful."

"Okay, you've lost me. What do you mean?"

"Never mind. We're off topic." Nicola waved her hand in the air dismissively. "If seeing someone she knew is connected to the motive for her murder, then we have to accept the fact that someone is lying to us all. If we accept this theory, someone knew Cindy before this weekend and lied to our faces about it."

CHAPTER 42

Nicola said, "Otis, I'm glad I caught up with you. I've been mulling something over in my mind and it's just not making sense. When something doesn't add up, my personality won't let me shrug it off or wave it away. My need for things to be orderly can't let go of things unexplained. I have to figure it out. That's how my brain works. I find it helpful sometimes, and sometimes it's damn annoying. I'd like your thoughts on something that's been bugging me ever since we found Cindy."

"Okay, what's up, Nicola?" Otis put down the rake he was using to tidy up the grounds. He removed his hat, wiped his brow, and replaced the Stetson. "Shoot, whatcha got?"

Nicola smiled at him, grateful for his time and attention. She could see the exhaustion on his face and in the slump of his shoulders. He was constantly working, but he didn't make her feel bad for interrupting all the chores he had yet to complete. They found some shade by the bench at the entrance and sat.

"You know how a group of people's memories of the exact same event can differ?"

"Yeah."

"Well, I think the same thing can happen with a conversation."

"Agreed. What conversation are you talking about?"

Nicola was suddenly nervous, unsure if she wanted to ring the bell that would change so much. "It's just that sometimes what people think they heard someone say, isn't what was said or, more accurately, it's not what they meant."

"I understand. Go on. Who are you talking about? What conversation?"

She hesitated. She knew if she shared her perspective, everything could change. There would be no backtracking. Damage would be done.

"Remember when Carter told us he was in the guys' cabin setting up an alibi for the prank when Kyra screamed? Well, Logan is adamant that what he told us didn't happen. Logan saw him about to enter the guys' cabin and not leave it when all hell broke loose. Logan told me that Carter always puts his own spin on things, and it can completely change the point of view to whatever he wants. It was easy for him to spin things, he's a charmer. I have a feeling he is very used to dealing with half-truths that involve subjective interpretation. He's just got that used car salesman smarminess about him."

Otis was quiet as he digested Nicola's information, and, after a few moments, he said, "So, that means Carter wasn't doing what he said he was but, it also means, neither was Logan."

"True. Jeez, that switches everything around. If they weren't where they said they were, then it alters everything about what happened just before Cindy died."

"I know. So, the question is why? Is this information important or irrelevant? Was it just a mistake or was it a deliberate lie?"

"Otis, that's what we need to find out. But we have to be very careful. We can't get caught."

"I agree, this is very dangerous. Once someone has killed, I'm guessing it's much easier to do it again in order to cover up the first crime. Nicola, we are in way over our heads. I think we have to bring Dickenson in on this." He met her gaze and they both were quiet for a moment.

Nicola sighed and said, "Sadly, I agree. I just want to make sure I wasn't off base before I reported this to Dickenson. He and I have an uncomfortable history, we've made peace with each other, but that peace is fragile. Our working relationship has never been great. There is something about the guy that makes my skin crawl. However, we are stuck with him for now. I'll call him and I'll keep you in the loop as to what he says and for any next steps."

She stood up to leave but Otis caught her arm.

He said, "Honestly, Nicola, my advice is that we don't take any next steps. Please keep this conversation between us and the detective. I'm not one to exaggerate, but this is dangerous territory and my advice is to bow out and leave the investigation to the police. Promise me that's what you'll do."

Nicola heard the concern in his voice and saw fear in his kind eyes.

She nodded her agreement.

CHAPTER 43

Mid-afternoon on Sunday, the group, still stuck together at the lodge unable to leave and hesitant to be alone, gathered for drinks on the deck, while the three youngest among them splashed in the lake.

Logan slammed his Caesar, on the table chomped on the large celery stalk garnish and said, "Christ, it feels like now we've gone from no one here could have done it to everyone here is a suspect."

Carter took a large gulp of his IPA beer and asked, "Well, then, let's go back again. Is there any possible scenario where it wasn't one of us? Can we identify a legitimate alternate motive for the murder? Let's think about it for a second. This crime is a violation. Yes, it's a horrific assault against a young woman but also an assault against this place. Who would want to defile one of nature's most beautiful settings? It's going to impact the entire area economically, as well as Otis's ability to attract visitors. It's hateful."

"So, who would hate a place like this?" Victoria asked staring at her untouched glass of wine.

Ethan spoke, "Well, there's eco-terrorists. Not to be confused with nature-loving preserve-minded folks. I mean the extremists. Maybe someone who didn't like tourists or development of the area were up to no good, and Cindy just happened to be in the wrong place at the wrong time."

"Doubtful. But I guess we can't rule anything out yet." Nicola said and thought of her stalker. The threat of the stalker never left Nicola. It simmered within her. Fear would escalate and then ebb slightly, but it was always present.

Brooke spoke next. "Hey, Otis, didn't you say something about Tyler's parents. Weren't they killed by a drunk driver on vacation?"

Otis looked at Brooke. "Yes, that's correct. But Tyler had nothing to do with this."

"How do you know that?"

"Because I know him."

Victoria looked at the worried, exhausted man beside her and gently asked, "Otis, do we ever really know another human being?"

Several minutes passed before Ethan asked, "Aren't some people just fuck ups? Everything goes wrong for them. They keep causing their own problems because of their bad choices and are mortified when they have to live with the consequences of their decisions. Cindy was like that, from what I've heard. I'm sorry she's dead, but I had no sympathy for all the pity parties she'd throw for herself. She never changed her behavior patterns that got her into all kinds of messes."

"So, I have a question," Carter said, taking a breath and letting it out slowly as if deciding whether or not ask it. He looked at Brooke and Jaclyn, both clearly upset about Cindy's death yet both trashing her and without a doubt doing what polite society frowns upon, speaking ill of the dead.

"Why were you friends?" His voice was soft and the tone was without criticism, but there was a confused look on his face. His kind eyes lingered on each of their faces searching for something that would make sense of what he was learning about the trio.

"Habit, I guess. It was just easier to go along with her annual plans. One weekend out of the year isn't a lot. I considered it community service," Brooke snorted and then caught herself.

"I said it before, we felt sorry for her. She was irrational at times, and I did wonder about her mental health but never in a dangerous way," Jaclyn added.

"What do you mean, dangerous way?" Carter asked. "Do you mean self-harm?"

"Maybe from time to time. But that's not what happened," Brooke said.

The hours moved slowly on Sunday afternoon. Lunch made everyone lethargic despite the circumstances. They split into groups; Otis, Victoria, Tyler, and Alex were outside on the deck looking at the lake and lost in their own thoughts while they watched Kyra and Ben dive off the floating raft.

Carter and Ethan were kayaking, explaining briefly their need to burn energy and get away from the site of the tragedy.

Nicola, Logan, Jaclyn, and Brooke returned to the girls' cabin. A further attempt at clean-up was underway. Brooke grabbed a broom from behind the door, and a piece of paper, stuck between the broom and the dustpan, fluttered to the ground.

Nicola picked up the thick piece of paper from one of the icebreakers. "It's a piece of paper, a note. Tyler's question is on the front but something is written on the back."

"That's Cindy's handwriting." Jaclyn whispered.

"Oh my God. What does it say?" Brooke dove across the space between the sofa and sank to the floor.

The handwritten note was almost illegible. With the help of good lighting from the table lamp and laser-like focus, Nicola was able to read the note aloud.

It is funny how society tells us it's not okay to lie, but a million times a day, in a million different ways, we all tell lies. That dress looks amazing on you (if the look of a stuffed sausage was the image you were going for). I love your new haircut (that looks like you lost a fight with a lawnmower). It's fine, I didn't expect you to give me a birthday gift (bitch), every day we tell different lies. But not me. I tell the truth. What I've discovered is that people don't like it. I tell the truth with the exception of the one lie I've been telling for years. But no longer. I'm done lying. You see my lie was for someone else, not myself. Everyone thinks I'm so selfish. They are wrong.

If you are reading this, something very bad has happened. I'm either dead or on the run from the man who ruined my life. The guilt almost killed me, but slowly, slowly I carried on despite my fear. Eventually, I made a life for myself, got a job, made friends, and tried to forget what we did, until today when I saw him. He calls himself by another man's name, but it's him and nothing remains secret and no one can hide forever.

Nicola shared the piece of paper. Brooke and Jaclyn confirmed the writing as Cindy's.

"She wrote this on Friday. She must have, it's on the back of the first icebreaker card. What the hell. . . she sees what, what secret?"

"I don't know, it ends there."

Logan took the note in his own hands to read and looked at Jaclyn as if she had an answer. She shrugged.

Nicola looked around the room and said, "This is the motive. We've been wondering why Cindy was murdered. This is why. This guy ruined her life, changed his name, disappeared, and then she found him. This is the reason she was killed. Here's the motive the police are looking for, she was covering up for what someone else did which must have been pretty damn bad."

"Did she say any of this to you?" Logan asked.

Jaclyn said, "No, but remember she got weird when we arrived. Everything was fine, JUGS weekend was underway, but then she got a weird look on her face and started acting like the crazy Cindy we knew. We've seen her like that enough times to recognize the early symptoms. Brooke and I usually just carry on, determined not to let her spoil our fun, until her bad mood passes, but this time it never did. She just got drunk, disappeared, and died." Jaclyn choked up, and Logan hugged her passing the note back to Nicola.

"Who was she talking about? Obviously, it's someone here. Male." Nicola stood up and began to pace.

"If that's true, there's only a certain number of men. Logan counted on his hand. "Otis, Alex, Carter, Ethan. I guess we should include Tyler and me. He held up both hands and then dropped one. "Six, well, five because it's not me."

"Well, it's not Alex either. Look, before we start pointing fingers, let's just think." Nicola rubbed her temples; the swell of pain signalled a headache was building. Cindy was obviously terrified and thought her life was in danger. Why else would she hide the note where, eventually, it would be found?

Jaclyn spoke, "Logan, you've known the other guys all your life, right? You're the bros, the brothers, the squad, the trio. I've heard all the names you called yourselves. You grew up together, I loved all your funny stories. You'd know if one of the others knew Cindy, right?"

"We are all of those things the nicknames describe, but we were a duo before we were a trio. Actually, Ethan and I are the ones who grew up together. We've only known Carter about four or five years but that doesn't mean anything. I can't remember exactly how we all met, I think it was at a raging party. You've met him, he's fun to be around, he made us laugh, and that's all you need to hang with us. Cindy is not his type. He can't stand high maintenance women. For sure, we would have known about her."

"I think it's Otis she referenced. There's just something about him that doesn't make sense." Brooke stated.

Nicola held up her hand. "No, no, let's go back to Carter. Where is he from? How well do you guys really know each other?"

Logan laughed and said, "Well, we don't sit around braiding each other's hair and talking about our feelings."

Nicola couldn't help but smile. "I get it, male friendships are different than female friendships. By the way, that's not exactly how female friendships work either. Every friendship is complicated whether they are life-long or recent. All I'm wondering is whether or not you all know each other well enough to vouch for each other in a murder investigation."

"Where's Carter from? Does he have family nearby?"

Logan frowned. "East coast I think, not really sure. He doesn't talk about his family; I think there's problems there. He's the guy you don't get into deep conversations with, not like Ethan and I do. When Ethan makes a friend, he wants to know your opinions and philosophies on everything. Not Carter. 'No hard questions,' he always says. And he always has lots of money."

"Where does Carter's money come from?" Nicola asked.

"Family, I think?"

Ethan entered the cabin and answered for Logan, "Probably drug money."

"Christ, Ethan, why would you say that?" Logan turned to Nicola and stated. "It's not from selling drugs."

"Okay, so maybe family money. Where is his family? Did you ever meet them?"

"He doesn't really talk about them. All I know is Carter's my friend. He's funny, humble, and generous, and you, Ethan, you are being a jerk. I had no idea you'd throw a friend under the bus so quickly." Logan stormed out, clearly pissed off.

Nicola saw what was happening. People were turning on each other.

Ethan turned to Nicola frustrated that Logan left.

"Please let me clarify. Carter always paid his way and was always very generous with us. I'm not proud to say this, but Logan is pretty cheap, and I'm a scholarship kid so, to have a buddy with seemingly unlimited money, I'm not going to lie, I found it appealing. Again, I'm not proud of this, but that's the truth. Carter bankrolled a lot of our fun including this trip. I guess some people might think that's strange, but I never ask too many questions. Carter seems to appreciate people not grilling him about everything. We get along great."

"What do you mean, Logan's cheap? He has pretty nice things?"

"Well, that's a story there for another day."

"No, not another day, Ethan. We may not have another day. Now. Tell all the stories now. The more we know about each other, the better." Nicola insisted.

Ethan shifted his weight and shrugged. "Well, you're right. He does have nice things, but I'm willing to bet he didn't pay for them."

Alex wandered in and sat down looking expectantly at this wife for an explanation of what was going on. "What's up?" He asked.

"We found a note Cindy wrote. Here." Nicola handed it to him.

Nicola was frustrated as she needed more information from Ethan and Alex was disturbing the flow.

Alex answered Nicola's question before she could ask it.

"Otis and Victoria are watching the kids and I can see them from here."

"Look, Alex, I'm just going over a few things about Cindy and,"

"Yeah, yeah, honey, I get it. I just came to tell you that I'm thinking of going white water rafting up near the falls this afternoon. That is, if the police allow it. Logan seemed interested. It's a bit pricey so I'm going to ask him to split the cost with me."

"Good luck with that. Just between us, I wouldn't count on Logan sharing anything, especially a bill of some kind. He's my buddy and I know him very well. Generous isn't a word I'd used to describe him."

"Why not?" Alex asked, took a big swig of the beer he was holding, and sat down next to Nicola on the couch of the girls' cabin.

"I'll tell you a little story about him, you judge for yourself. At a staff retreat a couple of years ago, I won a random draw for two tickets to one of the Stanley Cup playoff games. It was a huge prize for this lifelong hockey fan. I played the game since childhood. These weren't just any tickets, they were VIP seats, awesome seats. Logan was going through a bad time. He was working as a bartender trying to figure out what he wanted to do with his life. His girlfriend had just dumped him."

Everyone listening made themselves comfortable as it seemed Ethan's story was going to take a while.

"I thought treating him to the game would be a nice thing to do. His beat-up car was in the shop, yet again, so he asked if I could pick him up. Now, the unspoken rule with sports from my experience is, if someone springs for tickets, the other person arranges transportation but whatever. I picked him up, paid for our steak dinners before the game, and also for premium parking because the weather was crappy. He was drinking and laughing and having a great time. Logan was psyched, and I was sure he hadn't let loose in a long time."

Ethan paused, took off his baseball cap, rubbed his forehead, and replaced the hat. He seemed reluctant to continue.

"Here's where everything changed for me." His voice was quieter.

Nicola leaned a little closer as she watched Ethan tell his story. She noticed he pursed his lips and seemed to be deciding what to say next. A moment passed where Nicola wondered if he would continue with the story. Finally, he did.

"As usual with most major sporting events, on the way into the arena, volunteers were selling 50/50 tickets. This night the proceeds from ticket sales would be allocated to benefit inner city sports programs that provide equipment, lessons, and travel costs for kids who otherwise can't afford to participate in organized sports programs. The intent is inclusivity and to try to keep marginalized kids out of trouble. Stats seem to support the theory of keeping kids busy and engaged with team sports builds life skills and keeps them away from drugs and gangs."

"Yeah, of course," Alex nodded. "I buy 50/50 whenever I see them being sold. I buy them as a do-gooder, but I also want to win the stack of cash that accumulates at those games. Much better odds than any lottery and it's easier than ever now that it's mostly digital."

Ethan continued, "Yeah, so we stood in a fairly long line, and as we approached the ticket sellers, Logan suddenly announced he had to take a leak, and asked if I would get his tickets while he was gone. He said he'd give me the ten dollars when he returned. Convenient, I thought so I paid twenty dollars for the draw tickets, ten dollars each. He came back with two beers, and I passed him half the tickets and he gave me a ten.

"The game was great and it came time for the 50/50 draw in the third period. You know winners receive half of the amount of tickets sold. Miraculously, the numbers on one of the tickets Logan was holding was called. I can still hear him yelling, "I won, I won!"

He was so happy and so was I. They sold approximately $400K worth of tickets so the winner reaped almost $200K, a fortune to us at that time, it's still a fortune, even now.

"Cool, that's amazing." Alex said. Even though he often bought 50/50 tickets, he didn't know anyone who had won big.

"Not really. Logan kept all the money, every last cent, didn't even reimburse me for the dinner and parking."

"What? You're kidding, right?" Nicola's eyebrows met her hairline.

"As we were jumping up and down and people around us were patting him on the back, Logan announced he had to collect his money and he was gone. I waited for him to return, but he never did. As you might imagine, we had a major fight and, until this trip, we haven't seen each other much since. Carter did his best to mediate. He tried to convince Logan how selfish he was being. He encouraged Logan to at least split the winnings with me which would have helped my student debt load considerably. When Carter and I met him to discuss it, Logan said the money was all gone."

"What did he buy with it?

"Nothing, as far as Carter and I could tell. He still has a shitty car, he rents a crappy basement suite, and lives very frugally still working as a bartender. No assets, no ambition."

"He must have given it to someone," Alex suggested.

"Who do you give $200,000 to?"

"Beats me."

"Honestly, I think he kept it for himself, probably invested some and it's tied up. It sure would have helped me. So, now you see, why I said not to count on Logan's generosity."

Nicola picked up Alex's beer, took a swig, and said, "What a prick."

Ethan held her gaze and nodded.

CHAPTER 44

"Why won't you tell me what's wrong?" Tyler's head hung low as he slumped forward on the bench beside Kyra. "I can tell you're upset. If you don't want to talk, I can just hang out with you for a while."

Through eye contact and subtle gestures, they had signalled a meet up to each other. The two youth managed to make their way to the front entrance separately. As she walked through the lodge, from the back deck to the entrance, Kyra thought she saw someone but was relieved to see the area was deserted.

"I'm okay, really. My family is going through a lot right now. My Mom's been dealing with something really scary involving a creep that's bugging her. My parents don't know that I know about it. I overheard my parents talking about it at home a while back, and I heard my Mom on the phone a few times calling in for updates."

"Oh God, that's so awful. I'm so sorry this is happening to you guys. You must be so scared." Tyler slid over on the bench closer to her. They sat side by side, knees touching. Tyler reached over and wrapped his arms around Kyra and hugged her for a long time.

CHAPTER 45

Otis met with Nicola and Alex to discuss the pranks that took place at their cabin. They all agreed the fake squirrel and hammock pranks were strange, and the Hendersons wanted to know if Otis believed Tyler could be the culprit.

"No way." Otis shook his head.

"I wish I could be as certain, but I guess we'll move on. We don't need to mention it to him or anyone else." Alex looked through the dusty, streaked window of Otis's office at the two young people on the bench outside.

"I appreciate that, Alex. Tyler is a good kid given all that he's been through with a level of maturity far beyond his sixteen years. He doesn't feel sorry for himself even though he has every right to. He works hard and is a kind soul. I feel parental toward him even though we are not related, just a very good friend of the family. He may, in fact, have a crush on your daughter, but that situation would be an anomaly for Tyler. They are both teenagers. He doesn't cross lines and is usually a level-headed young man. I've decided to keep him busy so I assigned a couple of extra tasks that will be time-consuming and exhausting. He soon won't have the time or energy for much else other than work. Certainly not for elaborate practical jokes, although I'm certain he is not responsible. I really appreciate you both being so understanding. Thank you."

The Hendersons stood to leave, but Alex turned back and in a low voice said. "Otis, you don't think Tyler had anything to do with what happened to Cindy, do you?"

A shocked looked on the older man's face gave Alex his answer before Otis said, "Absolutely not. Now if you'll excuse me, there's somewhere I need to be."

His words were polite, but the look in the older man's eyes was not.

Jaclyn and Brooke left their cabin and walked toward the lodge.

Jaclyn said, "Cindy's identification is still missing. I thought maybe she had an emergency contact card. I know she has no family, but maybe she has someone listed but there's no wallet in her purse." Brooke shrugged.

"Maybe she didn't bring it which makes no sense because she drove here. Why wouldn't she bring her driver's license?"

Brooke shook her head. "She did have a wallet. I know she had it because she pulled it out at the gas station remember to fill up before we left." Jaclyn was holding Cindy's designer handbag upside down with its contents on the counter. "And she left it on the counter. Otis handed it back to her."

"Right, then where is it. Maybe she threw her wallet in her suitcase." Brooke went to search and returned shaking her head.

"Well, this can't be a theft gone wrong because all my cash and cards are still here. Yours?"

"Yup, nothing missing."

"What the hell?"

"I know, it's so weird. She could have left it in the lodge and someone picked it up. But you'd think, given what's happened, that someone would have mentioned finding it. Or, turned it into the police. Who would want to be in possession of a dead woman's wallet? There's probably a lost and found box, let's go ask Otis." The women locked their cabin door and rounded the bend heading toward the back deck of the lodge.

"The police would have checked already, besides, it's too late, he's a little preoccupied." Brooke nodded toward the pier on the lake.

Otis, holding two tall glasses of sweet ice tea, walked down to the end of the pier. Victoria was sitting on one of two Adirondack chairs looking out at the still lake.

"May I join you?" he asked offering a glass to her. She noticed he changed into clean jeans and a stylish white button-down shirt that suited him and emphasized his tanned skin and green eyes. He hadn't quite managed to tame his hair as long curls were pointed in all directions. Although his obvious attempt had failed, it may be accidently stylish these days Victoria thought with a smile.

"Yes, of course. Thank you." She took a sip and rested the glass on the wide arm rest farthest away.

They sat in silence, each deep in thought, staring at the water. Otis, put on his sunglasses, wiped away a bit of condensation that wet the side of his glass, and then wiped his hand on his jeans.

A few moments passed and then Otis asked, "Beautiful time of day, isn't it?"

"My favourite," Victoria followed his gaze admiring the blue sky and loving the warmth of the afternoon sunshine.

Otis reached for her hand.

"I remember, Fancy Pants."

CHAPTER 46

The group looked toward the end of dock with great interest. The sun glistened on the water and Victoria and Otis sat with their sunglasses on, holding hands, seemingly lost in thought as neither spoke.

"What's going on down there?" Ethan smiled and looked at Jaclyn.

"It appears a new, exciting, middle-aged romance could be blossoming."

Tyler left the Henderson kids in the water and was toweling off when he joined the guests. He looked at them and then at the couple on the dock. "Well, I guess it is middle aged, and it does look romantic, but it's definitely not new."

"What do you mean?"

Stunned, Tyler looked from one face to another. "Don't you know, didn't you figure it out? To be honest, it took me a while. It also involved a conversation with my Grandma. She recognized Victoria when she dropped the Henderson kids off after horseback riding."

"Figure what out?" A chorus of voices asked in unison.

"Otis and Victoria are a couple or were a couple," Tyler announced.

"I knew it!" Ethan said. He turned to the others and said, "Remember when she told us Otis doesn't drink. She had just arrived. We all had. How would she know something so personal about the owner of a lodge she chose for a vacation?" I remember thinking that was odd at the time and I've been watching them. I figured it all out."

"Figured what out?" The members of the *ad hoc* choir who remained in the dark asked again, in unison, louder this time.

Tyler tried to fill in the blanks. "Otis and Victoria are married. They have been for years. She's his wife that he talked about that one time. And he's her husband that she talks about all the time. She left him under tragic circumstances. It was their daughter who drowned at the waterfall ten years ago."

"No way, you're wrong" Brooke countered. She stood and began to pace. "Otis has a son, Sam, he told us all about him when he made his speech directed at Alex. Right, remember, Alex?"

"I remember it vividly. It felt like he was giving me shit for some reason. Anyway, Nicola, didn't Victoria tell you she lost her daughter and her husband. The daughter's name was Sherry or Shelley." Alex announced proud of himself for getting at least that right.

"Yes, she did." Nicola frowned trying to remember the details of the conversation. "She called her. . . um. . . Shelley Anne."

"Yes, Victoria talks about her daughter, Shelley Anne. Get it Shelley Anne McIntyre. The initials S.A.M."

"Oh my God," Jaclyn whispered under her breath. "She's dead. Her little girl is dead. Their little girl is dead."

"Victoria is Fancy Pants. Otis calls her Fancy Pants. Victoria is Otis' Fancy Pants." Jaclyn had the look of someone putting the last piece of a difficult jig saw puzzle together. Everything fit and the picture was complete, completely tragic.

They looked at one another and then at the couple on the pier. It was then the pride of piecing the information together was replaced by the realization of the monumental tragedy of the death of Otis and Victoria's little girl.

"How did their daughter die, Tyler?" Nicola asked.

"She drowned. Victoria and Otis hired a babysitter, and something went wrong, and the little girl wandered off and drowned. According to my Grandma, Victoria just couldn't stay here after Shelley Anne died and Otis just couldn't leave. This is where all his final memories of her remain. You are right, he doesn't drink. Not anymore. For the first few years, according to my Grandma, that's all he did, but he got sober, bought Mountain Shadows, and worked hard to make a go of this place, but Victoria just couldn't face it. This weekend is the tenth anniversary of their little girl drowning. I guess she felt she needed to be here and, from what I see, I'm glad she came back."

"I have some memories of her, but I was pretty young when it happened. Over the years, she's kept in touch with my family and occasionally checked-in with Otis, but this is really the first time she's been here since." Tyler turned and carried on his way eager to finish his assignments on time.

The rest remained in stunned silence.

CHAPTER 47

Following the revelation about Victoria and Otis, the group dispersed, and Nicola found herself alone with Logan. Her kids were with Tyler about to go kayaking, and Alex was on parental duty watching them. He was in charge of ensuring their life jackets were the correct size and secured snuggly. She turned to the young man across the table from her.

"Logan, I to need talk to you about something."

His brow furrowed as he recognized Nicola's serious tone.

"I heard a story about you and I judged you harshly without hearing your side of it. It's been bugging me so I'm glad we have this time to talk."

"Okay," Logan said warily.

"Ethan told my husband and me a story about you that I can't quit thinking about. It wasn't a very flattering story, and I can't quite reconcile what he said with the person you appear to be."

"Geesh, what the hell did Ethan say?"

"He told us about the 50/50 ticket and what happened after you won."

"Oh that, yeah, he's still a little pissed off about it."

It was Nicola's turn to be puzzled. "I understand why he'd be mad at the situation. I wouldn't be too impressed with you either. You didn't share the winnings from a ticket you wouldn't have been able to buy if not for being gifted a night out."

Logan shifted in his chair to face Nicola directly. He ran his hands through his long, shaggy hair that could really use some shampoo. It appeared as though he was choosing his words carefully.

A few moments passed and then he said, "I needed the money desperately. Ethan doesn't know why. It was none of his business, but now that he seems to be spreading negative stories about me and obviously carries a bit of a grudge about it. There is much more to the situation."

"I'm listening."

"My friend is a gambling addict. Poker, racing, machines, online. . . you name it, he would bet on it. He got in over his head and owed money to some scary dudes that take advantage of gambling addicts. Interest adds up and threats are made. I used the winnings to get my friend out of a dangerous situation without anyone having to know about it or go into financial ruin to bail him out. I helped him on the condition he went to rehab, and he's been okay ever since. When you have an addict of any kind in your circle, you always hold your breath a bit every day, probably forever.

"So, yeah, I kept that money and didn't tell Ethan why in order to protect my friend's reputation and to prevent anyone from learning about it. And I'd do that same thing all over again if given the chance." He smiled and shrugged.

"You need to tell Ethan all of this. He'll probably understand."

"I had no idea it was festering with him. I'll talk to him. Thanks, Nicola, for coming straight to me to clarify the entire story."

"I'm happy to clear it up. It makes sense to me now. I'm a pretty good judge of character. In my line of work, I see all kinds of people, and it just didn't fit that you were a bad guy." She laughed as she rose and went down the stairs to the beach to wave to the kids in the boat.

Logan stared at Nicola as she walked away.

He was no longer smiling.

CHAPTER 48

The kayaking excursion was a great success. There was splashing and laughing and, for a brief moment, some unexpected fun in the midst of tragedy. Exhausted, most participants returned to their accommodations to rest.

After returning to the cabin to change clothes, and with a promise to his parents to stay close, Ben went to play outside. Along the pathway, at the end of the row of cabins, Ben crouched fiddling with his walkie-talkie, trying to make a very important call to his Mom who had the other walkie-talkie. Within minutes, he was covered in dirt and one of his shoe laces was untied. He didn't care, he had urgent business to take care of, and, before he could finish his task, he heard footsteps and a branch break behind him.

He looked up at the shadow hovering above.

"Hey, buddy, whatcha doing?" Carter looked around in all directions as he approached the little boy.

"Nothing," Ben hesitated then stood up. He tucked something into the back of his jeans, under his hooded sweatshirt. "I'm not doing anything. I have to get back; my Mom wants me back at our cabin."

"Not so fast." Carter blocked the path. "You know Ben that doesn't sound like the truth to me. Are you lying, Ben? You lie quite a bit, don't you, kid? I have a bit of respect for that, I was kind of the same when I was your age."

Ben stuck his chin out and said, "I'm not supposed to talk to anyone alone unless they know the code word." He looked down at his dog who returned his gaze, lovingly.

Carter paused. "That's just for scary people you don't know."

"I only just met you." Ben looked at the dog, again.

Carter said, "I do know the code word. Your Mom told me it when you all arrived. Hmm, let me see if I can remember it."

Ben waited, unsure what to do, then reached to hug his dog.

"The code word is Barnaby." Carter guessed.

The little boy's eyes widened and he looked up at the man.

"Yup, that's it." Ben said quietly, disappointed and trying to make sense of why this man would know his family's code word. It was supposed to be top secret. Something didn't feel right, and his Mom always told him to trust himself. She said if he felt that something was wrong, it probably was, so listen to his feelings.

"You've been up to lots of things here, haven't you? But, sticking your nose into other people's business isn't polite. Haven't your parents told you that? I understand you've been telling the police we are all liars, is that right? That's not nice. That's not what friends do to each other, is it?"

Carter's voice was scary now, and Ben opened his mouth and was just about to yell "Stranger Danger" when Carter covered his mouth and grabbed his arm. Bennett bit Carter's hand.

"Ouch, you little shit. Don't you dare scream, and don't yell or I'll break your arm, understood?" Carter grabbed the walkie-talkie out of the boy's hand and threw it in the bushes.

The little boy nodded. His eyes darted everywhere, but there was nobody else around. He chose this place to hide because he needed to tell his Mom on the walkie-talkie what he found out about Carter. He just didn't get a chance to deliver the message. They weren't far from the edge of the walkways so maybe he could send a message somehow. He dug his foot in the sandy ground and tried to write BB without looking. He couldn't check because then Carter would see him and erase it. It didn't matter because it was too hidden for anyone to find. Ben began to sniffle, and he wiped the tears off his face with the back of his dirty hand.

"Hey, buddy, don't cry. Everything's okay, I'm just a little angry today. You have to listen to me because I'm the adult. You don't want to get into trouble by not listening, right? Let's just have a friendly conversation. Since you are so smart, tell me what you know. Go ahead."

"I'm not the one in trouble, you are. I know Carter isn't your first name, it's your last name, right, Adam?" His tone had a show-off air about it that angered the elder who tightened his grip on the young boy's arm.

"Oh, so you overhead Cindy and I arguing. When I heard what a little snoop you were, I was worried you may have heard us."

"Ow, you're hurting me and we're not friends," Ben twisted but had no chance of breaking free from Carter's hold.

"Quiet or I will hurt you. And I'll hurt your Mom and Dad. And I'll hurt that snotty sister of yours too. God, she's annoying. And then. . . you know what I'll do?"

Ben fought back tears and shook his head.

"I'll hurt that dog of yours." Carter's voice changed, it was deeper now, menacing. He grabbed the little boy's arm.

"Please don't hurt Mom and Dad. I won't tell anyone you have two names. Don't hurt Barnaby, he's a good dog. Don't hurt Kyra either. She can't help it if she's annoying."

"Okay, Ben, that's enough. I need you to tell me where Cindy's wallet is, okay? But we can't stay here. We are going on a little hike away from everybody else. You like hiking, don't you. It's fun. Maybe we'll make it as far as the waterfall." He gave the boy a push in the direction of the woods. It was not a request.

As he stumbled forward, Ben could see Kyra across the front area of the lodge. He held Barnaby as far away from Carter as the leash would allow.

Before Carter could do anything about it, Ben called out to his sister.

"Hey, Kyra, I'm not mad at you anymore. I wish you well. I care and I'll miss you." Ben wasn't sure his sister heard him. Ben caught the angry look on Carter's face, but Kyra couldn't see it. It didn't really matter because, under his hoodie, tucked uncomfortably into the back of his jeans, Ben still had the air horn.

CHAPTER 49

"Have you seen Ben?" It was late Sunday afternoon, a time when Nicola should be getting her family cleaned up and ready for supper. Fresh clothes, brushed hair. She should be complaining about all the sand on the kitchen floor and the mess her kids left while getting a snack. That's what she should be doing; instead, she was taking deep breaths trying to stay calm while looking for her youngest child. She saw Otis and Victoria holding hands and, instead of caring what was happening there, she ran down the short length of dock and interrupted them.

Otis stood immediately, a frown of concern appeared on his face to match the one approaching. "No, Nicola, I haven't seen him since they all came back from kayaking just after lunch. That was a couple of hours ago. Could he be with Alex or Kyra?" Victoria also rose and turned to see a mother's worry edge from slight concern approaching panic.

"We'll help you find him. I'm sure he's close by." Victoria said.

Nicola nodded and turned and the trio made their way back up the hill to the lodge where Jaclyn and Brooke were sun tanning on the lounge chairs. They lifted their sunglasses in unison when they heard the others approach.

For the second time within minutes, Nicola asked, "Have you seen Ben?" Her voice had a slight catch in it this time as she was losing the battle to remain calm.

Jaclyn shook her head, but Brooke responded, "I haven't seen him for a while. Last time I saw him he said he was going on a hike. I thought he was a bit young to go hiking and just assumed Tyler and Kyra were going with him."

"A hike? I'll strangle that kid when I find him if a bear doesn't get him first." Her hand flew to her mouth when she realized what she had said.

"Wait, Nicola." Otis caught her arm. "Where's Alex and where are the guys? They could all be together with Ben." He looked at the young women. "How about you two go inside and look through the lodge? Victoria and I will talk to the police officer to see if he's seen Ben. Then we'll search the grounds, and Nicola, why don't you go back and check your cabin. He could have returned by now. Let's meet back at the front entrance. Okay? Let's go."

Nicola flew down the path back to their cabin calling Ben's name along the way. She could hear the other members of the impromptu search party doing the same. She pulled the cabin door open and could tell Ben was not there. No one was. She was certain Ben wasn't hiding. Her sensitive boy would have heard the panic in her voice and appeared. She climbed up to his bunk bed and pulled his belongings down. His backpack was there, and Nicola dumped out his metal water bottle, a granola bar, binoculars, sunscreen, bug spray, and his notebook. She turned to the page where a picture of Ben holding Barnaby as a puppy served as a bookmark.

Barnaby. "He must be with Ben." Nicola whispered under her breath somewhat relieved to know they were probably together. Barnaby wouldn't let any harm come to her boy.

A scrap of paper fluttered from the notebook and Nicola bent to pick it up. Her son's meticulous, oversized printing stated, '*I wish I knew who hurt Cindy*.' The word wish was underlined.

"Mom," Kyra's call made Nicola jumped.

"Kyra, is Ben with you?"

"No." Kyra's eyes were big as she stood at the doorway and processed the mess her mother made in her shared room.

"What the hell, Mom? I mean heck."

Nicola crossed over to her daughter, grabbed Kyra by her shoulders, and bent to look her in the eyes. "Honey, this is very important. Have you seen Ben or your Dad this afternoon?"

"Yes."

"Oh, thank God, where are they?" Relief coursed through her body. She wiped sweat and wrinkles of fear from her forehead with both hands.

"Dad went for bike ride a while ago. I have no idea where Ben is but I saw him earlier."

"Where?"

"On the hiking trail."

"What exactly did you see?"

Kyra swallowed. Her eyes darted back and forth replaying the scene in her head. "I saw Ben with Carter." Kyra's frown caught Nicola's attention. It was different than her usual teenaged girl look of disgust.

"Okay, well, that's good he's with an adult. Come with me back to the front entrance. Otis and Victoria along with Jaclyn and Brooke are helping me look for your brother." Kyra had to jog to keep up with her mother who was retracing her earlier steps and turning her head left and right imagining Ben lying on the ground just out of sight. She looked over her shoulder and could tell something was troubling her oldest.

"What are you thinking about, Kyra?"

"Ben said something weird to me when he was leaving. He said he wasn't mad at me anymore. I didn't know, or care, that he was, but then he said that he wished me well. He's so weird. I didn't know what the hell, I mean, heck, he was talking about. I'm usually mad at him for something but not today. Not yet, anyway." She shrugged her thin shoulders and looked puzzled.

"When? When did he say this to you? Where was he?"

"I told you. When he and Barnaby were walking away with Carter, he turned and yelled the message at me. I guess about half an hour ago. It looked like they were going on a hike, but obviously, he didn't have his backpack."

Nicola began to pace. "Why would he go without asking permission? He wished you well? What for? What does that mean?"

"No idea and then Ben said something really weird. He said "*I care and I'll miss you.*" Super strange, right?"

"Well, it is actually kind of sweet, but your brother is still in big trouble. Grounding will be just the beginning."

"No, Mom, you really don't get it." Something in the tone of Kyra's voice made Nicola stop and look directly in Kyra's eyes as she continued to explain.

"When one of us goes somewhere without the other, we always say, '*I don't care and I won't miss you.*' It's our thing, like a joke. So why would Ben say the opposite?"

Nicola saw all search party members return without Ben. She shared what Kyra said, that Alex wasn't missing, that Carter and Ben had gone on the hiking trail, and Kyra added the strange message Ben said.

Nicola worked hard to control her panic. Her breathing slowed and sounds disappeared. All movement in her line of vision stopped. Her eyes engaged in a panoramic scan of the entire outdoor area near the front entrance of the lodge. Something was off. Something here was not right, but she could not pinpoint what it was that was bothering her. What was so disconcerting? With laser focus, she scrutinized her surroundings but was unable to identify the culprit. Now, she only cared about finding her son. She focused on the edge of property that led, not to the cabins, but to the vast, dense, forest. Could her baby boy be lost in the woods with a man who, in essence, was a stranger?

Otis stood in front of Kyra and asked, "How did they seem?" His voice was calm, but the intensity of his gaze told Nicola he shared her escalating apprehension.

"They looked like they were goofing around and then I saw Carter give Ben a little shove after he said that thing about missing me and wishing me well."

"He pushed my son?" Nicola asked.

"Not hard, Mom. If it had been a hard push, I would have jumped in, I would have said something. Why, what's wrong?" Not only could Kyra see her Mom was worried, she could hear it.

"Then what?" Nicola stood with both hands on her hips waiting.

"Then Ben saw me still standing there watching and said something I could hardly hear. When I didn't respond, he yelled something about wishing me well. Yeah, I remember now. I didn't know what he was talking about and that's when Carter shoved him and they went on their hike."

Brooke stepped forward and whispered. "He wished you well. . . wished you well. . . wishing well. If he said something about making a wish, maybe he was thinking of the wishing well." Brooke turned and pointed to the centre of the green.

Nicola's head snapped toward the quaint, white structure surrounded by red geraniums. "That's it, the wishing well. Maybe he wanted us to go to the wishing well. Why?"

"Just go," Victoria yelled. The others jumped at the unexpected, loud directive from this usually soft-spoken woman. "See if anything is there." They all ran.

Otis reached it first, but it was Nicola's arm that plunged up to her shoulder in order to reach the bottom of the empty well. The others arrived all trampling the floral border. Nicola felt an object covered in slimy leaves in the debris at the bottom of the structure. It was a rectangular shape and, a piece of paper on what felt like thick cardstock, was sticking out. Nicola pulled what she found into the sunlight. It was the expensive-looking, red leather designer wallet Cindy left at registration upon check in. Cindy's identification was still in it and, behind her driver's license, a corner of a small picture stuck out. Nicola removed it carefully and looked down at the back of a photograph. She saw swirly, pink cursive letters that read, *Adam Carter and*

I – First Date. She flipped it over the group huddled around her. Two young faces smiled back from photograph. They were the faces of a teenaged Cindy Elliott and a teenaged boy they currently knew as Carter Adams.

CHAPTER 50

"Oh my God, Carter is not Carter, he's Adam." Brooke's mouth was wide open. "Her Adam."

"Who? What?" Jaclyn asked.

"The imaginary boyfriend. Cindy's old boyfriend. I remember now, his name was Adam. She called him A. C. It makes sense how she reacted when we arrived. She saw her old boyfriend here calling himself by another name. She heard him say he was Carter Adams when he registered."

"Do you mean he's the jerk from the abusive relationship she talked about at the campfire?" Victoria's tone was now soft again, but as she looked over at Otis, he heard the seriousness in the tone of her voice.

Otis stood still. "Wait, I know that name. He was the boyfriend of our babysitter. And Cindy. Oh God, I didn't recognize. . ."

Victoria saw the shock on his face and heard the pain in his voice. "Yes, Otis, it's them. I invited them to meet me here. I didn't tell either of them the other one was also invited." She turned to the others and said, "Cindy Elliott was the teenager we hired one afternoon to babysit our daughter. Instead of watching our child, she called her boyfriend to join her and, at some point, our little girl wandered off on her own and plunged to her death."

"Why would you bring them back here?" The look of devastation on Otis's face was gut wrenching.

"Oh my God, Victoria," Nicola clutched her stomach as she felt an emotional shockwave wash over her.

"What? I still don't get it," Jaclyn's bewilderment was beginning to frustrate Brooke. She always required extra explanation and Brooke was not in the mood.

"Jac, think back to when we got here; we were distracted by our luggage and our chaotic arrival. I saw Cindy stand up straight and look in the opposite direction that we were looking. We faced toward the entrance and Otis, and she faced us. But she wasn't looking at us. I felt it. She was looking past us. At him. The guys were right behind us, remember? Cindy saw her old boyfriend and freaked out and didn't know what to do about him being here so she did nothing. Maybe that's why she stayed behind when we went exploring. She said she had a headache and we took off. What if she went to see him and that was the beginning of the end for her? Oh my God, where is he now?" We have to warn everyone. We could all be in danger."

"Ben. He's with Ben. Why would he take Ben?" Nicola doubled over with a guttural scream only possible from a terrified mother, and she turned and ran toward the path where the two were last seen.

Otis barked commands, "Brooke and Jaclyn, let the police officer know what's happening and tell them they probably need back up. He's helping with the search. Find him. Once you've alerted him, take Kyra with you and stay inside my office and lock the door. Update Alex if you see him."

"I'm coming with you. It's my fault he's here." Victoria said. No one argued.

"What do we do now? We don't know where to look for Ben. He could be anywhere."

A familiar ear drum piercing blast shattered the stillness. They all looked in the direction of the sound. It was coming from the most hazardous trail of the surrounding mountains.

"It's the air horn. Ben stole an air horn from the lodge." Kyra filled her Mom in quickly so she knew what she said was true, "I know, I was with him when he took it. It's him, Mom. It's Ben. He's sending us a signal for help."

Nicola pointed to a steep narrow pathway that she and Ben had tackled on the hide seek game when they first arrived. She knew how difficult the terrain was, and she took off running with Otis and Victoria right behind.

Nicola saw the BB half hidden, etched in the soil at the foot of the trail. Over her shoulder, she yelled at Kyra, "Tell the police what's happened and find your Dad."

CHAPTER 51

Nicola's anxiety threatened her ability to breathe and to run. Deep breath. She needed to keep going. One foot forward. Then the next. Faster. As she made her way up the mountain, panic over shadowed her logic. None of this made sense. A stranger had her boy, and she didn't know why. What did he want with Ben? Was Carter after her? Was he the one who sent the notes to her and took the picture? Nicola stumbled, and Otis caught her before she fell. Victoria was far behind them.

The lower branches of the tall evergreens began a rhythmic wave and the treetops swayed. It was getting late and the wind met the point where it crossed over from being a gently, refreshing breeze to becoming an indicator of bad weather on the way. And, it was getting dark.

Otis took the lead as he was familiar with the path. He knew it led to a cliff. And to a waterfall. And to heartbreak. And to grave danger. Nicola took up her position in the middle of the line-up, and Victoria fell into formation at the back and struggled to keep up with the others.

Winded, each experiencing burning, aching muscles, the self-appointed rescue mission, ascended the mountain. They continued to climb the nearly vertical terrain, each step more challenging and the air thinner. Their thighs ached and their lungs ignited with pain. The air's oxygen levels decreased shockingly fast, and it took bigger and bigger gulps for their aching bodies to access enough fuel to keep going.

After twenty minutes of climbing, they reached a small plateau and the struggling trio rounded a hairpin corner of the treacherous hiking path and froze. Before them was a ledge, less than two-feet wide, consisting of a mixture of sand and gravel and instability. Twenty feet ahead of them, leaning back into a narrow vertical crevice stood Carter, with his arm around Ben's shoulder, a knife pointed at the little boy's throat. Barnaby sat at Ben's feet oblivious to any danger.

A guttural cry escaped from Nicola and she pushed past Otis.

Carter yelled, "Stop. Turn around and walk away, and when I know you've gone, I'll let him go."

"I'm not leaving. Ben, it's going to be okay, honey." His big eyes looked back at her. She looked into the face of her terrified little boy and hoped her voice didn't sound as shaky to him as it did to her.

Otis stepped in front of Nicola and slowly extended his hand with his palm up as if he was a friend reaching out.

"Carter, we want to help you get out of this mess. We are here to help you. We know you knew Cindy and you lied about it. There is only one reason you would do that. Everyone knows. If you won't turn yourself in, just let Ben go. You don't want this. You don't want to hurt a child. Just hand him to me and get out of here, we won't get in your way. This is your chance to escape."

A flicker of emotion flashed across Carter's handsome face but was soon replaced with a crooked grin, "Ah, you're right, old man. I don't want to hurt Ben, I'd rather hurt you. You pissed me off the entire time I've been here but Ben will have to do. Now, back the hell away."

The blade was less than an inch from Ben's throat.

Victoria grabbed and pulled Otis' arm, and together, all three took a step backward. "Okay, okay, Carter," she said, "We're backing up."

The path was narrow, and their slow careful footsteps caused a series of small rocks to fall. They were all one wrong step away from disaster.

Nicola begged, "Please leave him and run away. We don't care what you've done. Just leave. We won't call the police." She prayed police vehicle sirens wouldn't reveal her lie.

The terrain was treacherous, and it was getting dark. Nicola could still see her son in the dusk, Carter's hand gripping his small arm as he dragged Ben higher up the rugged side of the mountain toward the highway. The cold and the fear that gave Nicola the needed adrenaline earlier now threatened to gurgle up inside her and explode. Otis was behind her helping Victoria navigate the climb. He stopped and yelled directions to Victoria, and he took off on a different pathway forged by glacier run-off. Otis bolted upward at a pace unexpected for his age. He continued to close the vertical gap but remained parallel to Carter and Ben. He was close enough for Carter to hear him.

"You have to stop running. We know about you and Cindy. It's over, Carter, or should we call you Adam?" Otis rejoined the women on the trail, grabbed the picture out of Nicola's hand, and waved it in the air. He wanted the attention away from the women and on him.

"Oh, that goddamn picture. She told me that first day she could back up her story if anyone doubted her. She said she had my old hair brush, and I'm a little embarrassed to admit that it took me a minute to figure out she meant she had my DNA. She could prove I was not who I claimed to be so I had to find it.

"She didn't tell me about the picture until I chased her down and caught her Friday night, but it was too late by then. I did what I had to do. Later, when everyone was lost in their own world trying to figure out who killed Cindy, I destroyed the girls' cabin trying to find the brush and the picture. I did find the brush and I burned it in the fire pit. Evidence destroyed, check.

"You see, I recognized Cindy right away too. I also knew Victoria invited me, not Cindy. Victoria put Cindy in charge of her child, not me. It was Cindy's responsibility to look after her. I believed Victoria when she said she wanted to move on from the past and needed to speak with me in order to do so. I didn't see her as a threat. Cindy, however, was a menace to me. She obviously was following my life, my limited social media posts, and probably my friends. I couldn't believe we were face to face. Why now? I knew it was no coincidence that we both ended up at the same holiday destination. A stench settled around me that day, a cloud of fear, a little of regret, but most of all a sense of determination. I had to fix this problem. I couldn't panic. I had come too far to lose everything because of that bitch."

Carter wiped the sweat from his brow with the back of his hand that was holding the knife. Despite his bravado, Nicola could see he was tired, but she was confused and needed to know more in the hope of placating him enough so he released Ben.

He continued his story, "The first day, before Tyler's orientation, I slipped away to try to talk to Cindy when I saw the other girls leave her cabin. She said she had faked a headache so she could talk to me, and I took the opportunity to confront her. She said she'd started looking into where I was and where I worked and saw where I lived. She was such a psycho.

"I started our conversation off nice and friendly like I didn't think she was out of her mind. I hugged her and gave her a kiss on the cheek. She seemed receptive so I thought maybe we could make this work, not romantically but as friends.

"I started by telling her how great it was to see her, how good she looked, but Cindy was smart and didn't fall for my bullshit or my charm. She announced that she was done with all the lies. I gently reminded her she had as much to lose as I did but she said her life was consumed with guilt, and she didn't care what happened to her, she was going to confess everything.

"Well, that's when everything began to spiral. At that point, I knew I needed to approach the situation a little differently. I grabbed a fist full of her ponytail, drew her face close to mine, and did my best to convince her to keep her mouth shut or I would shut it for her. I told her exactly what would happen if she told anyone. That got her attention." His eyes grew dark, and a frightening look crossed his face.

"I did try one more time to offer her a solution that would help us both and she seemed to go for it. You see, Nicola, Victoria appeared to accept our immense remorse, and Otis didn't recognize us. I told Cindy it would be best if we pretended to be strangers and just continue our lives like we had been doing. She agreed, I'm sure simply out of fear. So that's what we tried to do.

"Then later that first day during the ice breaker exercises and at the campfire, I saw her drinking, I heard her spewing veiled threats about truth telling and reconciling her past sins, and I knew what needed to happen. I could not trust her unpredictable behavior. I would never feel safe again. She had to die. But, then again, it turned out that I didn't have to lift a finger. . . not until much later.

"I will say I enjoyed my brief reprieve knowing for the first time since the real Carter died, I was truly free. The burden of what happened had lifted. Yeah, I botched the body disposal part, but what can you do, live and learn. It's all her fault, she just couldn't keep her mouth shut." He shrugged.

He was clearly a psychopath. There was no remorse. There was no regret.

"Let Ben go. You and I can talk. We'll figure something out together. Adam, you don't have to do this."

"I'm Carter." He yelled at Otis. "Adam doesn't exist anymore." His voice changed, deeper, angrier.

"Okay, Carter, yes, whatever you want." Otis said calmly. "We don't care what happened in the past between you and Cindy, but you have to know this is not going to disappear. We just want Ben released, and we won't follow you. You can run, we won't report you. It will be easier for you to get away without him slowing you down. Just give us the boy and go."

Barnaby started barking, sensing Nicola was close by, and, seeing her, broke loose from Ben.

"I will kill that fucking dog if you don't shut him up." Carter screamed back.

"Mom!" Ben's scream was for Barnaby's safety, not his own.

"I've got him, honey, he's okay," Nicola pulled the faithful dog next to her.

Nicola continued, "That's what first made me wonder about you, Carter. Everyone else seemed to be very intent on throwing suspicion on others, but not you. You were confident. You knew no one saw you or you would be under arrest. You could afford to remain calm and quiet and let the other young people point their fingers. I noticed that and it made me wonder why you were so sure of yourself. It wasn't natural to not be upset. That's when I first realized something was really wrong with you."

Carter's head jerked up, and it was clear he didn't like what Nicola said. He made a sound that was half cough, half laugh, "You probably aren't surprised to know that I've had people say that to me before. I heard them behind my back saying there was something off with me. We looked enough alike so it was easy for me to become my dead friend. Teachers, social workers, employers, girlfriends," he paused and wiped his mouth with the hand that held the knife.

"God help us," Victoria said, more like a prayer than a comment.

Otis stepped forward gently pushing Nicola away from the edge of the cliff. "Okay, Carter, you keep going. We won't chase you if you let the boy go. Come on, you know he's only slowing you down. Ben, stay calm buddy."

"Wrong. Hey, we were doing great until the little shit sounded the air horn. Christ that thing is loud. This kid is a great climber, aren't you? You never shut up about it." Ben started to cry, and Carter jerked his arm and pulled the child toward him as the path widened slightly.

"Okay, we get it, you're in charge. We know that." Otis kept his voice steady and his gestures nonthreatening. Otis saw his chance and moved laterally toward the two. He spoke in a calming voice and said, "I'm sure you didn't mean to hurt Cindy."

"It is true, I wasn't about to let her ruin my life by destroying everything I've achieved."

"Why? What did she do?" Otis tilted his position slowly. He needed to keep him talking. Let him tell his story.

"She was going to ruin everything. Why couldn't she just keep her mouth shut? Stupid bitch."

"You knew her?" Nicola asked trying to get him to keep talking. He was full of himself and was enjoying their attention. They just needed one moment of distraction. Just one moment. Otis understood what Nicola was trying to do so he asked, "Was Cindy your girlfriend?"

They knew the answer but needed to keep the conversation going.

"For a while. Until I didn't need her anymore."

"You told us what you did but you didn't tell us why?" Nicola's voice was soothing, motherly.

Carter glared at her and took a breath and he took the bait. "We got in a little trouble together back in the day and I needed to disappear. We went to university together, both of us on scholarships, and we met an exchange student from America with lots of inherited money and no friends or close family. He was a great guy, kind of looked like me and, get this, his name was the reverse of mine. I am really Adam Carter, he was really Carter Adams. We laughed about it when we met. The three of us hit it off right away I think it was because he was everything we wanted to be—rich and dependant on no one. For him, well, we were the human connection he desperately wanted. And, most importantly, he had a serious crush on Cindy. She and I filled in the friendship part for him, and she and I benefited by his wealth and loneliness. We did everything we could to help him spend his money." Carter laughed and wiped off the sweat on his forehead with the back of his arm.

The terrain was frightening and one wrong step would result in a fall into what appeared to be a bottomless gulch. Nicola was dizzy and her vision blurred. Deep breaths helped calm her panic but did nothing to help her son. She thought it couldn't be a worse situation so far up but immediately realized that it could definitely get worse.

In the distance, Nicola could hear water running, but she couldn't tell how far away. Ben could swim, but his little body would be no match for a fast-flowing mountain stream or, worse, a gushing waterfall. Nicola looked next to her and saw the extreme terror on Victoria's face and the pure rage in the eyes of Otis. Danger surrounded them.

Carter/Adam continued to talk. He seemed to revel in the attention from his captive audience, and his voice grew louder as the waters volume increased in both noise and size. He kept moving, albeit slowly.

"Cindy and I each had assigned dorm rooms, but Carter let us stay in his nice apartment off campus, at no cost, any time we wanted. Cindy was a good student. I was not. At school, instead of studying, I played a bit too much poker with a group of people from a part of the world you don't want to piss off. I realized too late that I was in over my head, and one night, when I couldn't pay what I owed, their goons came looking for me. Sadly, that was the night Carter decided he had enjoyed a night on campus a bit too much and asked to crash in my dorm room. I was out with Cindy at a movie but, when our friend, the real Carter, entered my dorm room, the bad guys thought he was me. They strangled him.

"It must have been quick and quiet as no one in the dorm admitted to hearing anything. That could be the truth, but more likely, they were all afraid. Cameras caught three thugs entering and leaving the building, but it was impossible to identify anyone. There were no cameras on the dorm floors. When Cindy and I returned to the dorm, there was nothing we could do to help our friend.

"They must have used a wire, I think they call it a garrote, at least that's what they call it in mob movies. I'll never forget the color of the mark the wire caused on his throat. It was a thin line, covered in dried blood. It was the color of rust on an old vehicle. All the cars in my neighborhood growing up were more rust than paint." Carter shook his head and then frowned as a memory crossed his face.

"So, with the exception of his small tattoo on his left wrist, Carter. . . the real Carter Adams, was gone. As far as the gang knew, they killed Adam Carter, the gambler who couldn't pay his debts, the real me. The police believed the same thing. Poor "Adam Carter" the gambler was a tragic victim of senseless violence, and nobody really seemed too upset about it. That pissed me off, but I shouldn't have been surprised. Somehow, through my magical charm, I convinced gullible Cindy into falsely identifying the body thereby solidifying the police's theory. I'm not sure if the case file is still open, but I'm pretty sure no one has been charged with my murder if you get what I mean."

"Barely, what you are telling us is so confusing." Nicola knew it was important to keep him talking.

"No shit. Imagine how we felt. Cindy and I stayed up all that night trying to figure out what to do. We thought about going to the police, we racked our brains trying to remember any reference he made to family but didn't think anyone would miss him. There was a former nanny he told us was his emergency contact, but he hadn't been in touch since his arrival months earlier. Then a glimmer of an idea began to form, I'm not sure who said it first, but we were both on the same page. Wouldn't it be easier if it was poor Adam who died and rich Carter who lived just like the gang believed? Me. . . poor, scholarship me. . . lucky-to-breathe-the-same-air-as-these-rich-assholes me, could just disappear with more money than any one person deserved."

"So then what happened?" Otis asked he took a small step forward as he asked.

"Cindy got cold feet, panicked, and said if I promised never to come near her again, she'd keep all of this a secret. I believed her as she would be clearly implicated if any of this was uncovered. She also received a steady stream of money from a dead man's bank account to ensure her silence. She said she'd only take what she needed and didn't care about the rest of the money. She said it probably carried bad karma or some bullshit like that."

He laughed then. "Perhaps the little bitch was right. Anyway, as planned, Carter Adams dropped out of school and with some storytelling lies from Cindy to the few people who would question the situation, it was done.

"I thought accessing his banking accounts would be a challenge, but in this digital age, it was easy. The guy wasn't so bright when it came to online security and password protection. I left the accounts open. I just drained them almost dry through a series of spaced-out e-transfers to a new bank account in a bunch of different locations. I spread the money around just in case everything went tits up. If there was any fall out afterwards, I was long gone and so was Cindy.

"So off I went with access to all my dead rich buddy's accounts and began my brand-new life as Carter Adams. It was shockingly easy.

"I became a different person. . . a completely different person. I morphed from life-long loser Adam Carter into wealthy, golden boy Carter Adams, the poor little rich boy with no family or friends. Adding to We looked enough alike so it was easy for me to become my dead friend. I updated my identification as I moved around. Driving his car and wearing his clothes helped. Changing my tattoo helped. My original wrist tattoo was my accurate initials, AC, but I added an E and created my own nickname ACE."

Nicola's head was spinning with fear for her son and disgust for what this monster had already done. There was no way she could let him out of her sight. By his own admission, he was a thief and a kidnapper. She slowly looked over at Otis while he listened to Carter bragging about how clever he was and knew the older man was keeping him talking in order to distract him. Both Nicola and Otis were waiting for the same thing, a brief moment of distraction. It was unspoken, but she knew she would grab her son, and Otis would grab the monster.

"Cindy and I never saw each other much after the night the real Carter was killed. We came up with the plan surprisingly quickly and, because she was scared for her life too, she went along with it. She was also in danger from the gang I owed money to, just by being my girlfriend. It was a win/win situation, but that all came crashing down the moment I saw her here Friday afternoon.

"Cindy being here threatening to expose everything I worked five years to build. It was no coincidence we were here together. I understood the reason. I didn't know Cindy couldn't live with the guilt and wanted to come clean. I couldn't let that happen.

"Just before the orientation meeting on Friday afternoon, I walked over to the girls' cabin and saw Jaclyn and Brooke leave. It was my chance to talk to Cindy without anyone else around. I was always able to get Cindy to do what I wanted, but she had changed. She told me her plans to confess to the police. I reminded her that she also had a lot to lose as she falsely identified the body and she was definitely part of the impersonation plan. She had no difficulty spending the stolen money I accessed. She said she didn't care. She said keeping the secret was killing her. So she sealed her fate. What I didn't expect was what happened next."

Carter shifted his weight from side to side. His breathing became heavier. Telling the story was upsetting him. He was no longer bragging about his cleverness. His tone was angrier. Recounting the details of their twisted agreement heightened his agitation.

"Cindy was adamant she was going to the police and admitted to tracking me down to warn me. Apparently, she never did get over our relationship and never recovered from something that happened a long time ago."

Carter laughed when he said, "Since she knew my fake name, it was pretty easy to find me on social media. I didn't post often, but just enough to not cause anyone to wonder why I didn't have an online presence. It's a bizarre world where, if you don't post pictures of your meal or a beautiful sunset, it's suspicious. That's the same reason I got a job. It would have been weird not to have one. Believe me, it was a necessary evil, so to speak. She told me she befriended my new friends using a fake name of her own and was then able to monitor what I did and where I went."

Nicola kept trying to engage fake Carter in conversation even though she no longer understood what he was saying. He seemed to want to talk so she asked, "Did Cindy reach out to you online?"

"No." The questioned angered him. "That would have been the smart thing to do. She was useless, and she had become a legitimate problem for me. I don't like problems." With that, he looked down at Ben who was frozen with fright.

"Legitimate. That's an odd word for you to use. There is nothing legitimate about you." Otis crossed his arms and stared at the young man. He could see his words landed hard.

"I don't think you want to throw shade my way, old timer. I'm the one calling the shots here. I had no choice; I couldn't let her ruin everything. It wasn't just because of the crime of impersonating someone else and stealing his money. I reminded her there were very bad people out there who, if they heard about the identity switch, would still want me, Adam-The-Gambler, dead. They would find out about the cover up, hunt me down, and kill me whether I was in prison or not." Stress showed on his handsome face. It was evident in his voice and in the way his shoulders slumped. Nicola saw the signs of his exhaustion, and it fuelled her body.

"I don't believe you. None of what you just told us is plausible." Nicola was emboldened and needed to keep him talking.

He waved the knife in Nicola's direction and said, "Do I look like I give a shit whether you believe me or not?"

"In this day and age, it's pretty damn hard for someone to disappear off the face of this earth and nobody notices. It makes no sense."

"Ah, that's where you are wrong, again. Nicola, you are mistaken because no one disappeared."

"Well, you just told us, the real Carter did."

"Well, he died but no one really knew that, other than me and Cindy," Carter shifted his weight, and his foot slipped on the dirt on the border of the trail, but he quickly regained his footing and continued. "I told you, I notified the school, and then I got in touch with a few contacts pretending to be him. There was no one close other than a former nanny and a tennis coach. . . old acquaintances. Kinda sad really. I had his mail forwarded to a post office box, and I returned any correspondence as required. I will admit the issue of income tax filing was becoming a bit of an issue for both Adam Carter and Carter Adams. The tax department in both countries had been in touch. I'll tell you, it's a little freaky filing your own death certificate. However, the blessing of bureaucratic red tape, along with everything moving at the molasses-like speed of government, worked to my benefit. Even though I was able to dodge it for a few years and had a bit of breathing space, the issue is eventually going to heat up. Someday."

Nicola and the others saw that Adam Carter was taking the bait provided him. His ego needed to belittle Nicola. He had an audience and needed to demonstrate his brilliance. No narcissist could pass up such an opportunity.

"Look, I didn't come here planning to murder anyone. Even when I first saw her, that wasn't my plan. She made it impossible. I was no longer able to get her to do what I wanted. You have no idea how much that pissed me off. Someone was going to die, either me or her."

Carter shook his head to get his blond curls out of his eyes in order to meet the older man's glare.

He continued, "The answer to how Cindy and I ended up at the same mountain resort, after all these years, is simple. We were invited."

"Why did you accept the invitation?" Otis snapped.

"Well, I couldn't resist, Otis?"

Otis looked at Victoria. She refused to meet his scowl.

Otis turned back toward Carter, closer now. He lifted his chin and lowered his voice, "All I know is that you killed a young woman."

"You are wrong, Mountain Man. I didn't kill Cindy."

The sneer on Carter's face displayed his enjoyment of what he said next.

"Isn't that right, Victoria?"

CHAPTER 52

Victoria collapsed to her knees, sobbing. Otis made no attempt to help her. Nicola, stunned at what she just heard, stared at the woman she thought was her new friend.

Carter continued. "I should have known that, even in death, Cindy would be a pain in the ass. I witnessed the showdown between Cindy and Victoria. All Victoria wanted from us was our accountability for the death of her child. She never received it from Cindy. I gave my apology to Victoria as soon as I arrived. I played up my sadness and remorse over what happened, and my haunting regret, to the hilt and the old lady lapped it up. Cindy, however, continued to be belligerent and unapologetic and denied full responsibility for the kid's death. She blamed Victoria for not teaching her daughter to not go near the falls. So, on Friday night, after everyone was back in their cabins, I saw Victoria lose her mind. I saw her chase Cindy because I was right behind them. I had to know what was happening. Cindy hid in the bushes in the dark, but Victoria, who is surprisingly fit, was familiar with the terrain and eventually came up behind her, grabbed the back of her hoodie, and knocked her on her ass. I almost clapped. When she stomped on her arm, I couldn't believe it. Victoria had gone psycho, and I was a little scared myself. Cindy almost reached a big rock with her good arm to use as a weapon, but Victoria beat her to it, and it was lights out for Cindy-Yell-A-Lot. Good riddance."

Stunned silence greeted Carter when his story telling paused. He took a breath and continued.

"That's when I arrived on the scene. Victoria was in a trance it seemed. I needed her on my side so she'd shut up about my new identity that I assume Cindy told her about and everything that had gone on, so I offered to help. I sent her back to her cabin to change as there was a little blood spatter on her clothes. I rushed to grab a tarp that was covering the nearby kayaks.

I ended up having to move the body more than once. It really was Cindy that Kyra saw late Friday night on the path. I heard Kyra scream, and I needed more time but, no such luck. I had a sliver of an opportunity to take Cindy's body from the path to the cellar in the lodge. I couldn't believe I needed to move her again, this time to the rain barrel. Not ideal, but I had no choice. Victoria and I made a pact to pretend none of it happened. Unfortunately, Bennet, the little superspy, ruined everything. He pretended to be sleeping, but he was actually a witness to me moving Cindy. When he said everyone was lying, I knew he meant me especially."

Ben looked down at the wet mark at the crotch of his pants and the small puddle forming between his shoes.

Nicola was stunned at what she heard. She felt like a horrible mother. Her son had witnessed the cover-up of a murder and kept it a secret. Her daughter had come across a dead body, and no one, including her own mother, believed her.

"Wait, what? How could you have had time? Kyra was only gone from the pathway a couple of minutes later."

"I know. You should have seen me haul ass." Carter spoke as though he was regaling a funny anecdote to a group of friends at a party. "We were pulling a lame prank on the cowboy, and I made sure that I was assigned the set-up of an alibi. That would allow me time to grab Cindy and drag her out in the woods as originally planned. When I heard your kid scream and saw her run back to your cabin, I knew I had to do something else with the body to bide more time. When Tyler and Otis ran out the back door and down the path, I had Cindy over my shoulder and went in the front door of the lodge where no one saw me.

"I was unprepared and I'm never unprepared. I had to move Cindy's body to the root cellar in the lodge. She was covered in a tarp, and I just heaved her over my shoulder, threw back the rug, opened the lid, and threw her down the stairs. I barely got away with it. I guess didn't really because Ethan's camera captured everything. I was able to get my hands on Ethan's confiscated camera and hide it in our cabin, but, apparently, not well enough as it wasn't there when I went to retrieve it."

Victoria gasped at his callousness but was ignored. She no longer had a right to be indignant.

Carter looked at his accomplice and continued, "Imagine my dismay when I heard about the homemade goodies that were going to be served and realized the storage area Otis talked about was not only storing pickles and jam but also a dead body. I needed more time to figure out what to do so I knew I had to move her again. I had no idea Tyler and the kids were making ice cream in the kitchen when I retrieved her the next day. I heard their voices just as I was leaving. I didn't have time to put the furniture back properly.

"So there I was, walking around with dead Cindy over my shoulder again, and no one saw me. As careful as I was when I placed her body in the rain barrel, I still got soaked so I pretended I'd been swimming. I stashed my tee-shirt, socks and shoes in the garbage bin so you all saw me walk up with wet shorts and hair. I retrieved my stuff from the bin before the body was discovered. I also knew I could count on Victoria helping me with any alibi I needed. It was simple."

Nicola flinched at the heartlessness of the scene he described. He was a sociopath, perhaps even a psychopath, but he was also something else. The real Adam Carter was evil.

Nicola took a step closer to her son, maneuvering as close to the knife as possible without upsetting Carter. She needed an answer from this criminal.

"Carter, have you been sending me threatening notes? Have you been terrorizing my family here?"

"What the hell are you talking about? No, I haven't. I just met you." Carter shook his head and seemed genuinely confused.

Nicola sensed his reaction was real. There was no reason for him to deny it unless it wasn't true. He wasn't her stalker.

"So," Carter said, "Here we are. You all need to remember, Adam's supposed to be dead, so you can keep calling me Carter. In fact, I insist you do because no one will ever learn what I just told you. You can even keep Victoria's secret, and I'm not talking about lingerie, if you choose to. I only care about me." He looked down at Bennett and back at the Nicola, and the implication was clearly understood. They had possession of his secret, but Carter had possession of her child.

"Victoria?" Nicola's eyes searched the face of the woman she thought she knew.

Victoria held up a hand in surrender and whispered, "How could I let that girl live when I learned what kind of a nasty bitch she turned out to be? There was no remorse in her. How could I let her fall in love, have a family, have a future. . . grow old? I didn't plan it but don't regret it. Carter, I did you a favor by getting rid of Cindy. Now it's time for you to repay me by letting the child go."

"Not happening."

Ben started to softly cry.

Nicola reached toward him and said, "It will be okay, honey. We'll figure something out."

A minute passed as the group absorbed what was said. Two people were dead, both linked to this cunning, selfish, dangerous man who held her son hostage. Otis looked at Victoria as though she was a stranger.

Throughout the storytelling, positions shifted, and Nicola lessened the distance to Ben as all eyes were on Victoria as she spoke. Nicola wanted to grab Ben but couldn't take the chance. Nicola knew she could touch her son but might not be able to free him. It would be deadly, at this point, to try. Nicola no longer knew if she could count on Victoria for help.

Carter was clearly mentally unstable and increasingly agitated. Nicola looked into her son's eyes trying to convey that everything would be okay. Her little guy never took his eyes off of her, and all she saw was his fear. Carter pulled Ben closer into him. Ben's narrow back was against Carter's body, and the man's forearm was pinned against the little boy's chest. His grip tightened on Ben's slim wrist. The boy was going nowhere.

Carter turned to face Otis. By doing so, the trio managed to separate. Otis moved beside Carter, while Victoria and Nicola remained slightly behind. In their triangulated formation, Carter was as close to being surrounded as possible on a treacherous, narrow pathway, halfway up a mountain.

CHAPTER 53

Nicola was reeling from the fact that her child was in grave danger and genteel Victoria was a murderer. How could Victoria fool everyone? How could she pretend to be innocent?

Nicola summoned everything in her being to remain calm in an insane situation. On the ascent, Nicola hadn't noticed how narrow the ledge was and how high they had climbed. She pushed through her fear of heights, it was nothing compared to the thought of losing Ben.

Help had to be on the way, it was now a matter of how long it would take to find them. Would the police take the correct trail? Would they understand the BB signal Bennett left as a clue? She knew Alex and Kyra would understand. She had to remain calm. She looked at Victoria whose pallor indicated shock. Nicola knew she could not count on her for any real help. The solution to this nightmare would be up to her and Otis. She locked eyes with him.

Carter laughed again when he saw Otis and Nicola processing everything he told them. Nicola became increasingly concerned that Carter was no longer thinking rationally. She felt her knees begin to quiver and prayed her voice didn't shake.

"Look, Carter, give me my son. You don't need him anymore. He'll slow you down. It will take at least an hour for us to get back to the lodge. Maybe longer in the dark. You head toward the highway, flag someone down. I don't care. You go your way. We'll go in the opposite direction." She needed to convince him this was his best chance to escape. Their pace would be much slower than that of a young, fit man running for his freedom. She also knew it is impossible to reason with someone clearly out of their mind.

"Cindy crossed a line with me. I was no longer her college boyfriend, Adam. She realized a little too late that I enjoyed being the new version of Carter, and I wasn't going to let her fuck that up." He tightened his grip on Ben. He blinked as if his eyes stung and wiped the sweat dripping into his eyes. "Do you see now why I wanted to stop her? I built a new life and then she appeared, and it would all be ruined. I couldn't let that happen. But I wasn't the only one with a grudge against her so I lit an emotional fire under Victoria telling her a few lies and igniting the grief-stricken mother inside her and Victoria did the rest."

"I understand," Otis locked eyes with Victoria and lied. He turned back to Carter and said, "There's a way out for you now. You look exhausted, Carter. Are you thirsty? I'm sure Ben is." The little boy tried to nod, but his chin touched the metal blade and his crying grew louder.

"It's okay, buddy." Otis continued and took two steps forward.

"Get back."

Victoria spoke up. "Here, Carter, I'll toss the canteen to you." She secured the lid and tossed it. It landed three feet away from Carter and Ben.

"Nice try, Vic. Did you think I'd let him go in order to get water. Ever the maternal figure, right? Such a caregiver, aren't you, Victoria? Except when it mattered most, isn't that right? Mother of the Year Award for you. They think your daughter fell in near here. At the waterfall, right?" They all heard the rushing water nearby.

His words cut Victoria deeper than any knife could. Seeing the devastation of Victoria's face, Otis lunged at Carter yelling, "You bastard, you aren't getting away with anything."

"Stop," screamed Nicola.

Victoria knew what needed to be done. She needed to be the one to sacrifice herself and confront this madman. She stood and faced Carter. "You're correct. Everything you said is true. How clever of you to have the grieving mother solve your problem with Cindy. But what you need to know are two things. Nothing you say to me is worse than what I've said to myself, so your words cannot hurt me. Second, I will not see another child die here. So, take me instead. Trade me for Ben. I won't slow you down, and I'll do everything you say." She took a step forward.

"No," Otis grabbed Victoria by her shoulders and twisted her behind him rushing to within a foot of Ben and Carter who then jumped backward causing more mini landslides. Their running shoes were dangerously close to the loose gravel at the edge of the path.

"Whoa," Carter looked down at Ben. "Close one, eh buddy?"

"You're not my buddy, jerk."

Nicola recognized Ben had understandably hit his limit and could do something that would cost him his life if she didn't act quickly. She knew she needed to distract both Ben and Carter for very different reasons. She inched closer to them and tried a different tactic.

"Victoria is right, you are very clever. So how did you figure everything out in order to avoid suspicion on you or Victoria?"

"The old-fashioned way, I took a page of this little guy's book, and I eavesdropped on a few conversations. By the way, your daughter has serious issues. I'd keep an eye on that hot mess."

Carter poked at her, trying to cause more pain. He succeeded.

She continued. "The rest of the guests are on their way to help. They are following us, any minute they will come around that corner." She indicated the treacherous bend they had just trekked over. It was barely visible.

He shook his head in pity. "No, Nicola, nice try. Maybe by now they all got permission to go home, and they probably couldn't pack up and leave fast enough. They are likely all on the highway and halfway home by now."

Maybe he was right. She didn't know.

Carter took a deep breath; he was reaching his limit too.

"Enough," Carter pointed the knife at Nicola. "This is over, we are leaving now. You are turning around and going back to the lodge. Young Bennett here is staying with me. Once I manage to flag down a car, I'll let him go. Trust me, he has been a little bastard this whole time. But, if you try to stop me, I will throw him over this cliff."

This was her chance.

The knife was no longer at her baby's throat.

"Never." Nicola screamed, lunged forward and grabbed Ben's arm, and yanked him into air, and he landed behind her at the edge of the cliff. She may have dislocated Ben's shoulder. He cried in pain but held onto a tree root with his left arm.

"Mom! Help me!"

Otis scrambled to pull Ben to safety before Nicola could move. Otis, almost falling over the cliff himself as he lay on his stomach, overextended his reach. He held the child's good arm and heaved him upward to safety. The sound of rocks, loosened by the commotion, bounced off the sides of the crevasse and disappeared into the gulch below.

Otis scrambled to pull himself up from the cliff's edge, and Victoria wrapped her arms around Ben shielding him from the horror before her. Despite the boy's protest, Victoria pulled Ben back down the mountain toward the lodge, away from the danger with Barnaby running behind them. Otis stood between the two groups. On one side, Victoria and Bennett were still in sight but on their way to safety, and, on the other, Nicola and Carter were in the middle of a showdown.

Carter pounced on Nicola. She raised her arms in defense position, and the knife slashed her forearm but not before she managed to grab the collar of his shirt. She dropped backward and sat down perpendicularly on the narrow ledge with the top of her head hanging over the edge. She pulled her knees up to her chest, looked up at the sky, and silently asked for divine help. Blood poured from her arm but she managed to pull Carter down toward her.

He was off balance.

Out of control.

He dropped the knife.

She dug both feet into his groin and hoisted him above her. With one smooth motion, she released his shirt collar and, extending her legs and, with every muscle fibre she possessed, she catapulted him in a backward somersault over her head and into oblivion.

Everyone froze.

The only sound was his scream.

Then nothing.

CHAPTER 54

MONDAY

The guests and staff assembled in the main room of Mountain Shadows Lodge. Dawn was breaking over the mountaintops. They had been up all night, only the children slept, intermittently, on the cots nearby.

"Before the death, before the betrayal, we were happy. The beauty of this special place thrilled us each time we visited. Our last trip began as usual. We arrived together filled with excitement. Days later, we parted, at different times, in different ways. Shattered." Victoria explained.

"Our daughter drowned here, at Mountain Shadows, playing at the edge of the waterfall, where Shelley Anne was never allowed to go. It was Cindy's fault, and Adam's, and ours for leaving her with them. I'm referring to him as Adam from now on as the real Carter was an innocent victim. When Ben went missing, my first thought was, please God, not another child in danger here. I went to Otis; we knew we had to do everything we could to help."

The group was shocked, angry, and numb. Jaclyn and Brooke refused to look at Victoria, but the rest wanted answers. "I called Detective Dickenson this morning and confessed." She nodded to the constable who was about to arrest her. "Dickenson said he'd be here as soon as possible, once his senior officer arrived for the day. He knows I'm not a flight risk."

Otis spoke, "Helping to save Ben gave us the chance we never had to help our Sam. Carter wasn't the only one surprised to see someone from his past arrive at Mountain Shadows on Friday afternoon. I couldn't believe Victoria was here."

Logan spoke, "I'm still struggling to understand." He glanced at Jaclyn who stared out the window. "My brain can't handle it. I was in shock when I saw the camera video of Carter, I guess I should call him Adam, running with something over his shoulder, but I had no proof it was Cindy so, like a coward, I said nothing. All I knew was Carter, I mean Adam, lied."

Logan crossed the room to stand beside Jaclyn who reached over to hold his hand. Nicola was still surprised at the perfect match this odd couple created.

Otis added, "We hadn't seen each other for a few years, and I had no idea why Victoria was here. We decided right away that sharing our history would be too painful so we chose to pretend to be strangers. That's what we were discussing when Adam almost hit Ben with the Jeep."

"So, Victoria, who are you really?" Alex asked, it sounded harsh.

"I'm really Victoria Shea and I am who I said I am, for the most part. It's just that Shea is my middle name and my last name is McIntyre. I'm still married to Otis."

In unison, the adults' heads turned from Victoria to Otis standing by the fireplace. He looked different, Nicola thought, softer, sorrowful. There were no scowl lines creasing his forehead, only sad eyes resting on the woman he obviously still loved who was a murderer.

"I knew it all along." Ben announced. He was drinking hot chocolate with one arm in a sling. Fortunately, Otis determined that the little boy's shoulder had not been dislocated, only sprained, when Nicola grabbed him from Adam. Ben was in some pain, but everything seemed a bit better when Otis made a special sling for the brave young man.

"Bennett, not now," Alex admonished him.

"No, really, I knew because when all of you were talking to each other, I watched Otis bring Victoria coffee with cream in it. How did he know that she wanted cream in it? She didn't say to put cream in it. He just knew. Then, another time, Victoria brought him coffee. But she didn't put cream in it. She put two sugar cubes in it. How did she know that was how he liked his coffee? I didn't hear him ask for sugar. So, because I'm a detective now, I knew then that they knew each other and were friends. Yup, I figured you knew him when you fixed his coffee the first day and knew Otis liked it black with two sugars. I saw that. How would you know that if you weren't friends?" Ben tapped his temple with his forefinger.

"Yes, smarty pants, I realized you noticed and wondered if you'd say something but you didn't." Victoria smiled. "I guess you can keep a secret."

"So, I'm smarty pants, Kyra's bossy pants, and you're fancy pants. Ha-ha, that's funny." The little boy's giggle was contagious. They all needed a little comic relief.

Nicola's thoughts turned to the damage discussion of murder would have on her children.

"Ben and Kyra, I need to you to go outside please. We need to have some adult talk, okay?"

Kyra didn't argue. "Sure, Mom, c'mon, Ben."

Brooke turned and looked at Otis. "We didn't even blink when you said you had a daughter, and we thought Otis had a son. Who would have guessed?"

Silence and sadness descended on the group.

"After we lost her, I couldn't wait to run away. Sadly, Otis couldn't bear to leave the last place where we all were together and happy. We've seen each other periodically, but it was just so devastating seeing the shared pain in each other eyes. It never leaves. It's not something you ever get over, it's something you try to get through. Eventually, we decided to just live separate lives. To put one foot in front of the other and, after a long while, it was easier not to think about what happened here. Until this past Friday, I hadn't been back so imagine the shock Otis had when I pulled into the driveway. He even called me by his nickname for me at one point, and I thought Tyler heard it."

The summer student nodded. "I thought it was just a comment on your beautiful car, not your nickname. I didn't recognize you, or know who you were, until I talked to my Grandma."

"Forgive me for asking," Nicola spoke softly. "Why did you come back now? What were you thinking, inviting Cindy and Adam here?"

"For three reasons, ten years had passed and I needed to honour Shelley Anne's memory. Second, I needed to see Otis. I was finally strong enough to face him and to face this place. Third, and most importantly for me, I needed to confront Cindy and Adam. The police declared Shelley Anne's death an accidental drowning, but I wanted the two of them to acknowledge they were to blame. I did not plan to kill Cindy. I did lose my mind, but I will plead guilty, and I'll serve my time. Nothing can be worse than the punishment I've been living with for the past decade."

The missing pieces of the story of the earlier death were now fully explained. The missing pieces of the story behind the current death were still evolving.

The previous evening search and rescue teams returned to the lodge to report they found Adam Carter's body, battered but recognizable enough for Otis to identify. The sun was casting eerie mountain shadows over all of the inhabitants in the area. For the second time that weekend, the group gathered and watched the Medical Examiners van take away someone from their group. This time Nicola felt nothing when she saw the coroner's body bag zip closed. No regret, no sadness for the young man, simply anguish for all that happened. Another young life ended, and she was numb.

Detective Dickenson was right when he said secrets were like water, difficult to contain and always seeking an escape. There were no more secrets involving Cindy, but there was one involving the last moments of Adam Carter's life and Nicola hoped it never found its way out. Only three people knew what took place on that cliff at the very end and one of them was dead. She was thankful Victoria took Ben and ran down the path and around the corner with him. He'd never know exactly what happened at the end.

After Nicola flipped Adam backward and sent him flying over her head and over the cliff, he tumbled and then grabbed a tree root and was splayed vertically against the mountain side. His feet moving frantically trying to land on an earthy ledge. His left shoulder drooped, probably dislocated, so with his one good arm, he grabbed the root and looked up at Otis and Nicola.

Quietly he said, "Help me, please."

They heard Adam's plea but neither moved. The real Carter was dead. Cindy was dead. Ben could have been next. Otis and Nicola paused. The truth of what happened next took place between those moments. It was unspoken, it was mutual. In that moment, neither Nicola nor Otis was willing to risk their life to save this monster. Maybe they could have, maybe they eventually would have.

Maybe not.

Within moments, Adam plummeted to his death, and the decision was made for them.

Adam's body hurled down the mountain bounced off several rocks and disappeared into a deep gorge.

Now they were all safe from him.

A police vehicle driven by Inspector Lancaster, accompanied by Detective Dickenson, arrived and Victoria was arrested. She was stoic as she was helped into the back seat, refusing Otis' offer to accompany her.

Those left behind, who share an unexpected, traumatic experience, automatically form a bond that goes beyond the event itself. After Victoria's arrest, both guests and staff, united by tragedy, busied themselves by making breakfast together and solemnly gathered around the outdoor table. They were somber but also relieved.

Nicola, more than anything else, was grateful. Her boy was safe, her family intact, and she was headed home with renewed strength and determination. Earlier that morning, she phoned Glen's cell for an update on her case. He told her there were no stalker incidents at her home while she was gone. There were no hidden cameras in her home. There was no one lurking in the neighborhood, and no additional notes were delivered to her home address or to the station. The consensus was that, without the thrill of causing terror, the perpetrator didn't get whatever kick he or she was seeking. Therefore, the culprit had likely moved on to another victim. Nicola didn't wish the fear she experienced on anyone, but she felt the tension she held between her shoulder blades ease.

When combining the known facts and bits of information Adam bragged about, they now had a full picture of what happened on the night Cindy was killed.

Logan asked Nicola to go over the scenario in detail as he was struggling with the realization he was friends with a psychopath.

Nicola spoke, "Adam watched Victoria chase Cindy down to the beach and back into the bushes where she hit her with a rock. He didn't try to stop Victoria; he wanted Cindy to be eliminated. He offered to help dispose of the body if Victoria kept his false identity a secret. Victoria, in her state of panic at what she had done, agreed. Adam carried Cindy's body up to the bushes and thought he had hidden her near the pathways. His plan was to move her once everyone was asleep. Kyra did see Cindy's crumpled, body underneath a tarp on the side of the path. She was not moving and was covered in blood, but it is unclear if she was dead at that point. Carter heard Kyra scream and, when Kyra ran back to get her mom, he had seconds to grab Cindy and run. He didn't want her discovered so quickly, if at all. He told us on the cliff that he needed more time to create an alibi. As Tyler and Otis and Ethan ran out the back stairway at the sound of the scream, Adam circled through the front. He remembered Otis mentioning the old dirt root cellar under the great room in the main lodge. He took a gamble, flung back the rug, opened the door on the floor, and threw her body down the ladder steps. It was the image of Adam running with Cindy over his shoulder that Ethan caught on camera but didn't witness as he was looking, and running, in the other direction."

Softly Tyler spoke, "I guess I didn't see a Sasquatch after all. Poor Cindy."

"What Adam didn't know was that Tyler and the Henderson kids were in the kitchen making ice cream the next day when he went to retrieve Cindy's body from the root cellar to dispose of her. Tyler heard a thud but didn't have any idea of its significance. He didn't realize Adam dropped the cellar latch door and ran out the front. He took so many risks. Reckless. Earlier, Tyler shared his observation of the furniture out of place and reminded them of his discovery of a drop of blood on the carpet. Forensics followed up taking a sample of the stain that remained despite the young man's cleaning attempt. It matched Cindy's blood."

Nicola shuddered when she heard the missing pieces of the story as she realized how close her children and Tyler came to witnessing Adam move the body from the cellar to the rain barrel. Adam only had a brief window of time to move Cindy as he knew Otis was heading down there in preparation for lunch. Otherwise, who knows how long Cindy's body would have remained there in the cold cellar or, eventually, out in the forest to be destroyed by wildlife.

Nicola spoke softly, "I believe Victoria tried to do everything to keep Otis out of this nightmare. Part of the problem has been about who we say we are, versus who we really are, and the damage it causes when the truth comes out."

The others nodded in agreement each lost in thought.

Brooke spoke first. "I think we are all a bit shaky still. There is a disconcerting feeling that comes from finding out someone you knew, however briefly, has done something horrific. I can't believe Victoria did this, I never would have suspected her."

"I guess we really don't know anyone fully, do we?" Logan's level of shock exceeded Brooke's.

"Maybe that's true, but that's not always a bad thing, and usually, it's not this kind of effed-up situation." Ethan helped himself to more toast and spread a mound of homemade raspberry preserves on top. He shrugged when he noticed Jaclyn recoil and he added, "It's not like Cindy's body touched the jars. Everyone relax, I got this from the kitchen fridge."

Eventually, the conversation over breakfast evolved from the discussing their shared harrowing experience to the recovery from the experience. Everyone's upcoming plans were outlined along with promises of continued friendships that were formed during this unforgettable long weekend. They would see each other again. Contact information was shared, and Brooke and Jaclyn promised to keep everyone updated regarding Cindy's memorial service, but they were not finished trying to make sense of everything that happened.

Brooke spoke, "Cindy told a lot of lies, but the most harmful were the ones she told herself. Lies that she wasn't worthy of love, that everyone wanted something from her, and that she didn't deserve to be happy. Those messages caused a lot of damage over her short lifetime. They shaped the decisions she made as an adult, including not being able to say no to Adam's scams. I believe she wanted to but, due to past trauma, was not able to trust anyone to help her."

Jaclyn added, "I always thought her college boyfriend story was fake. There were no pictures of them together. It's now clear that either Adam destroyed the rest of them or wouldn't allow them to be taken in the first place. If Cindy hadn't kept that one picture of them, hidden with her confession, in her wallet, we would never have known about them. Victoria wouldn't have said anything. Cindy had a conscience after all. So it was Adam, not a wild animal, who tore our cabin apart. He was looking for the picture in the wallet she told him she had and, thank God, Cindy was smart enough to hide it in the wishing well."

Kyra, followed by Ben, bounded up the steps and helped themselves to the sausages and eggs at the buffet table and covered them both in a mound of ketchup. Nicola watched her daughter and noticed something had changed within Kyra. There was a lightness about her. She pulled out a chair beside her mom and reached into the pocket of her jean shorts.

"I found a note but decided not to show you until we were leaving. Oh, I thought I put it in my pocket but I guess not."

Nicola looked at her daughter and then met the gaze of her husband. Something started to bubble up in her chest. The familiar hint of the pressure of anxiety was trying to take over. She took a deep breath and waited for her daughter to continue.

Kyra explained. "I got a note on the first day telling me not to look under the bed, but I knew it was Tyler trying to mess with me."

Alex asked, "So, did you look under the bed?"

"Hell no. I mean no, not then. I took off. I was a little creeped out. Later I did, there was nothing there, not even a dust bunny. Someone must have dusted under there, or. . . Oh My God. . . maybe someone was hiding under there when I was in the room. Maybe Tyler wanted me to look and to find him."

Kyra paused and then pointed to the handsome young man who looked confused. "Nice try." She flipped her hair in an exasperated, yet flirtatious, move.

Tyler looked up from across the table and struggled to finish chewing his toast and peanut butter.

"I didn't send you a note." Tyler's face was sincere and he shook his head.

"I didn't say you *sent* me a note." Kyra rolled her eyes. "You left it on the second page of the note pad on the nightstand in our cabin where no one else would see it until later."

"Kyra, I'm telling you, I didn't do that." Tyler stared at the girl. He was adamant he wasn't involved, and his handsome face seemed upset at not being believed.

Otis put his hand on the young man's shoulder and said, "If Tyler says he didn't do it, then he didn't do it." It was clear Otis was in full protective mode and increasingly concerned about what he was hearing. If true, that meant someone had been in his cabins without permission.

"Okay, then what about the fake dead squirrel and the twig family?"

"What are you talking about?" Tyler dropped his knife on his plate and everyone jumped at the sound.

Kyra told the story of putting out seeds she thought were provided by Tyler or Otis and then finding the fake dead animal in the dish that she believed to be real at first. She told everyone about the twig figure, leaving briefly only to find the hammock swaying and the four decapitated stick figures upon her return.

Everyone at the table stopped eating.

"When did this happen?" Ethan's question was ignored. The others remained quiet and stared at the troubled young girl.

"That's sick and cruel. I'd never do something like that and I'm insulted you think I would." Tyler said.

Kyra looked at his earnest face and knew he was telling the truth. "I'm sorry, I didn't know what was going on. Well, if you didn't do it. . . Ben, are you sure it wasn't you?"

"Nope," Ben answered with a mouth full of scrambled eggs. Barnaby remained close by hoping for any food item to drop. Even the dog knew this was the spot where food was most likely to fall.

Ben swallowed his food and added, "You know, I was thinking, Carter's nickname was A. C. but it should have been Ass." He pushed his small chest out, proud of his statement.

"Ben, language." Alex glared at his son.

Nicola, still holding her fork mid-air asked, "Do you still have the old note. Kyra?"

"Yes, like I said, I kept it. I must have thrown it in my backpack so no one else would be freaked out. My backpack is in the van."

"It's unlocked. Go get it," Nicola's voice had an edge to it. Kyra pushed away from the table as she recognized her mother's tone and didn't argue.

Logan took a bite of bacon and eggs and, with his mouth full, asked, "You are a popular lady. Did you get that other note?"

"What other note?" This time it was Alex who was asking. The look on his face made Logan chew and swallow faster than usual.

"The blue one, with Nicola's name on it, pinned to the bulletin board in the glass case out front. I saw it when we were wondering where Ben went, but with everything going on, I just forgot to mention it. I'll go grab it."

"No," Alex shouted and turned to Nicola. "Stay calm. I'll get it, honey. Stay here with everyone else. Ben, stay put. Kyra, get back here. Nobody moves. I'll use a napkin, in case there are prints." All those around the table froze. Even Ben stopped eating.

"That's what it was, another note." Nicola spoke softly to herself. She knew something wasn't right. She felt it in the mad scramble to find Ben. Subconsciously, she knew something was out of place, something didn't belong. That's what caused her senses to react. In the frenetic moments scanning the property, panicked over Bennett missing, she must have seen the fully visible note but, subconsciously, dismissed it.

Alex returned to the table, out of breath from running and worry, and handed the note to his wife. It was covered by a clear plastic document case readily available at office supply stores. Presumably, the plastic was meant to double protect the message from the elements if the glass case failed.

Nicola's hands shook. Instinctively, she knew the note was from her stalker. The others watched as she carefully peeled back several layers of clear tape from the paper envelope trying not to rip it. She lost the end of the tape several times and used her fingernails to continue. The last layer of tape revealed the envelope inside had not been sealed by licking it or wetting the adhesive. No DNA.

Kyra returned from the van with the message from the bedside notepad and handed it to her father. His worrisome reaction made her ask, "What's going on? What's wrong?" Nicola shook her head and didn't answer. She could tell immediately the handwriting on both messages matched the other notes she received.

He found her.

Nicola stood up, spilling her coffee on the table. She tried to control her breathing as she pulled a single sheet out of the envelope, her eyes tried to read the lines on the page, but her head was spinning and her vision blurred.

She blinked. The words came into sharp focus like when an optometrist flips the correct lens into place during an eye exam.

Blue always looks so pretty on you.

She looked down at the blue shirt she was wearing. Her heart clenched. She continued reading.

Tell Kyra thanks for the couple of pictures she posted. She's turning into such a beautiful young lady. She filled out those cute little shorts and crop top nicely. What a great singer at the campfire and I was so impressed with how she handled that big horse. She was bossy and in charge. Like mother, like daughter. Your son sure had fun here too, didn't he? It was quite the adventure he went on but everything ended happily. Now it's time for our adventure.

A Polaroid fell out of the envelope.

A photo of Nicola, taken that morning, drinking coffee, talking to her kids.

Nicola screamed and the onlookers jumped, confused looks on all their faces. They didn't know what was happening. Nicola hadn't told any of them about her stalker. No one knew.

Alex put his arms around Nicola and reached for the photo in her hand. He took a moment to look at it. He flipped it over and back again and slowly put it in his shirt pocket. There would be no fingerprints. Nothing to protect as evidence.

Nicola knew.

It was from the stalker.

It. Was. Him.

He's been here the whole time. Watching. He heard Kyra sing the first night at the campfire; he saw her on the trail ride the next day. The stalker must have followed the kids when they went horseback riding and, by doing so, avoided being caught during the police search. He knew about the ordeal with Ben. He saw what Nicola was wearing this morning. He took a picture of her with Kyra and Ben.

Nicola saw what was on the other side when she flipped the note over. There was only one word and two symbols.

Soon. XO

The End

AUTHOR'S NOTE AND ACKNOWLEDGMENTS

Writing my debut novel began as a personal challenge. I had no idea the amount of work, and joy, it would bring. I started and stopped writing multiple times, over multiple years. I now know how *not* to write a book.

When I finally committed to finishing, that's when the magic happened. There are no short cuts. I believe it takes three things to write a novel—imagination, a bit of talent, but, more than anything else, it takes discipline.

Mountain Shadows was written while I travelled all over the world. One of the great things about writing is you can do it anywhere, at any time.

Many friends and family members helped me along the way. I'm sure they grew tired of hearing about my writing journey. Special thanks go to my husband and daughter, my first readers, who were asked bizarre, random questions and read messy first drafts.

Thank you to my extraordinary beta readers, Kim, Denise, Sherry, Carol, and Christi, who questioned plot, found typos, and fixed the glaring errors I could no longer spot. I appreciate all your incredible work.

I'm grateful for the suggestions received from retired police detective, Mike. All errors in the book are mine alone, and certain plot choices were made for dramatic purposes.

This is a work of fiction. All of the characters, organizations, and events portrayed in this novel are either products of the author's imagination or are used fictitiously. The amazing real life Just Us GirlS (JUGS) group is nothing like the ones described in the book.

I extend my deep gratitude to the brilliant authors in the crime fiction world who have entertained and inspired me for decades. I've been lucky to meet some of my heroes and they did not disappoint.

Lastly, most importantly, to you, my readers, thank you. I hope you have enjoyed *Mountain Shadows*. Please know the second book of the trilogy will be available soon. To keep updated you can follow me @lauriemclurewriter on Instagram.

Happy reading!

Laurie